THE TEMPTATION BEGINS . . .

He was too close. The words were almost a whisper in that hypnotic voice of his. "Close your eyes," he said, and his voice sank into her bones. "Stop fighting, just for a little while. It won't hurt, I promise. Just lean back against the wall and let go."

She was tempted. Oh, God, she was so tempted. She closed her eyes, her fierce will helpless against the siren lure of his voice.

"There's peace here, Rachel. No more battles. Life has been a battle for you, but you don't have to fight any longer. You can just let go. Surrender. You can't win all the battles. You can't slay all the dragons. Let someone else do it for you. Just this once."

His tone was even more evocative than his words, and she felt herself slipping, against her will, her skin tingling with longing and awareness.

"You can have it, Rachel. No more fear. No more anger. You can just let go. Can you feel it? The peace floating through your body? The wholeness spreading through your body?"

She couldn't open her eyes. She was helpless beneath his spell. She couldn't speak, couldn't move, trapped in ~~~~~~~~~~ that she didn't wa~

"Do I have yo~ ~~~~~~~~~~~~~~~~~ ody and soul?"

RITUAL SINS

Anne Stuart

AN ONYX BOOK

ONYX
Published by the Penguin Group
Penguin Books USA Inc., 375 Hudson Street,
New York, New York 10014, U.S.A.
Penguin Books Ltd, 27 Wrights Lane,
London W8 5TZ, England
Penguin Books Australia Ltd, Ringwood,
Victoria, Australia
Penguin Books Canada Ltd, 10 Alcorn Avenue,
Toronto, Ontario, Canada M4V 3B2
Penguin Books (N.Z.) Ltd, 182-190 Wairau Road,
Auckland 10, New Zealand

Penguin Books Ltd, Registered Offices:
Harmondsworth, Middlesex, England

First published by Onyx, an imprint of Dutton Signet,
a division of Penguin Books USA Inc.

First Printing, October, 1997
10 9 8 7 6 5 4 3 2 1

PUBLISHER'S NOTE
This is a work of fiction. Names, characters, places, and incidents either are
the product of the author's imagination or are used fictitiously, and any
resemblance to actual persons, living or dead, events, or locales is entirely
coincidental.

For Barbara Keiler and Judith Arnold,
two of my dearest friends.

For Richie, who keeps me sane.
And for Maureen Walters and Susan James,
who take such very good care of me.

RITUAL
SINS

PART ONE

SANTA DOLORES, NEW MEXICO

1

Rachel Connery didn't want to be there. At the age of twenty-nine she'd made it her policy never to do anything she didn't want, to always have a choice in matters. She was here by choice, she reminded herself grimly. It was simply a choice she wished she didn't have to make.

The taxi had already pulled to a stop outside the sweeping expanse of Santa Dolores, home base to the Foundation of Being. Seventeen miles away from Albuquerque, it sat beneath the New Mexico sun like the peaceful retreat it was purported to be. A compound devoted to meditation and enlightenment, combined with a hospice center to care for the dying.

Her mother had sought enlightenment behind those walls. Her mother had died there.

The cabdriver had already opened her door,

and she slid out, brushing imaginary dust off her silk suit as she glared up at the compound. She didn't want to be here, she thought again. And *they* knew it.

"I can handle it from here," she said, taking her leather suitcase from the driver and handing him a generous tip.

"Blessings," he murmured.

"What?"

"Blessings. You're one of Luke's People, aren't you?" The driver seemed momentarily confused, but his fist closed tight over the money in case she was inclined to snatch it back.

"No," she said shortly. "I'm not." And she marched toward the beautiful forged gate, her high heels firm in the dusty drive.

Luke's People, they called themselves. She'd managed to blot that particularly ugly thought out of her mind, but now it was back. There was no more hiding from things she didn't want to face. She'd never met the man, only seen him from a distance. But even across a crowded courtroom she could feel the poisonous strands of his charisma, like a spider's web reaching out toward any stray creature who wandered in its path.

Luke Bardell, ex-con, convicted murderer, founder of what some people called a philosophy, others called a religion, and Rachel called a cult. The man who had mesmerized her dying mother into leaving twelve and a half million dollars to the Foundation of Being. And not a damned thing to the only child she'd ever had.

Ten years ago Rachel might have simply curled up in a tight ball and wept. But not now. She'd fought back, hard. Only to have her lawsuit thrown out by the first judge, her lawyers quit on her, and defeat wash over her like a bitter shower of acid. You can't sue a religion. You can't accuse a saint. Stella Connery was of sound mind when she made her will, she knew she was dying of breast cancer, and she'd made her decision and disinherited her daughter.

And the Foundation of Being had been nauseatingly gracious in triumph. Surely Rachel would want to make a pilgrimage to the place where her mother had spent her final peaceful days, to the spot where she was buried? She could see the good that Stella's money was doing, make peace with what the courts and her mother had chosen. The Foundation, and Luke's People, would welcome the chance to share the blessings that had come their way.

Rachel would have rather eaten fried caterpillars. They certainly weren't about to share the money that they'd wheedled and tricked out of a vain, dying woman. Stella and Luke had been lovers, Rachel had no doubt about that whatsoever. Stella had gone through men with a voraciousness that had left her only child awed and frigid in response. No good-looking man had been immune to Stella.

Luke Bardell, the messiah of the Foundation of Being, was a very good-looking man indeed. And he'd been paid well for sleeping with a dying old lady.

If Rachel had been willing to accept defeat she would have refused their offer of hospitality. A sensible woman would have accepted the fact that the mother who'd abandoned her on almost every level had finally finished the job. She could find a new job, make a life for herself, choose not to be a victim of a distraught childhood.

Choice, again. There was that word. She could choose anger and revenge. Or she could choose to get on with her life.

If it hadn't been for the letter from a stranger she might have made the wise decision. But once the creased, scrawled letter arrived in her mailbox with its hints and accusations, she had no real choice.

Your mother never had cancer. She was murdered by one of Luke's People. Maybe by Luke himself, or at least he gave the order. At the end she knew what was happening to her, but she couldn't stop them. Come to the center and I'll help you find proof that will bring him down.

No real choice. The letter was unsigned, written

in a childish scrawl, but it rang with truth. Or at least, the truth she wanted to believe.

At that point, anger and determination kept her going, and they carried her straight to Santa Dolores, to the Foundation of Being. And to Luke Bardell.

"She's here, Luke."

He didn't move. He'd heard them shuffle in, that odd group of middle-aged and elderly professionals who'd found the answer to life's questions with the Foundation of Being, and used their financial expertise to make it thrive. They were called the Grandfathers, even though there were several women in the group, and they ran the organization like a blue-chip company.

And Luke ran them. He lay flat on his back on the cool tile, arms outstretched, eyes closed, as he inhaled the sweet, sharp smell of burning sage. He could feel the energy tingling, rushing, flowing through his body, every nerve taut, every vein pumping with blood, with life, pulsing, throbbing. That energy was his power, his gift, and he used it carefully, never squandering it.

For a moment he wondered who they were talking about, and then he remembered. Stella's daughter. The skinny, pale, sour-faced woman who'd had the astonishing gall to try to take his money away. She'd gotten nowhere, of course.

The Grandfathers thought she should have been paid off. After all, lawsuits and accusations, no matter how farfetched, were bad publicity. And the Foundation of Being preferred little or no publicity. They weren't looking for converts. Those who needed what they offered would find their way to Santa Dolores. Sooner or later.

But Luke hadn't wanted to pay her off. He'd watched her, with her patrician face and her fuck-you eyes, her designer clothes and her utter contempt, and that old feeling rose in him, one he thought he'd squashed down. Here was a challenge, when nothing had been a challenge for years. Here was a soul who would fight him, tooth and nail, before he could claim her. Here would be a battle that would test his rusty skills, prove that there was no one immune to the power he could exert, when he chose to focus it.

He would bring Rachel Connery to Santa Dolores and he would seduce her. Spiritually and emotionally, he would strip her, ravish her, drain her, and own her. As he did all the others.

He had no qualms about it. He could take that sour look on her pale face and turn it into the placid expression of bliss that surrounded him twenty-four hours a day. All without laying a hand on her.

He never slept with his followers. As far as they knew, he never slept with anyone at all. Luke

Bardell was celibate, vegetarian, drug- and alcohol-free, purity personified. It was all part of the tools of the trade. They all wanted him. He knew it, and he used it. He slept with no one, and they believed they could all have him, men and women, young and old. As long as he remained out of reach it kept them blind and focused and needy.

The way he liked them.

It would be interesting to see just how long it would take him to bring about that change in an angry disbeliever like Rachel Connery. He'd converted others before, it should be a simple matter.

Except that she was different, he'd felt it, even from a distance. Her anger ran deeper. And it called to him, a challenge that he had no intention of refusing.

He opened his eyes and sat up, fluidly, brushing his long hair behind him as he crossed his legs and stared back at the Grandfathers. "Blessings," he said.

"What do you want us to do with her, Luke?" Alfred Waterston had been chief of staff at one of the leading cancer research institutes in the country. He'd taken early retirement to follow Luke's way, in the meantime taking charge of the Foundation's complex finances. Alfred's attention to detail was impressive to the point of obsessive.

"Make her welcome," he replied in his gentle voice that he'd trained to carry to the farthest corner of any room. Another tool, one he used wisely.

"She's expecting to see you. I told her you were meditating, and she just laughed. I'm afraid she'll be a disrupting influence, Luke."

Luke simply nodded. "Not for long, Alfred. See if she'll submit to purification before she approaches. What's she wearing?"

"City clothes," Alfred said with a dismissive sniff.

"Bring her some of our things. She'll be more comfortable in them."

"And if she refuses?"

"Then I'll deal with it, Alfred. I always do."

She'd refuse, of course, even though the ritual bath was simply the private use of a hot spring that was wonderfully enervating. She'd probably insist on cold showers during her stay. She'd refuse the loose cotton clothing that they all wore as well, but he'd see to that in good time. The phrase rang in his head, *Strip her, bathe her, and bring her to my tent*, and he smiled serenely.

"Blessings," Alfred murmured, with no idea what his saintly leader was thinking.

"Blessings to you all," Luke replied, lying back down again.

It had been three months since he'd been laid. He'd grown used to the long periods of celibacy—if he were to keep up the image of purity, then he had to be very careful how and when he took care of his needs when they became overwhelming.

But he'd learned to channel that frustrated sexual energy into a kind of burning power that reached out to everyone. And he lived inside that volcano, inviolate.

Santa Dolores was a safe haven for all, based upon trust and love and freedom. It also worked extremely well due to an advanced surveillance system that gave Luke visual access to certain rooms on the compound. He sat up again, alone in the pale, cavernous room, and rose. He would retire to his private meditation chamber, the one place where no one, not even Calvin, would disturb him. He would draw aside the thick black curtain and stare at the banks of television monitors. And maybe he might get a chance to see whether Rachel Connery was as pale and sour and skinny without her clothes on.

The first thing she noticed was that there were no children around. Apparently this cult catered to the unencumbered. The better to extort their money, Rachel thought. The main house of Santa Dolores was built along fittingly Southwestern lines—cool tile floors, adobe walls, plain dark wood on the windows and ceiling.

They'd put her in a room far at the end of one

hallway. The woman who'd shown her there was pleasant enough, and to Rachel's annoyance she didn't appear to be particularly brainwashed, despite the pale cotton outfit she wore, which resembled a cross between men's pajamas and a karate gi. She tried to press one on Rachel, something she flatly refused, and tried to lure her to a hot springs for purification.

"Not in the mood," Rachel had drawled. "I took a shower this morning."

"You'll feel wonderful. Like a new person," the woman, who'd identified herself as Leaf, said.

"I like the old person just fine," Rachel said. "When do I see Luke?"

"When he's ready. He spends most of the day in prayer and meditation. I'm certain he'll grant you an audience as soon as he's able. In the meantime he would want us to make you welcome at Santa Dolores."

Rachel looked around her, at the plain walls, the kiva fireplace, the narrow bed with the white cotton coverlet. "Not very sybaritic, is it?" she observed.

"We aren't here to indulge our senses," Leaf replied. "We're here to fine-tune them. To open ourselves to everything."

"You can't do that on a single bed."

Leaf smiled at her. "We do not indulge in drugs,

alcohol, sex, or any toxins. This is a place for purification and learning."

"No sex?" Rachel echoed. "What about husbands and wives?"

"They welcome the chance to concentrate on
their spiritual rather than their physical needs."

"Great," Rachel said. "My mother never spent
a celibate week in her life."

"Celibacy is not a requirement," Leaf said. "It's
merely a suggestion. If we wish to follow the
master, then we should emulate him."

It took a second for this to sink in. "You're
telling me Luke Bardell is celibate?"

"Of course."

"Of course," Rachel echoed in disbelief. "You
know, there's a problem with celibate religions.
No little followers to keep the faith going. The
Shakers found that out."

"We aren't a religion, we're a philosophy. And
children aren't allowed here. They're too young
to understand our teachings. Luke says we must
take care of our worldly responsibilities before
we nurture ourselves."

"A cult leader with a republican conscience,"
Rachel muttered. "What next?"

"It's not a cult."

"Yeah, I know. Not a religion, not a cult, just a
way of life," Rachel said, tossing herself down on

the bed. It was narrow and hard, like a bed of nails. It suited her mood.

"Dinner will be at six o'clock. We're all vegans here, but our cooks are very skillful. I know you won't mind."

The only thing worse than a vegetarian diet was its stricter form, vegan. Rachel sighed. "It'll be fine. I don't really care much about food. In the meantime I think I'll take a little rest."

"Perfect," Leaf said. "I'll come back for you at suppertime."

Rachel lay very still on the bed, listening as Leaf's sandaled feet disappeared into the thick silence. She'd left the damn uniform behind, and Rachel stared at it, wondering if she had the energy and the anger to dump it in the trash. She didn't.

She looked at the wood-paneled ceiling overhead. She'd done her research well—this facility was less than four years old, built with the best that money could buy. It was worth millions, all thanks to the spiritual leadership of a man who'd spent three years in prison for killing a man during a barroom brawl.

Luke Bardell had risen far and fast in the twelve years since he'd walked out of Joliet Prison on parole for manslaughter. And now no one could touch him, no one would even dare try, including the parole board who should have thrown him back in jail for violating the rules of his parole long ago.

No one would dare try to touch him, but Rachel Connery. And she was going to bring him down.

As soon as she found out who her ally was. Who had sent that warning letter.

She'd worn high heels as a stupid little act of defiance. She wasn't going to go exploring in them, she wasn't going to put on those damnable sandals that Leaf had left behind either, even though they looked like they might fit. She would go in her stocking feet, roaming the empty halls of Santa Dolores, and see whether she could come across the elusive Luke Bardell. She wasn't going to await his summons for a papal audience. She was going to find him, now. And remind herself just how human he was.

She should have known it would be a waste of time. She passed a good half dozen of the brain-washed—people who looked a her and smiled and murmured some crap about "blessings." But Luke Bardell was nowhere to be found. No one stopped her from going into any room, including the large, stark room that looked designed for large meetings or human sacrifices. But there was no sign of their mysterious, illustrious "master." And no sign of anyone who seemed to know or care who she was.

By the time she gave up and headed back for

her room her mood had not improved. She was hungry, she was hot and tired, and whether she liked it or not she was going to change out of her city clothes into something more comfortable. She wasn't certain that she'd brought anything suitable, and she'd go around stark naked before she'd dress up like the karate kid, but a shower would revive her for her quest. A quest she had no intention of failing.

It was late afternoon, and her room was filled with shadows when she reached it. There was no light switch on the wall, and she cursed beneath her breath as she stumbled into the gloom, the door swinging shut behind her, sealing her in.

"Goddamn place," she muttered. "No goddamn light switches, no goddamn meat, no goddamn messiah when you go looking for him." She flailed around for a lamp on the bedside table. She found one, only to discover that it was an oil lamp.

"Shit," she said out loud. "And no goddamn electricity."

The flare of the match was dazzling in the inky darkness, and Rachel uttered a little shriek, mesmerized by the light as it traveled toward a lamp. A moment later a dim illumination filled the room, growing brighter by the moment, and the man shook the match out and tossed it in the round stucco fireplace.

"You were looking for me?" Luke Bardell said.

She would never forget nor forgive her initial moment of panic. She'd gone in search of him, to face the lion in his den. And instead he'd invaded hers.

He was as mesmerizing close up as he was from a distance. It wasn't something as simple as physical beauty, though he had that in abundance. An elegant, narrow face, wide gray-blue eyes that looked at her with astonishing compassion, a nose and chin strong enough to give his angelic face masculine character, and a mouth that could seduce a saint.

He sat on her bed, ignoring the straight-backed chair, his long legs stretched out in front of him. He was wearing one of those baggy cotton outfits, though his was pure white instead of the pale colors the others wore. He had one of those tall, lean bodies that looked almost gaunt, and yet only a fool would underestimate the strength and power beneath the loose-fitting white tunic. His hair was very dark and very long, and it flowed down his back, and he watched her with his large, elegant hands folded quietly in his lap, watched her with faint curiosity and not the slightest hint of apprehension.

"How'd you get in here?" she demanded, not caring how hostile she sounded. "You scared the hell out of me."

"We have no locks at Santa Dolores," he said in

a tranquil voice. "We don't use harsh or profane language. It's an infectious poison, just as surely as drugs and alcohol and animal flesh are."

She resisted the impulse to tell him to fuck himself, she wasn't sure why. "Sticks and stones may break my bones," she murmured.

He raised his eyes to look at her, and she met his gaze with complete self-control. No wonder he was able to have otherwise intelligent adults eating out of his hand. Those eyes of his could make an iceberg melt.

But Rachel was frozen harder than an iceberg, and thoughtful looks and soulful eyes left her unmoved.

"You're very angry with the Foundation of Being, aren't you?" he said, not moving from her bed. "You think we took advantage of your mother."

"No." She began unfastening her silk jacket, determined not to be intimidated by him. "I think *you* took advantage of my mother. You seduced her, convinced her to leave her money away from her only child, and then you act as if you're the misunderstood victim."

His smile was slow and oddly unsettling. "I'm celibate."

"So they told me. I don't believe it."

"You were asking, Rachel? Why did you want to know?"

The dark wouldn't show the faint color that

rose to her cheeks, she thought with sudden gratitude. "They volunteered the information."

"How very odd," Luke said, swinging his long legs around and rising from her bed. He was very close to her in the small room, and she realized he was quite a bit taller than she'd realized. She didn't like tall men. But then, she didn't like short men, or average men either, she reminded herself. There was nothing to be nervous about. "They must have divined somehow that you wanted to know. There are no coincidences in this life. No accidents."

"Life is nothing but one long accident," Rachel snapped, immediately regretting her impulsiveness. "If my mother hadn't met you, she wouldn't have fallen under your influence, and I wouldn't be a pauper."

"Yes," Luke said gently, reaching up and touching a strand of her short-cropped hair. It was an oddly intimate gesture, one that left her frozen in place. "But you still wouldn't have your mother, would you?"

She was still standing there, minutes after the door closed behind him.

2

They met in secret, the Grandfathers, with solemn faces and dignified demeanor. All of them, men and women alike, sat cross-legged on the rough floor, hands turned upward toward the sky as they waited for enlightenment. Even the outsider, the one who would never belong to their exalted group, sat in respectful silence.

They could be seen, perhaps, if someone tried hard to find them. But they couldn't be heard. The Grandfathers met often, to discuss the financial well-being of the Foundation of Being, the uncertainty of the future, the wondrous change Luke Bardell had wrought in their lives.

As they did now. Alfred Waterston looked at the Grandfather next to him, his jowly face serene and determined. "How are we going to arrange Luke's death?"

And the outsider carefully, politely, raised his hand.

So he'd won the first encounter, Rachel thought, staring at the rough wooden door. It made no difference. If she were a quitter she wouldn't have come to Santa Dolores in the first place. There were things she couldn't let rest in peace, and the occasional setback was nothing she didn't expect. Besides, somewhere among these happy smiling people she had an ally.

He was right, of course, there were no locks on the doors. She wedged the straight-backed chair under the door handle, closed the shutters on her deep-set window, and began to strip off her clothes. If she viewed it objectively, it might not even be considered defeat. She hadn't responded to the mesmerizing effect Luke Bardell was supposed to have on most people. She hadn't even been tempted. She'd faced the enemy and survived. That in itself was a triumph.

The bathroom was small and utilitarian, a stall shower, toilet, and small sink, but the hot water was plentiful, and she stood beneath it for long, sybaritic minutes, letting it sluice over her, trying to soak away some of the edginess that threatened to consume her. She didn't want to lose the tension and anger that fueled her, but she needed calm and control above all things. Luke Bardell and the Foundation of Being were formidable enemies. She needed every advantage she could muster.

The pastel cotton pajamas had disappeared during her foray, and she wondered who had taken them. The mint-green had never been her color in the first place, and she pulled on jeans and a T-shirt with a certain amount of defiance, finger-combing her short-cropped hair. The rooms at Santa Dolores didn't come equipped with mirrors, probably to discourage vanity, but Rachel knew exactly what she looked like without having to check. Her clothes were deliberately shapeless on her too-thin body, her face pale and makeup-free, her eyes viewing the world with doubt and suspicion. There was nothing to inspire interest or desire in any but the most desperate, the most perverse.

She was out of place in this dream world. That in itself was nothing new. There was no longer any place on this earth that felt like home to her. From her earliest years she'd felt like a guest in her mother's various apartments and townhouses, and the series of boarding schools she'd attended hadn't been much better. She hadn't the gift for making friends, unwilling to trust anyone enough to get close to them, so there'd be no other families to visit. From the time she'd left college she'd lived in a series of apartments, each one more spacious and anonymous than the previous one, ending up in a large, empty set of rooms in Manhattan's East Seventies.

Less than a year ago it looked as if things might change. Her MBA from Harvard had stood her in good stead, providing her with a series of managerial jobs that she'd undertaken with cool efficiency. She'd just resigned her most recent one, emerging with a healthy savings account to augment the trust fund she'd grown up with, and she'd done one of the few capricious things she'd ever allowed herself. She'd packed a small bag with only the bare necessities and taken the next, shockingly overpriced flight to Spain.

It made no sense—Spain had never held any particular interest for her. But she'd arrived on a blisteringly hot, sunny day, rented a car, and driven until she was too tired to drive any longer, ending in a tiny village at the tip of a small peninsula. She'd found a house for rent, and there she'd stayed, hidden from the world and from her mother, for three long, glorious months, doing nothing but lying in the hot sun and eating fresh fruit and bread and cheese, letting the years of fear and anger bake out of her until she was dangerously close to being happy.

The house, belonging to an elderly grandmother in Andalusia, was for sale. And Rachel returned to New York full of an unlikely hope. She would make peace with her critical mother. She would liquidate some of her stocks, buy the house in Spain, pack up her spartan belongings, and move back to the first home she'd known, with the first friends she'd ever had.

But her mother had already left New York for the cloistered solitude of Santa Dolores, refusing all communication with her only child. And for good reason. The trust fund, set up by Stella's third husband, had already been stripped of everything Stella, as trustee, had access to. Stella's Park Avenue condominium, with its fortune in artwork and antique furnishings, had been sold, and even the few good pieces she'd given Rachel over the years were missing from Rachel's apartment.

Her healthy rage had carried her along for a number of months while she tried to recoup her shattered finances, searched for another high-paying, soulless job, and contemplated revenge on her uncaring mother.

The late night phone call from Santa Dolores had changed everything. The words, the voice, still echoed in Rachel's head when she least wanted them to. "Your mother has taken her final journey," the woman who'd introduced herself as Catherine had murmured over the phone. "Blessings, my child."

Rachel had slammed down the phone, standing alone in her empty apartment, shivering slightly in the chill night air. "Blessings, my ass," she said aloud. And then she began to cry.

As far as Rachel could remember, it was the last time she'd cried. She cried so seldom in this life that she could remember each and every rare, painful occasion. She had cried over her mother's final, irrevocable loss. By the time she heard about the disposition of her mother's substantial estate, including the pilfered trust fund, she'd gone far beyond tears to a blinding fury.

That fury still sustained her. But it required fuel, and she couldn't remember when she last ate. It was close to six, the appointed hour when dinner would be served, and Rachel was feeling weak enough to eat anything, up to and including fried rats. Except that Luke Bardell's little cult were vegetarians. In a few days fried rat might start to look tasty.

She wasn't expecting the soft knock on the door. She moved the chair and opened it, half expecting her nemesis to make a reappearance, but the person standing there was a far cry from Luke Bardell's unsettling, lethal presence.

She looked like the kind of mother Rachel had always secretly dreamed of. Plump and grayhaired, with kindly eyes and a sweet expression on her elderly face, the woman exuded warmth and concern. The kind of thing Rachel knew she should automatically distrust.

But anger seemed to be taking too much of her energy. She looked at the sweet old lady and felt a treacherous, sentimental longing.

"I'm Catherine Biddle," the old woman said in a soft, gentle voice. "We spoke the night your mother died. My dear, I'm so very sorry I wasn't able to give you more comfort at that sad time."

Rachel tried to summon forth her caustic tongue, but her efforts were mild. "I wasn't in the mood for comfort at that point," she said.

"And you aren't yet, are you?" Catherine said wisely. "Never mind, my dear. All things in their due course. I was hoping you might join me for dinner."

"Here?" She knew she sounded doubtful.

"Where else would we go? All the answers we need are here with Luke's People. We all share our meals—Santa Dolores is communal living at its purest. But if you care to join us at our table we would welcome you most happily."

"Everyone eats together?" she asked warily. Despite the fact that her mysterious ally would be there, she wasn't in the mood to confront all the happy campers of the Foundation of Being en masse. Particularly their leader.

"From the newest follower to Luke himself."

"I'm not a follower," she said sharply.

"Of course not, dear," Catherine said comfortably. "I didn't mean to imply that you were. But you've come to learn our ways, haven't you? To see how your mother's generous bequest is helping others less fortunate? You've come with an open mind and a willingness to partake of the peace and tranquility only Luke's way can offer?"

The very thought filled her with horror. But Catherine Biddle looked so sweet and hopeful, so trusting, that something kept Rachel from being blisteringly frank.

"I've come to learn," she said with complete honesty. And she would learn everything she could. Of course, she intended to use her newfound knowledge to strip the Foundation of her mother's money as well as anything else she might manage to get away with. And to see Luke Bardell in hell if she could manage it.

"Of course you have," Catherine said approvingly. "And learn you shall. And all the Grandfathers will be glad to help."

"I don't want to get anywhere near the Grandfathers," Rachel said, following her into the hall. "I spend as little time as I can with old men in suits."

"Grandfather isn't a particularly descriptive term for our group of leaders. Most of them are old, but they're not all men." Catherine appeared faintly amused. "The Grandfathers dress as everyone else does here. You can tell what people do by the color of their clothing. Newcomers wear green. The Grandfathers wear gray."

Catherine's tunic and pants were a pale dove-gray. "Oh," Rachel said.

"We're nothing to be afraid of, Rachel," Catherine continued in her soft, friendly voice. "The Grandfathers are like everyone else here, using their life knowledge for the good of humanity. We'd really like to show you some of our ways."

For some reason the cynical response that rose to Rachel's lips stayed there, unspoken. She may have been fiercely resistant to Luke Bardell's mesmerizing tactics, but Catherine's maternal warmth was a more potent threat.

She compromised. "I expect it will all be very interesting," she said carefully.

Rachel hadn't been paying attention to her sparse surroundings as they walked. Catherine had stopped by a pair of thick, plain doors, and she looked up at Rachel, her gray hair coming askew from its casual bun at the back of her head. "You don't trust us," she said in a cheerful voice. "I don't blame you, my dear. At your age I was just as easily hurt, just as suspicious. But we'll win you over. I know that we will." She threaded her arm through Rachel's, and she was surprisingly strong beneath the loose-fitting shirt. "Come and be welcome," she said, and pushed open the door.

Catherine had been an inspired choice, Luke thought as he watched the two women. Everyone turned to Catherine for warmth and mothering, and a young woman who'd had very little mothering in the first place would be an easy mark. All the more so because Catherine's motives were pure. Her maternal instincts, stunted for years, were entirely natural, and Rachel Connery's cynical mouth was already softening.

Would he have as easy a time with her? He wondered if she would be likely to see him as a maternal figure. It was an entertaining notion. He usually managed to be all things to all the people in his flock—father, mother, child, and lover—all the while keeping his emotional distance. He might make a bet with Calvin, the one person here who really knew him, to see how long it would take him to subvert one angry young woman.

He'd taken her mother, and he'd taken her money, all with the angelic innocence of a saint. He'd take Rachel as well.

She hadn't seen him yet, though he could tell she was trying to look. Catherine was taking her over to the Grandfathers' table, and the others were eyeing her with distrust beneath their benevolent smiles. His followers were almost pathologically protective where he was concerned. They had no idea he had her well in hand.

He was sitting in the midst of the penitents tonight, their soft yellow clothing blending with his white tunic. He always sat with the flock, eating little, his presence a powerful stimulant. The penitents were almost trembling with excitement, unaware that all his attention was focused on the stubborn outsider.

"Will I ever find true understanding, Luke?" Melissa Underwood, a skinny blonde with a sexual addiction problem, edged closer. She had spent the last year trying to turn her formidable sexual energy into some kind of search for peace, and he smiled at her benevolently. He wasn't a man who wasted his energy on anything as capricious as a conscience, but if he ever had to face a judge again, in this world or the next, Melissa would be a point in his favor. Here she wasn't courting death and disease, going through men and women at a voracious pace. At Santa Dolores she was living in quiet contemplation, paid for by her generous divorce settlement.

Bobby Ray Shatney was another one. He sat cross-legged at the end of the table, staring at his hands. Not many people knew that Bobby Ray, at the tender age of thirteen, had gone on a killing spree that had wiped out his entire family, three neighbors, a UPS man, and a cocker spaniel. He had the clear-eyed innocence of a child, his murderous rages washed clean from his body for as long as he was protected from the society that asked too much of him.

He looked up, catching Luke's contemplative

gaze, and smiled in drugged-out bliss. Besides, he was too tranked to hurt anyone, even if he was tempted.

Things would be different when Luke left. When this all came crashing down, and Luke had no choice but to decamp, he'd be leaving Bobby Ray and a few other lost souls like him to wreak havoc on the world and the other innocents who filled Santa Dolores. There would be no one to drug them into complacency. No one to control them with their childish belief in messiahs and salvation.

Luke Bardell knew what it was to kill. There wasn't a day he spent on this earth when he didn't remember the feel of the knife sliding past flesh and fat and muscle, sliding deep. The rich, black color of arterial blood, the rattle of death that came with shocking quickness. The smell of it.

They said it got easier. The more you killed, the more you wanted to repeat the act. Again and again. You could even grow to love it.

He didn't want to find out. He preferred his nightmares, the haunting that never quite left him. It was his own penitence, and the people around him recognized it without words, strengthening his hold over them.

But he would have to do something about Bobby Ray Shatney and the others before he left.

Rachel was seated between Catherine and Alfred

Waterston, and the two of them were exerting their usual well-bred charm. Catherine came from mainline Philadelphia, one of the oldest families in the country. She carried herself with patrician good cheer, the last of a line of harmless dilettantes whose unspoken breeding instilled awe in most of his nouveau riche followers. Alfred was just as impressive, combining the stuffy bedside manner of a cancer specialist with the sharp-brained diligence of a financial wizard.

Rachel was succumbing to Catherine quite nicely, coming dangerously close to smiling. He suspected a smile would transform that pale, unhappy face. He wasn't sure he wanted to discover just how much. A challenge was one thing. A weakness was another. Not that he counted much in this life as a weakness. A good steak, maybe. A plump, tender woman who asked him no questions and made no demands. And they weren't weaknesses, merely some of the things he occasionally allowed himself. When no one was looking.

She turned in his direction, but he'd already looked away, guided by that preternatural instinct that had saved his ass on more than one occasion. He smiled benevolently at Bobby Ray, mentally calibrating the dose he'd need to keep him peaceful. Maybe just a simple overdose when the time came. Murder by remote control. He could do it if he had to.

The time was coming closer, and Luke knew it. Stella Connery had been a herald, and Luke had always been a man to pay attention to signs and omens.

Her daughter's arrival was the beginning of the end. The end of the soft, cushy life he'd been living. And it wasn't coming a minute too soon.

The Grandfathers wouldn't like it. He didn't make the mistake of underestimating them—at least Alfred would have noticed his restlessness. They'd be making contingency plans, to keep the Foundation going, to keep the money rolling in, keep the faith alive without their charismatic messiah.

He wondered what they had planned for him.

Evil was all around, in this large, peaceful room, full of gentle, passive people. Evil was an old enemy, a close companion.

Maybe it was time he introduced spoiled, angry Rachel Connery to its hungry grip as well.

Georgia Reginald closed her eyes, smiled, and slipped peacefully closer to death. It had been a long wait, it seemed, since she was first diagnosed with that particularly virulent form of cancer. Thank God she'd already been a follower. Luke had shown her the way, and when the doctors at the Foundation hospice had made their devastating discovery she found she'd almost welcomed the news.

She'd never been in any pain, and she knew she could thank her newfound faith for that. She never would have guessed that cancer had invaded and spread throughout her seemingly healthy, sixty-year-old body. After all, there was no cancer on either side of her family, and she'd always prided herself on how well she took care of her health.

Ah, but fate had been a trickster, as Luke and his disciples had warned her. The cancer had come with no sign, no warning, as it had to so many of her friends. They'd done everything they could, the poison, slash and burn of cancer treatment, and nothing had helped. She was weak now, and ready to go, but she wanted to see Luke one last time.

They'd sent for him. If she could just hold out for a little while longer, she could look at him and dream that she was young again. That those eyes were looking only at her.

She wanted to be the one to tell him about the money. The Grandfathers knew, of course. Particularly Alfred, who'd overseen her care. He'd helped her make the arrangements, but she knew that Luke paid no attention to the financial aspects of the Foundation. His mind and soul were settled on higher things—that was why he had the Grand-fathers around. To take care of business.

Her estate would help take care of a lot of business, and it was the one thing that brought her joy.

There was a scraping sound, and she used the last of her energy to open her eyes. Luke stood there beside the bed, his face almost obscured by his long hair, and she wished she could reach out and stroke it, when no one was ever allowed to touch him. Surely he'd allow her that much.

She tried to lift her hand, but she had no strength. There were others in the room—she couldn't quite focus, but it didn't matter anymore. Just then she wasn't interested in anyone but Luke.

She opened her mouth to speak, but nothing came out. She felt Luke's warm hand pressed against her icy skin, but it was too late to warm her.

"Time to let go, Georgia," he said, his rich, deep voice washing over her in waves of elegant longing. He held her hand, as someone drew closer, dressed in the pale blue colors of the medical personnel. The needle was cold in her arm, filling her veins with death.

She opened her eyes wide, looking for Luke. But all she saw was emptiness.

3

Calvin Leigh was fifty-seven years old and was often mistaken for a child. It wasn't just his height—at four feet nine he didn't quite qualify as a little person, but he came close. His youthful face added to the effect of innocent agelessness, as well as his light voice and his seemingly sweet manner. Over the years he'd learned to use those physical traits wisely.

It hadn't been easy growing up on the South Side of Chicago. His ancestry was a racial mix of such varying backgrounds that it was almost impossible to recognize a dominant strain. Which meant, of course, that everyone hated him. Hated him for being black, white, Hispanic, Asian, and Jewish. Hated him for his stunted growth and his strangeness.

It was a wonder he'd survived the regular,

vicious beatings that were part of his home and street life. But he had, and it wasn't until he was in his late forties, doing time for passing bad checks, that he found out why.

He'd met Luke Bardell, and known peace. He'd been put on this earth, given these various trials and challenges, to prepare himself to be Luke's helper. It was all he'd ever asked in life: a purpose. A cause. And Luke Bardell was that cause.

Not that he had any illusions about the man he chose to follow, out of prison and into the richest con game a man could ever imagine. He knew Luke better than anyone. He was privy to the secrets, the needs, the plans that no one else could even imagine of their sainted leader. He knew where the money was, both his and Luke's share. And he knew the escape route by heart.

But he also knew Luke better than Luke knew himself. Knew that his strength, his ability to draw people to him, to move them, was more than a con man's ultimate gift. It went beyond that into realms so bizarre that Calvin couldn't attempt to understand it, and he didn't try. It was simply something he felt with his heart.

Something Luke himself denied.

Calvin had known Stella Connery was trouble, and he'd welcomed her death with unholy relief. Only to find it wasn't that simple. Her daughter was a far greater threat.

One that had to be neutralized.

She was here now, and he could see the way Luke watched her. Calvin prided himself on being more attuned to Luke than anyone, and he could practically read Luke's mind. He wanted her. Despite or perhaps because of, the threat she posed to everything they'd worked for, he wanted Rachel Connery.

And Calvin meant to see he didn't have her.

He wasn't squeamish about death. He wasn't squeamish about anything; he did what needed to be done. He would do it again.

Before Luke could make one mistake too many.

Considering the fact that she was sick to her stomach by the time she finished the meal the Foundation provided for her, considering she was feeling restless, edgy, and resentful, it seemed odd to Rachel that she slept well in that narrow bed. Perhaps it was simple relief that she hadn't had to deal with another confrontation with the leader of this odd group of people.

Except that she had to admit they weren't that odd. Alfred Waterston wasn't that dissimilar from several of the wealthy men her mother had married, although he seemed kinder. And Catherine seemed unquestionably friendly, helpful, and even maternal, with a genuine warmth that was almost unsettling to someone of Rachel's emotionally deprived background.

The other Grandfathers were familiar as well—decent, stable, slightly stuffy men and women who seemed more at ease in a boardroom than seated around a table full of lentils and soy. They were the kind of people she'd worked with in New York, the kind of people whose greatest flights of spirituality usually concerned a bottom line. What they were doing dressed in matching cotton and following a charismatic con artist was beyond her comprehension.

Because that was what Luke Bardell was. Everyone else in this place might be blinded by his otherworldly air, his aura of saintliness, but Rachel wasn't other people. She had come for Luke Bardell's head, and she wasn't about to be blinded into thinking he was anything but evil incarnate.

Everyone in that huge room had seemed equally, stupidly devoted to their leader, from the Grandfathers to Luke's strange-looking companion, Calvin. If her secret cohort was there, she wasn't able to hazard a guess as to which follower was really a pained disbeliever.

She couldn't remember her dreams, which was nothing new in itself. She wasn't the sort who paid much attention to her dreams if she could help it—what she did remember of them was always unsettling. She knew by the way the sheets were twisted around her body that her dreams that night had been disturbing. It was little wonder. There was death here. She could smell it in the dryness of the air, feel it through her sweat-damp skin.

There was a new set of cotton clothing for her, this time in a pale shade of blue that was slightly more flattering than the green they'd offered her before. She ignored them anyway, and by the time she emerged from her shower, dressed in jeans and a loose cotton shirt, they were gone from the foot of the bed and her door was ajar. Obviously the chair she'd wedged under the handle was useless.

The hall was deserted. She was in desperate need of caffeine, and she would have sold her soul for one mug of it, strong and black. She wondered if Luke Bardell would consider that price too high.

She was about to find out.

"Looking for breakfast?"

There was nothing sinister in the question, or the soft tone of Luke's voice. She didn't like the way he seemed to materialize in the empty corridor without any warning, but for the possibility of coffee she was willing to be pleasant.

Rachel stopped, guarding her expression. "I suppose coffee might be too much to hope for?" she said. "Or do you allow caffeine in this place?"

"We have a grain beverage that's quite energizing."

"I should have known." She didn't bother to disguise the disgust in her voice. "You know that when people are deprived of caffeine they become irritable and unpleasant?"

"That should be quite a change for you," he murmured without blinking.

"And they get terrible headaches," she added, undeterred.

"Let me know if you develop one and we'll do a healing for you."

The very notion filled her with horror. "No, thank you. I can take care of myself."

"But isn't it better to accept help from others?"

"Not particularly," Rachel said.

He wasn't that close to her. Luke Bardell wasn't a man who crowded his audience, who used physical intimidation to gain his power. He didn't need to. He was several feet away from her in the empty hallway, seemingly relaxed, at ease, almost ethereal. "Ah, Rachel," he said, "you have so very much to learn from us. I'm glad you didn't wait too long to visit."

"Learn from you?"

"That's why you're here, isn't it? To learn everything you can about the Foundation of Being? You want to know our ways, our philosophy, follow our teachings for a while. Don't you?"

That was about the last thing Rachel had in mind, but if he was so blindly egocentric to think so, then she wasn't about to enlighten him. "Of course," she said.

"I know perfectly well the only reason you'd want to learn our ways is to destroy us," Luke continued in the same calm voice, leaning against the stucco wall. "That's a risk that Catherine and the Grandfathers are completely willing to take."

"I don't want to destroy anyone!" she protested, looking at the man she wanted to bring down.

"Then why are you here?" The question was simple and unanswerable, except with a lie.

Rachel knew how to lie when the situation called for it, and she could be very convincing. After all, she'd learned from a master—her mother. "You invited me," she said.

"And we're not afraid of anything you may discover. Stay with us, Rachel, learn from us. And if you can find any proof, any sign of wrongdoing or evil, then we will learn from you."

It was a lovely little speech, simple, graceful, calculated to make her hang her head in shame. Too bad it was wasted on a recalcitrant soul like Stella Connery's daughter, Rachel thought. Too bad it came from the mouth of a murderer. She mustn't forget that fact, ever.

She managed a convincing smile. "That's what I'm here for," she said.

"And where do you want to start?"

"With coffee."

She didn't like his smile. She didn't like the fact that he was tall, that his voice was gentle, that his eyes were feral. Most of all she didn't like the fact that he made no effort to intimidate her. As if he already knew the arcane influence he held over everyone, including her.

She didn't believe in pacts with the devil. She didn't even necessarily believe in evil. But if there was a devil, then Luke Bardell had partied with him and prospered.

He pushed away from the wall and she stood her ground. "With the right diet, you won't need artificial stimulants, Rachel," he said. He held out his hand to her, patiently, like a hunter trying to tame a wild beast. "Come. We'll feed you well, and start your training."

He had beautiful hands. Long, elegant fingers, narrow wrists, blue-veined and strong-looking. There was a tattoo encircling each of his wrists—a rough, ink-blue bracelet of thorns, like a martyr's crown.

There was no way in hell she was going to touch those beautiful hands. "Training?" she said, skirting out of his way.

"Classes will begin at sunset. A very peaceful time here in the Southwest—I think you'll find it conducive to the meditative state. Where would you like to work?"

"Work?" She sounded like an idiot parrot. He'd

started down the hallway, expecting her to join him. She did so, keeping a safe distance.

"Everyone works at the Foundation," he said. "You can choose what you'd like—physical or mental labor or a combination of the two. You can scrub toilets, work in the kitchen, or help on the grounds."

"I'm not much on manual labor." She managed to sound almost disinterested. "What about office work? It's what I'm trained for."

"Ah, Rachel, your sweet faith touches me," he said. "But I don't think so. I'm not certain I want you delving into the Foundation's records." He paused at the double doors to the dining hall.

"Afraid I'll unearth your dirty secrets?"

He took her barb with a faint, annoying smile. "What secrets? The fact that I'm an ex-con, who killed someone in a bar fight? That I did time in prison, and might very well have ended up back there, or dead in the next fight, if it hadn't been for enlightenment? No, Rachel. Everyone knows about my past. We're a trusting group here, but for some reason I wouldn't put it past you to plant something incriminating in our computer."

"The thought hadn't occurred to me," she said with complete truthfulness. She had very little doubt about her own ability to ferret out the truth behind Luke Bardell's idiot followers, and faking evidence seemed an unnecessary complication.

There was proof here, proof of monstrous evil, she just knew it. If they'd really killed Stella, then they might have killed others as well. Other rich, foolish women who could be flattered and seduced out of their money. And Rachel wouldn't rest until she found that proof that had been dangled in front of her nose by the anonymous letter, like a carrot in front of a stubborn mule.

"You'll need to learn to be more devious if you're going to go into battle against the devil," Luke murmured.

"Is that what I'm doing? Is that what you are?"

He looked down at her, his eyes dreamy and far away, his wide, disturbing mouth curved in a holy smile tinged with mockery. "God only knows, Rachel."

He told himself he should be disappointed. She was ridiculously easy to read most of the time, and he'd wanted a challenge. She wasn't afraid to show her hatred, though, which was a refreshing change. He was getting mortally tired of people looking up at him with glazed adoration. Only Calvin dared contradict him, and he did it in private. Everyone else was willing to lay down their lives for the mere gift of his smile. Or at least they told themselves they were.

Rachel Connery was probably willing to lay down her life for his head on a platter. She wasn't going to have to pay that price, and she wasn't going to win that prize. He still wasn't quite certain what he had in store for her in the long run. Maybe just the perverse delight of seducing her soul and then disillusioning her as he made his escape.

She still refused to wear the Foundation clothes, but that wouldn't last much longer. He might miss the sight of her long legs, her trim ass in jeans that were too loose for his taste. But he'd be able to console himself with the knowledge that the body beneath the soft cotton clothes would belong to him if and when he wanted it.

He knew where he'd start her off, even though Catherine had voiced a protest and Calvin, when he'd heard, shook his head in grim disapproval. She wasn't ready for the hospice center—it would remind her of Stella and strengthen her rage just when he wanted to demoralize her. He could send her to the meditation center to scrub toilets, but slave labor wasn't how he wanted to bring her down.

No, he had a much nicer place for Miss Rachel Connery with the broomstick up her ass. He'd send her to the psycho ward, and let her see what happened to those who doubted the power of the Foundation of Being.

He glanced down at her as she stood outside the refectory. Not his kind of woman. Too angry, too upper-class, too lean, and too fierce. But she smelled damned good. And even her skinny little body called to him, even as she glared at him, making little attempt at superficial courtesy. He wondered what she would do if he pushed her back against the wall and put his hand between her legs?

She'd probably scream her patrician little head off, he thought with dark amusement. She was a far cry from her mother, with the hungry appetites and the taste for trash. Princess Rachel wouldn't be interested in dallying with the devil. And he doubted she needed Stella's money. People like her came equipped with generations' worth of money—she didn't need Stella's, and he did. It was just that simple.

She just wanted to screw him. Figuratively speaking, of course. He smiled down at her, using his sweetest smile, the one that melted most of his followers, the one that left Rachel stony-eyed and glaring.

"Are you afraid of illness?"

"I'm not afraid of anything," she said.

"Aren't you? Well, you're young," he said, deliberately dismissive.

"I suppose you think that when I get to your advanced age I'll be wise enough to be frightened," she snapped, obviously irritated by him.

He wanted to keep that irritation alive. It amused him, and it made her vulnerable. "Somehow I can't imagine you ever being as old as I am," he said.

"I did my research, O Great White Spirit," she said sarcastically. "You're somewhere in your late thirties. You think I'm not going to make it another ten years?"

"Oh, I imagine you'll live to a ripe old age, unless you annoy someone enough to kill you. But you'll always be an angry child, spoiled and fretful." He waited patiently to see her reaction to that particular salvo.

It wasn't what he expected. She didn't go pale with rage or denial—she seemed more amused at his description. "You think so?" she murmured. "And what will save me from such a horrible fate? Wearing pastel cotton pajamas and listening to your pontifications?"

"I seldom pontificate," he said. He'd misjudged her, not a mistake he often made. He'd viewed her as a spoiled little rich girl, wanting her own way. He was beginning to suspect things weren't quite that simple. What else had Stella said about her? He couldn't remember, and details like those were too important to overlook. "You might start with an open mind."

He'd managed to move closer to her without her realizing it. She was amazingly skittish, considering how determinedly confrontational she was. "An open mind?" she echoed. "I suppose I could try it." Her smile was incredibly snotty. "There's a first time for everything."

He wasn't about to rise to her bait. "Including a grain beverage for breakfast and a hard day's labor," he said, pushing open the refectory doors. "I think we'll start you out in the east wing of the hospital, helping the caregivers. You'll feel at home there."

"Sounds lovely."

"I'll leave you in Calvin's capable hands. He knows more about the running of this place than I do, and he'll get you settled in your work. You can even see if he'll divulge all the dark secrets behind this pristine exterior on your way to the east wing."

She glanced over at Calvin, waiting calmly by the table, and he had to admire her sangfroid. She didn't even blink. "What's in the east wing? The nonbelievers?"

He bestowed his sweetest smile on her. "No. The mental patients."

Calvin's loyalties and goals were clear, and they had been since the day he'd first set eyes on Luke Bardell. He didn't like to remember that time—it had been a bad stretch for both of them, and he was a simple man with simple needs. Dwelling on fear and pain was a waste. Particularly when things were going so well right now.

Not that it was safe. Things were never safe, and Luke ought to have known that, but after years of people telling him he was perfect, the man was starting to believe it. Until Calvin set him straight.

Luke had enemies. More than that stuck-up bitch who wanted to get her hands on her mother's money. Fat chance of that—in the years he'd known Luke he'd never known him to willingly give up anything he'd earned, stolen, cheated, or lucked into. Not if someone tried to take it away.

Rachel Connery was far from the worst of Luke's problems, but she wasn't harmless either. If he started ignoring the little threats, underestimating them, then sooner or later he would lose it all.

Calvin didn't intend to let that happen. He needed Luke too much. He needed Luke's gift for conning money out of the most unlikely sources. He needed Luke's cool, wise, sensible attitude toward a life that started out bad and had taken too damned long to get comfortable. He needed Luke's love and friendship. And there weren't any lengths he wouldn't go to, to protect those things he needed.

Including disposing of an inconvenience like Rachel Connery. He'd done it before and he had no qualms about doing it again. An ugly necessity. Luke had never been able to make peace with the ugly side of reality, and it was up to Calvin to look out for him. He protected his own, and he knew a threat when he saw one. He just wondered if Luke had lost that particular ability.

Rachel Connery was a threat all right, he thought, as he led her across the compound beneath the bright New Mexico sun an hour later. "How long have you known Luke? How did you happen to meet?" she asked in a light, innocent voice that didn't fool him for a minute.

He was tempted to tell her, just to see her reaction. Pretty little rich girl with her safe life, she wouldn't know a thing about . . .

"Long enough," he said.

"You're not like the others."

He looked at her. "I'm not the only freak here," he said. "You stay here long enough and you'll run into people even stranger than I am."

She didn't instantly deny he was a freak, which raised her a small notch in his grudging esteem. Calvin knew who and what he was, and polite, politically correct responses didn't make it any better.

"I meant you aren't sweet and saintly like the others," she said. "Everyone else seems like something out of a *Brady Bunch* rerun."

"I wouldn't know," he said. "When I was growing up there wasn't much time for television." He pulled open the heavy carved door of the restoration center and started down the hallway, knowing she'd follow. "Gretchen's the caregiver in charge—you just do what she tells you and you'll be fine. But remember to keep away from Angel."

"Angel?"

"Most of the patients are safe enough. They're suffering from various forms of sickness, and with enough healing they'll be better. But Angel's beyond our help. She's delusional, and dangerous. She'll be leaving here tomorrow, but in the meantime don't go anywhere near her room. It's kept locked, so you shouldn't have any problem."

"Is she really a danger?"

"To herself, and to everyone else." He glanced at her. She was taking it all in, rising to the bait like a starving guppie. "She thinks there's a conspiracy going on. That Luke's just using everybody, stealing their money, and then murdering anyone who gets in his way. Particularly the old ones who didn't have that long to live. She thinks he helps them along. Imagine that?"

"Imagine," Rachel echoed faintly.

"She'll try to wheedle her way around you. Don't listen to her. It's all a pack of lies." He rapped on a heavy door with a high, barred window. "Isn't it, Angel?"

"Go to hell." Angel's voice floated through the barred window, sharp and level.

"See what I mean?" Calvin said. "She sounds as sane as you or me. But don't believe it." He raised his voice, pitching it toward the locked door. "I'm leaving a new helper, Angel. Her name's Rachel, and she'll get you anything you need. Just don't go

playing your tricks, trying to fill her head full of
your lies. You hear me?"

Her response was succinct and obscene, and
Calvin laughed. "I'll come back for you just before five," he said. "That's when you start your
training with Luke."

"Whoopee," Rachel muttered, glancing toward
the locked door.

"Don't even think about it," he warned her.
"She's dangerous."

"I'm not interested in endangering myself,"
Rachel said with great dignity.

Sure you're not, he thought. He only hoped he'd
done a good enough job priming her curiosity.
If Rachel Connery proved true to form, he could
count on Angel to take care of the rest. And he
could meet Luke's accusing gaze with relative
innocence.

He loved it when things fit together.

It took Rachel forever to get to Angel. The
woman didn't make a sound behind her heavy,
locked door, and Gretchen, a long-haired, middle-
aged woman in pale green pajamas, kept Rachel
reasonably busy, reading to one patient who barely
seemed to listen, rolling yarn for another who kept
knitting the same square over and over again and
then pulling it out. It wasn't until late afternoon
that she had a few moments to herself. Gretchen

had gone for a cup of green tea, a refreshment that filled Rachel with horror.

The corridor outside Angel's room was deserted. The window was low enough that Rachel could peer inside, and the sight that met her eyes stunned her.

It was no madwoman curled in a corner, drooling and babbling. The woman who sat at the table, writing in a journal, looked neat, sane, and even pretty, her thick blond hair curling on her shoulders, her face determined.

"Angel?" Rachel whispered.

The woman lifted her head, staring at the door. Her eyes were clear, calm. "What do you want?"

"It's Rachel. Stella Connery's daughter. Did you know my mother when she was here?"

Angel put her pencil down. "I knew Stella," she said. "They killed her."

Rachel froze. "Are you the one who wrote to me?" she asked urgently.

"Wrote to you? I don't even know you. I knew your mother. They killed her." There was the madness, and yet she sounded so matter-of-fact, so reasonable.

"Why would they do that? She was dying anyway."

"So they say. Maybe she really did have cancer. Maybe they hurried her along to put her out of her misery. Maybe that's what they did to all the others."

"All what others?"

Angel rose and came to the door. She was a tall, slender woman, with strong-looking hands. "All the people who've died here. All the rich people who've come here to follow Luke's way, only to find they have a terminal disease that no one can help. They die. They die very quickly. And they leave all their money to the Foundation."

"How do you know this?"

Angel's mouth twisted in a bitter smile. "Why do you think I'm locked in here? You think people are really nutcases like that little weirdo Calvin said? They're trying to silence me. I found out too much, but they don't dare kill me. Yet."

"Are you going to have your parents do something about it . . . ?"

"Parents? My parents have been dead for years. That's just another one of Calvin's lies. I don't know what they have planned for me, but by tomorrow I don't think I'll be caring. Unless you help me."

"How can I help you?"

"Let me out of here. Give me a chance to get away from them. You don't know how bad they really are, how evil. You don't know what they're capable of. I have all the proof I need right here in my journal—times, places, names of victims—but they'll never let me keep it." She paused. "I could give it to you. That way if something happens to me, at least it won't all be covered up. You'll do that for me, at least, won't you? Keep the journal, make sure it gets to the right people?"

She didn't even hesitate. Who was she to trust, Luke Bardell's right-hand man, or a woman much like herself, who knew just what evil was going on beneath the saintly exterior of the Foundation of Being? Yet she denied being the author of that chilling letter. And if she wasn't, who else knew of Luke's horrific sideline? How many people were in on it?

"Does anyone else know what's going on? Is there anyone else I could talk to about my mother?" she persisted.

"Your mother was a believer. Almost until the end. There are others who've begun to suspect, but they keep us separated, locked up if they can."

"Surely she must have had friends here . . . ?"

"Stella was only interested in what Luke could give her."

That was her mother all right, Rachel thought grimly. All her life had centered around whatever man she currently slept with.

"Let me out," Angel said. "And I'll give you the names of people who might know something about your mother."

It was too much to resist. "Yes," she said.

Angel didn't move. "You have to open the door," she said patiently. "I can't slide the notebook underneath. You'll need the keys."

Rachel looked around her, ignoring the prickle of uneasiness. "I don't know where they are."

"In the drawer. Second drawer down on the right. Help me, Rachel. For your mother's sake. And help those poor souls who've already died."

The key was there. It fit into the lock easily enough, and when Rachel pushed the door open Angel was standing a few feet back, a relieved smile on her face, the journal open in her hands.

"You see," she said. "This has all the answers."

Rachel looked at the open pages of the book. Word after word of scrawled obscenity, senseless, wandering across the paper, totally insane.

She took one step away, one small, infinitesimal step back from the woman who towered over her. But it was already too late.

"Oh, noooo," Angel whispered, her face still eerily calm. "You're one of them, aren't you? I should have known. You were sent to tempt me. I won't allow it. He sent you. But he's mine. Luke is mine. You won't have him!"

Rachel had half turned to run when Angel's body slammed into her, throwing her to the ground, knocking the air out of her. Those strong hands closed around her throat, and even as Rachel clawed at them, she could feel her breath slipping farther and farther away, as Angel shrieked obscenities, slamming her head against the floor.

And in that moment Rachel knew she was going to die.

4

They convened once more, the Grandfathers, and their faces were grave in the reflection of the firelight. "We're running out of time," the outsider said.

"Disrespectful," George Landers hissed in disapproval. He cherished his power, and disliked allowing a mere penitent into their closed meetings. But George was a physical coward. Willing to let others take the real risks, while he played with stocks and bonds.

Alfred held up a restraining hand, and the noise subsided. "This woman is dangerous," he said. "Her presence here is a disruption. She's forcing our hand, and the last thing we want to do is be precipitous. We need to take our time, make sure we don't make any mistakes. We need to get rid of her as quickly as possible."

"I'm working on it," said the outsider, ignoring George. "I have everything well in hand."

"And you aren't going to tell us?" the old woman next to him asked in a soft voice. She was sleeping with the outsider. She probably already knew the answer, Alfred thought with a disapproving sniff.

"The fewer people who know, the better. She'll be taken care of. Punished."

"And Luke?" George demanded, glaring at him.

"All in good time, Grandfather," the boy said with mocking courtesy. "All in good time."

It was dark when Rachel awoke, and there was pain. Warmth pressed down around her, cushioning her, and she kept her eyes shut against the wavering light that teased in the corner of her consciousness. If she opened her eyes she would have to acknowledge the pain, and she was afraid. Afraid there was too much for her to handle, afraid she would be vulnerable once more, when she'd spent so much of her life trying to fight her vulnerability.

She'd learned, early on, that people hurt you if they possibly could. She tried to make it very clear that no one could hurt her, ever again.

But someone had. Her throat was on fire, her head throbbed, and her entire body felt as if it had been trampled on by elephants. She didn't know where she was, or how she'd gotten there. She only knew she had to escape.

She blinked, unwillingly, finally giving in to the need to open her eyes. The room was murky, filled with a pungent smoke that ripped at her sore throat. For a moment she couldn't remember where she was, or what had happened.

The faint flute music that drifted from a distance was her first clue, though she was certain she'd never heard it before. She was in New Mexico. Land of enchantment, though the retreat center at Santa Dolores was leaving her far from enchanted.

She gradually realized she was lying on the floor, on some thin pallet in a dark, cavernous room. The flute music was coming from somewhere in the distance, the pungent smoke surrounded her. Her clothes were loose, comfortable, and she didn't have to look to know that Luke had eventually gotten his way. She was wearing one of their damned sets of pajamas.

She tried to lift her head, but the pain was so intense she let it sink back to the pallet with a groan. She could remember Angel now, the ill-named creature who'd tried to kill her, her strong hands around her throat, choking her, as she smashed her head against the hardwood floor.

Stupid, stupid, stupid, she berated herself. She'd come away with nothing but a bruised and battered body and a crazy woman's ravings. A pack of lies. Much as Rachel wanted to believe the worst of Luke Bardell and his followers, on reflection the notion of wholesale murder was far too melodramatic. There were easier ways to extort money from gullible people—con men and evangelists had known that over the centuries. They didn't have to resort to anything as messy as murder.

Rachel shifted, biting back the instinctive cry of pain. Lying on the floor wasn't her idea of comfort, and the incense-filled darkness felt more threatening than soothing. Even the knowledge that she was alone, to lick her wounds and mend, was little comfort . . . especially as she suddenly realized she wasn't alone at all.

She turned her head, slowly, carefully, the throbbing intensifying. In the misty darkness she could see him, sitting cross-legged, his hands upturned, resting on his knees, his eyes closed, his face serene. He looked like a lean, benevolent Buddha, though Rachel had no illusions. That meditative grace was purely for show. And she was far from an appreciative audience.

"We don't believe in the concept of sin." His voice was soft, deep, and his eyes didn't open.

"Convenient," she tried to say, but her voice was no more than a strangled gasp of air.

He opened his eyes and smiled at her with

annoying benevolence. "Very convenient," he agreed, though there was no way he could have understood her word. "It's an antiquated Judeo-Christian concept used to engender guilt and obedience."

He turned his hands flat, stretching out his long legs. "I'm not particularly interested in obedience from my followers. Which is fortunate, since I imagine obedience is the last thing I'll get from you. And I know you're not a follower," he added, before she could wreck her throat with a protest. "Not yet."

She sat up at that one, trying to speak, but her throat was so raw it brought wicked tears to her eyes. He watched her, unmoved.

"We believe in character defects instead of sin. Flaws that we try to mend, or accept if there's no changing them. You already know one of your major defects is pride. You were so certain you could control Angel, that you were right and the caregivers were wrong.

"Fortunately one of my flaws is a dislike of being kept waiting. Which worked out well for you, since I had someone go in search of you when you didn't arrive for your five o'clock training session. Otherwise I imagine Angel would have smashed in the back of your skull before too much longer." He sounded completely unmoved by the prospect.

"That would have solved your problems." At least that was what she tried to say. What came out was a harsh mumble.

"You might as well not bother," he murmured. "You'll just aggravate the damage, and no one can understand you anyway."

You can, she thought defiantly. *You know exactly what I'm thinking.*

His faint, cool smile was answer enough. "Lie back and close your eyes, Rachel. The caregivers have said you should rest your voice for twenty-four hours. They've given you herbs to help the pain and bruising. What you need now is rest."

There was no way she could disguise the alarm in her eyes at the thought of what Luke Bardell might think of as herbs. As usual he was a step ahead of her, reading her perfectly in the murky light. "The majority of the caregivers are licensed professionals who've chosen to follow a new path, Rachel. They're doctors and nurses and therapists. Alfred oversees them, guides them. Their care, combined with the healing forces of the believers, work miracles. Now lie down."

She glared at him in silent defiance.

"Lie down," he said again with great patience, "or I'll put my hands on you, and that's the last thing you want, isn't it?"

Her mute alarm was answer enough. She lay back on the pallet, noticing belatedly that for all its thinness it cushioned her bruised and aching body quite nicely.

"You're not afraid I'll hurt you," Luke continued in that voice that was perhaps one of the most dangerous of his very real weapons. "You know better than that. You're frightened of the alternative." He lifted his hands and looked at them absently, as if they belonged to someone else. Rachel looked too. They were such beautiful hands, strong, with their encircling tattoos of thorns, and for a brief, mad moment she wondered how they would feel, touching her.

She lifted her gaze, to look into his deep, unreadable eyes. There was no way he could guess what she'd been thinking, she told herself. But his faint smile, devoid of mockery, was unsettling.

"There's nothing to be afraid of," he said. "No one will hurt you, I promise."

Her body felt heavy, useless. She had no defenses, not even her voice, and he knew it. She couldn't move, couldn't speak, and her eyelids were so heavy she couldn't even glare at him. She sank back, mentally cursing him, cursing whatever drugs the benevolent caretakers had pumped into her system, cursing Angel, but most of all cursing herself for her stupid arrogance and pride in not recognizing the danger Angel presented. She'd been warned . . .

Of course, that warning had been couched in

deliberately provocative terms. Anyone with a rudimentary knowledge of human nature, Rachel Connery's in particular, would know that she would find the challenge irresistible. There was no avoiding the humiliating truth—she'd been set up. Offered to the homicidal Angel as a virgin sacrifice.

She didn't think they'd really wanted to kill her, or she'd be dead. It must have been along the lines of teaching her a lesson. She had no doubts whatsoever that the command had come from the man sitting beside her in the smoky darkness. Calvin would have been just carrying out orders.

Naturally, she'd been rescued in time. Bloody but unbowed, wasn't that the phrase?

She was so sleepy. Drugged, of course. She tried to rally her anger to keep her mind alert, her body awake, but it was no good. The flute music in the background was low, insinuating, sliding through her veins on tendrils of melody, and the incense burned in her eyes, her nostrils, cleansing, purifying.

She let herself sink, unwilling to fight any longer. Tomorrow would come, and she'd be stronger. Fueled with her righteous rage, she could fight then. For now she could float.

Luke stared down at her. He'd warned them to be sparing with their use of drugs, and in return he'd watched her struggle needlessly against their effects. She needed the healing powers his caregivers could provide. She needed the healing powers he could provide.

He'd first become aware of his odd gift while he was in prison, and he counted its appearance as the start of his new vocation as messiah. The notion always amused him. He had no explanation for what happened when he focused his energy on some wounded creature. Calvin would have been dead if it weren't for Luke, holding his hand, willing the strength back into him after he'd been savagely beaten and raped in Joliet.

Rachel wasn't going to die, no thanks to Calvin. Luke had no illusions about who had set Rachel up. Calvin had delivered her to the psycho ward, and if it weren't for Luke's instincts it might have been too late.

Calvin would have felt no regrets, and nothing Luke could say to him would instill any kind of conventional sense of morality. He considered Rachel Connery a threat to Luke. And when it came to his self-appointed need to protect Luke, Calvin could be entirely ruthless.

Rachel needed to be neutralized and disposed of, as quickly as possible. On that point Luke agreed with Calvin completely. They were simply at odds as to how to best go about it.

It was as simple as their disparate natures, that

Calvin would choose murder by proxy, and Luke would choose seduction. And obviously he wasn't going to be allowed the luxury of doing it leisurely.

She was breathing deeply. They'd stripped her when they'd brought her to the trauma center, and like the rest of the followers she wore no constricting underwear beneath the loose cotton robes. She was too thin, but he wanted to see her breasts. It would be a simple enough matter to unfasten the tie and expose them to the air.

Unfortunately there was a small cadre of followers in the corner, meditating devotedly for her recovery. He'd have to wait for a more private time to see her, touch her. He leaned over her, his long hair obscuring his face in the darkness, and he let his hands skim her face.

She didn't move, didn't quiver, lost in a drug-induced dream. He expected those dreams were erotic.

Her skin was flushed beneath his cool hands. He let his thumbs stroke her eyelids, his long fingers cradle the back of her head, moving down to the back of her neck. Her mouth was open slightly, and he let his thumbs trail over her lips. Soft.

Even in the murky light he could see the bruising on her throat. She didn't like being mute—it made her furious, and it gave him a wickedly unfair advantage. If she continued to be unable to

speak there was no way she could cause trouble—
she'd be trapped here, at his mercy.

Ah, but she was already at his mercy, though
she hadn't quite realized it yet. She was already
trapped. And he didn't want this to be too easy. He
put his hands on her bruised throat, easily encircling it, his fingers covering the marks of Angel's
strong hands, and he felt the energy flowing from
him, into her.

She jerked, as if she'd had an electric shock,
and he released her immediately, sitting back on
his heels. She was abnormally sensitive to his
touch. Good.

They were watching him jealously, longingly,
from their corner by the incense brazier, watching as he put his hands over her. Waiting for him
to finish. He wouldn't disappoint them.

He stretched out over her, only their clothes
touching, as he held himself a few scant inches
above her, his muscles taut with the effort. It had
been a long time since he'd been tempted to give
in to his powerful appetites, to let his body sink
down on top of a woman's, to touch and taste
and take. He wasn't sure if it was simply that he
was coming to the natural end of this odd period
in his life, or whether it had something to do with
Rachel herself.

He doubted it was Rachel. He liked women.
Liked their curves and their scents and the sweet

noises they made when he fucked them. He liked their temper and their intelligence and their nurturing. But he'd never found a woman who could make him risk anything he'd gained in this life, and he wasn't about to start with a cool bitch like Stella's daughter.

She was warm, the heat rising from her body, and he was so cold. In her drugged stupor she looked younger, gentle, capable of healing a man with a wounded soul . . .

He levered himself away from her, almost too quickly, collapsing beside her in sudden exhaustion. If she ever found a man with a wounded soul, a man fool enough to trust her, she'd flay him alive with that tongue of hers.

Lucky for him he needed nothing and no one. Lucky for him he'd met hundreds of Rachel Connerys in his life. Rich, spoiled, searching for some kind of meaning. They didn't know the secret of the universe, and he wasn't about to tell them if they hadn't figured it out on their own. That life was essentially meaningless.

She was breathing more easily now, the rasp in her damaged throat quieted. He stretched out beside her on the hard stone floor, not touching her, letting the music flow around them as he concentrated on gathering his depleted energy.

Few people would dare approach him in those circumstances. He could feel their intrusive presence, and he knew it had to be Calvin or Catherine. He guessed it was Catherine—Calvin already knew the sting of Luke's displeasure.

He didn't move, didn't bother to open his eyes as Catherine knelt down by his head. She was a smart old lady; there were times when he wondered just how much she knew, or guessed, about the secret workings of the Foundation of Being. She reminded him of Granny Sue, the old woman who'd taken him in when he first arrived in Chicago, a tough-talking, chain-smoking ex-hooker who'd taught her daughters how to turn tricks by the time they were fourteen. There was a similar ruthlessness about the two of them, though Catherine, with her blue blood and her perfect manners, hid it better than most. She was more than a match for some of the worst cons he'd known. More than a match for Calvin.

She waited in respectful silence, and he held it long enough for her to get restless before he opened his eyes. "Blessings, Catherine," he said. Rachel didn't move, still lost in a deep, dreaming sleep.

"You're going to have to do something about Calvin," Catherine said. "He's become unstable."

"I thought it was Angel McGuiness who was unstable," he murmured.

"She's no longer an issue. Calvin, on the other hand, is becoming more of a problem. You don't deny he's responsible for this? That he deliberately endangered Rachel?"

"I don't deny it. I'm just not certain why he did it."

"He must think she's some sort of threat. Which is ridiculous, of course. We have nothing to worry about, no secrets to hide. Rachel is a severely troubled young woman, looking for meaning in life. We can help her find the answers she needs. If Calvin would keep his murderous tendencies to himself."

"Calvin can be a bit . . . overenthusiastic where I'm concerned," Luke said. "I hadn't realized he was worried about her presence here. I've spoken to him. He expressed the proper shame and repentance."

"So it won't happen again?" Catherine persisted, forgetting, as she often did, that she was in the presence of her spiritual master. Generations of old Philadelphia money made subservience difficult.

It was easy enough to remind her, with the touch of his cool hand on her dry, aging flesh. She jumped, startled, suddenly contrite.

"Forgive me, Luke," she murmured. "I'm just an old woman who worries too much. Of course you've got things well in hand. I'm just concerned about the girl—she's a sweet thing, despite her anger."

He controlled his amusement at the notion of Rachel's alleged sweetness. "Of course she is, Catherine. And I know that we can all help her basic goodness and gentleness come through." *As long as Calvin doesn't try to off her again,* he added to himself. *And assuming there's any goodness and gentleness there to be brought out.*

"You'll show her the way," Catherine murmured.

"I'll try," he said, wondering just how drugged Rachel was. He wanted to look at her. Touch her. Let his bare skin rest against her. He wanted to fuck her, but having sex with a comatose woman wasn't particularly appealing, even if it was the only way he could have her for now.

"I'll leave you," Catherine said. "She's already looking better—I think her color's improved. Shall I make arrangements for her to be brought back to her room? Or do you want her in the infirmary?"

"Later," he said. "Take the healers with you. I want to concentrate on her without any distractions."

"You're too good," Catherine said in a husky voice, rising with surprising grace given her age. Within moments they were gone, all of them, and he was alone in the murky, cavernous room with Rachel Connery, so deep in sleep that she'd never remember a thing.

No one would dare interrupt him. Only Calvin, and in his current disgrace he wouldn't show his face until tomorrow at the very earliest. Luke had hours to himself, and a surprisingly sensual woman to play with.

It was a good thing he was such an amoral bastard, he thought, propping himself up on one elbow and surveying her. Other men might have qualms, scruples, all those strange, crippling moral dilemmas that had never bothered Luke Bardell. Other men would be shocked at the very notion of taking advantage of a drugged woman who'd just gone through the kind of ordeal Rachel had.

Fortunately Luke wasn't other men. Never had been. He reached out and began to untie the knot that held the loose tunic top closed over her breasts.

His hand shook slightly, which surprised him. He must be hornier than he thought. It hadn't been that long, but there was something about the night, and the woman, that made him feel dangerous.

Her skin was a pale white-gold in the darkness, and she seemed almost peaceful. He knew it was an illusion. She was driven, determined, Stella had told him, on one of the rare occasions she'd talked about anything but herself.

He knew what was driving her now. Her determination to destroy him. The very thought amused him as he pushed the jacket off her shoulders. Narrow shoulders, oddly defenseless-looking. People had tried to destroy him since before he was born, starting with his grandparents' attempt to make his mother abort him, his so-called father, on through the gangs in prison, the cadres of lawyers, the angry young woman who lay motionless, sleeping, beneath his impassive gaze.

And no one could. He had a gift for survival, for escape when things threatened to get too bad.

But there was no need for escape right now. For the next few hours he could enjoy himself with his new toy. And if she remembered anything the next day, it would all seem like an erotic dream, one she'd be ashamed to admit she'd had.

He let his fingers skim down her flat stomach to the drawstring of her pants. Smooth skin, silky.

And he leaned down to taste it.

5

Rachel dreamed again, a shifting mélange of blood and violence. Of an angel, screaming in her face as she wrapped strong fingers around her throat, closing off her breath, her life, and somewhere in the distance was the faint sound of the flute.

Her eyes refused to open, no matter how hard she struggled against the heavy veils of sleep. And the murderous creature straddling her, strangling her, the long hair falling in Rachel's face, was now a fallen angel, a creature of light and darkness. Even as she recognized the threat, the hands no longer punished, they caressed her throat, her neck. And everywhere they touched, healing followed.

The fallen angel was a man, Lucifer, kicked out of heaven for wanting too much power. He would rather reign in hell than serve in heaven. But was she in hell now, or floating somewhere in between?

He touched her with his mouth, and she shivered in the darkness, resistant, aching. Her hands were by her sides, held down by someone far stronger as he leaned over her, blotting out what little light there was. She was hot, burning up, and he was cool, and sweet, a calm bastion of healing and serenity. He was what she wanted, what she needed so desperately.

He would give her love. He would give her peace. And total, eventual destruction.

Bobby Ray Shatney lit a cigarette, cupping it in his hand to keep the wind away from the match. It was late, pitch-dark outside, and if anyone bothered to look out a window they'd see the glow of his cigarette, and they'd go running to Luke like self-righteous little snitches.

He didn't think Luke would be surprised. He knew everything. All he had to do was turn his eyes on Bobby Ray, and his soul was naked before him. Luke knew his weaknesses, for cigarettes and pussy, for pain and for redemption. He knew Bobby Ray would die for him. Would kill for him.

It was a special bond.

He didn't even need Luke's words—there was a magical thread of communication between the two of them. Bobby Ray knew when Luke wanted him to punish someone, for the sake of the community. Everything Bobby Ray did was for Luke. Every drag on his cigarette, every woman he fucked, every person he killed, he did it for Luke, on Luke's unspoken orders. And in return he had Luke's unspoken gratitude and approval. Which was reward enough for Bobby Ray.

That new one, though. He wasn't sure what Luke wanted done with her. That little gnome Calvin had almost gotten her killed, a stupid move, but then, what could you expect from a midget ex-con? If he'd been trying to anticipate Luke's needs he'd blown it, for all of them.

She was a complication, a danger, and had been since Alfred had finished with Stella. Stella had hated her own child, something Bobby Ray understood only too well. Bringing her here, luring her here, was the least he could do. He did what he was told, to a point, and Catherine had told him to do this, for Stella, and for Luke.

Rachel reminded him of his older sister Melanie, with her spoiled mouth and her attitude. He'd killed Melanie first, before the others got home, taking his time with her.

He sucked the smoke deep in his lungs, then blew it out, peering through it with half-closed eyes. It danced in front of him, shifting and drifting, taking form slowly. He watched it, waiting for a sign. Which way should he go?

The smoke dispersed, drifting into the New Mexico night, and there were no answers. Bobby

Ray cursed, stubbing out his cigarette. He'd have to wait for a sign, and he didn't like waiting.

Maybe she'd know the answer. She could guide him. He pushed away from the stucco wall and headed for the west wing of the rehabilitation center. He knew he'd find her there.

Luke waited until she opened her eyes, watching as she frowned, trying to focus, trying to remember where the hell she was, and how she'd got there.

It would be interesting if she remembered what happened afterward, Luke thought wryly, leaning back and watching her, his legs crossed. She already hated him with an almost murderous passion—if she remembered what he'd done to her restless, responsive body her rage would know no bounds.

She turned her head, her eyes narrowing as they focused on him. He was half in the shadows, but she wouldn't mistake him for anyone else. With a sudden nervous gesture she clutched at her chest, but the tunic was neatly fastened once more, covering her securely.

"What am I doing here?" she demanded, her voice still scratchy.

"Being healed."

"Bullshit."

"A couple of hours ago your throat was so

bruised you couldn't speak. Bruising doesn't heal that fast without special help."

"Bullshit," she said again.

"I wonder if we can reverse the process," he murmured, half to himself. "I think I liked you better mute."

"I'm sure you did." She rolled onto her side, gingerly, and he could see she was still stiff and sore. "You like all your women silent and obedient."

"All my women? Are you one of my women?" he taunted softly.

She sat up at that, as he knew she would, trying to stifle a groan of pain. "I thought you were celibate."

He watched her, deliberating how best to handle her. His casual taunts were keeping her off balance—if the others heard him they'd be shocked by their saintly messiah.

But he was tired of being a saint. And he liked the way she jumped every time he poked at her.

Besides, the brief, wicked taste of her body had only whetted his appetite. He wasn't going to be satisfied with a moral and spiritual seduction, as he was with the rest of his followers. He needed total capitulation in her case, and nothing less would do.

"You don't really believe that, do you, Rachel?" he said.

Her reaction was priceless, her eyes widening. "You're admitting you aren't the saint everyone here thinks you are?"

"No one is a saint, particularly those who think they are. What do you think?"

"I think you're a con artist who preys on neurotic people and rips them off. I think you seduced my mother, got her to leave all her money to you, and then . . ." Something, some vestige of restraint, stopped her.

"And then?" he prodded. "What did I do then? Have her killed?"

"Did you?"

He laughed, knowing the sound would irritate her. "You've got a hell of an imagination, Rachel."

"I thought the Foundation of Being disapproved of profanity," she shot back.

"Rules don't apply to me."

"Did you?"

"Did I what? Seduce your mother? You must not have known Stella very well if you think she needed seduction. Part of her therapy was to confess her character defects, and sexual voraciousness was one of her major ones. She wasn't the kind to wait for a man to make a move."

"So she seduced you?"

"Why are you so passionately obsessed with my sex life, Rachel?" he asked softly. "Don't you have one of your own to keep you busy?"

"We're not talking about me," she said. "We're talking about your sins."

"Not a concept we agree on, remember?"

"You're not going to deny you're a con man?"

"I'm not going to deny anything."

"Including that you cheated my mother out of her money?"

"Your mother's dead, Rachel. She has no need of money where she's going."

"Then you cheated *me* out of her money!" She was up on her knees, moving closer. All he had to do was sit there, legs outstretched, and lure her closer. It was child's play. He liked her awake, alive, furious. He wanted to taste her angry mouth when she could fight back. She would, he knew it. But she'd eventually surrender, making it all the sweeter.

"Why do you think you deserve it?" he asked. "You couldn't have been very close. She never talked about you. You'd think if there was any warmth or affection between the two of you she would have at least asked for you on her deathbed."

"And you're telling me she didn't?"

He could hear the pain in her voice. He'd learned to soothe pain, to heal it, through lies and half lies and even, occasionally, truths. Healing her pain would avail him nothing. Hurting her more would throw her off balance, make her more vulnerable. Vulnerable to him.

"Not a word. You must have let her down very badly in this life."

For a moment he wondered whether he might have gone too far. He had known Stella Connery very well. He knew the deep, ingrained selfishness that had ruled her life, and he had little doubt that if, in truth, anyone had been abandoned in that tiny, dysfunctional family, it had been the angry young woman staring at him with hurt and denial in her eyes.

She was shaking, he could see it, so furious she was almost beyond speech. She crossed the space that separated them, on her knees, catching his tunic in strong hands and yanking at him in blind rage. "How dare you pass judgment on me? You don't know anything about me and my mother. You admit she never said anything about me. What makes you think it was my failing, and not hers? Did she strike you as the maternal type? The sweet, caring mother that every child deserves? Did she?" She yanked at him, and he let her, surveying her out of half-closed eyes, fascinated by her passion and sudden fearlessness.

He reached up and covered her hands with his. His were much larger, enveloping hers, and she released the soft cloth of his shirt in sudden panic. But he wouldn't release her, no matter how her fists squirmed in his enveloping hands.

"Let go of me," she said fiercely.

"Let go of Stella. She's gone. She can't be your mother, and all the money in the world won't make up for it."

"It's a start," she shot back. Her bitter, angry mouth was very close, irresistibly so. Yes, he definitely liked her better this way. Furious with him. He wanted to taste her fury, swallow it.

He didn't move, keeping her fists captive. She was leaning over him, balanced precariously on her knees, and he could watch the knowledge of her vulnerability dawn in her eyes.

"If you try to pull away," he said in a deliberately lazy voice, "you'll lose your balance."

"Is this the way you treat all your followers?" she demanded.

"But you're not one of my followers. Are you?" He decided he didn't want to wait. He tugged, lightly, and she went sprawling across him in a tangle of arms and legs and soft, small breasts.

For a moment she lay absolutely still, straddling him. If she stopped to think about it she'd feel his erection, though how she'd react was a mystery.

She stared up at him, breathless, shocked, so close he could put his mouth against hers before she had time to realize what he was doing. He could feel her heat and anger, vibrating around him. Feel her fear. He never thought a woman's fear would be erotic. Rachel's was.

He didn't move, considering the notion, considering her. She was afraid of him. Afraid of having sex with him. It was small wonder he'd find that obsessive fear fascinating.

"Let go," he whispered, his voice low and persuasive. "Stop fighting me. Stop fighting yourself."

Uncertainty darkened her eyes. And then she scrambled away, and he released her, reluctantly. A prize worth having was a prize worth waiting for, he reminded himself. And he was beginning to think that Rachel Connery would be a prize indeed.

He could still smell the scent of her on his fingers, and he wanted to bite her. Instead he leaned back, deliberately, infuriatingly at ease.

"You won't win, Rachel," he said.

She was leaning against the wall, staring at him like a cornered animal. An apt comparison. But there was still fight in her.

"You think I should give up?" she said. "Forget about the twelve and a half million dollars, go back to New York, and get on with my life?"

"Is that the only reason you're here?" he said softly. "The money? I thought you were looking for your mother."

It didn't quite finish her off, but it came close.

Her angry eyes grew bright with unshed tears, and for a moment her full mouth trembled.

And then it hardened again. "Bastard." She spat the word out succinctly.

"Definitely. In spirit as well as fact." He'd gotten enough out of her for one night, and he surged to his feet with his usual fluid grace, towering over her in the murky light. She wasn't a large woman, and in her current pose, huddled against the stucco wall, she looked deceptively frail.

He was usually kind and gentle with frail women. Nurturing with those who were suffering from emptiness and loss, filling them with serene, asexual comfort that soothed and healed.

With Rachel Connery all he wanted to do was prod the wound and make her bleed.

He looked at her, the fragile, well-defined bones of her face, her slim body. He knew just how little weight she carried, and it bothered him.

"You don't eat enough," he said abruptly.

He'd managed to startle her. "I don't like the food here."

"I bet you don't eat enough at a four-star restaurant either."

"I don't see why that concerns you."

He couldn't quite see it either, but it did. He suddenly wanted her to be like the others, peaceful and undemanding.

But Rachel wasn't the kind of woman for easy

answers, for blissed-out acceptance of the unacceptable. She couldn't make peace with herself and her past, and he wasn't about to help her. She needed to do it for herself.

And whether or not she came to terms with her mother was the least of his worries. He was more interested in whether she would come to terms with the fact that he wasn't going to give up one penny of the twelve and a half million dollars Stella had left the Foundation. And whether she was going to let go of that shell of anger and protectiveness long enough to let him get her into a real bed, where she could react, respond, take him deep inside her and . . .

He shut off the erotic thought with ruthless efficiency. "You need to sleep," he said, the taunting drawl out of his voice. He could already hear the others, beyond the door, stirring to life as they heard him. He'd grown used to this life, to having a half-dozen people waiting and eager for his slightest whim. He'd grown used to it, and he hated it. There were times when he wanted nothing more than to be back in a tumbledown house in the backwoods of Coffin's Grove, Alabama, Jackson Bardell passed out on a cot, no food in the house except for a box of oatmeal. But there'd been no one to watch him, no one to worship him. He was getting so damned tired of being worshiped.

Maybe that was why he was so irrevocably drawn to the angry young woman staring up at him. Maybe he just really needed someone to hate him for a change. Maybe he needed the challenge. Or maybe it was a twisted nostalgia for a time when nobody loved him.

She rose too, and the door at the end of the large room opened, with three acolytes silhouetted in the broad entrance. She came up to him, knowing she was safe, knowing he wouldn't touch her while there were witnesses. "You killed her, didn't you, Luke?" she whispered, and the certainty was so strong in her voice that it shook him.

She didn't give him time to answer. She knew that he wouldn't. She simply walked toward the open door and the waiting helpers, her back straight, her neck oddly vulnerable beneath the close-cropped hair. He'd put his mouth there, on the soft nape of her neck, and then he'd bitten her. He wondered if he'd left teeth marks.

They took her back to her room, the three of them, all solicitude and murmured concern. Catherine was one of them, her face flushed, her silvery hair coming loose from its bun. Leaf was another, her serene face unmoved. The third was a man, a boy really, with a sweet face and the faint whiff of cigarettes about him. Rachel didn't smoke, but the scent of the forbidden made her warm to the angelic-looking boy.

They lit her oil lamp for her, covered her with a soft blanket, and left her, with that incessant murmur of "blessings" ringing in her ears.

Luke had almost admitted it. There was very little of the saint about him, even if everyone was blinded by his remarkable charisma. He was a user, a manipulator, and for some reason he didn't mind showing Rachel his true nature. Probably because he knew it would be useless to try to convince her he was anything other than what he was.

Damn him, why did he have to touch her? She didn't like being touched. She'd never developed the knack for it—there'd been no one to touch her during her childhood, no one to snuggle up with, to hug her and soothe her and tell her she was safe.

Touching meant pain. Shame. Blame and anger. She shivered in the warm room, suddenly chilled, as unwanted memories swamped back over her. Of her mother, screaming in her face, twisting her arm. Of her stepfather, pale, guilty, silent, as he watched the melodrama unfold.

Everything works out for the best, she'd always told herself. They sent her away then, at thirteen, and she'd never come home again. She had no home. But even for the first thirteen years of her life it had been a battle zone, not a haven.

Her only haven was when she was alone. And even that had been defiled by Stella's greed.

He'd touched her, and she hadn't liked it, but she couldn't get it out of her head. His hands closing over hers, enveloping them so that her own smaller ones had disappeared within his. The crown of thorns around each strong wrist. The feel of his body when she'd tumbled against him, bone and flesh and muscle, warmth and solid strength that was somehow terrifying. The closeness of his mouth.

She didn't like to be touched.

She didn't like the way he looked at her either. There was none of the saintly compassion he seemed to emit for the masses. His clear gray-blue eyes watched her with the intensity of a predator. He was very still, scarcely moving, and yet she had no doubt as to what kind of threat he could be. He'd taken her mother, he'd taken her money, he'd even taken from Rachel the illusion that Stella had an ounce of feeling for her. And he would take more, if he could. He would destroy her, and he would do so without a second thought. If she was weak enough to let him.

She lay in the lamplit darkness, tense, angry, confused. Her throat still hurt, though not with the fiery ache of earlier, when she could barely force air through the rawness. Her body felt bruised and aching and the pain in her head had subsided to a dull throbbing.

But there was something else disturbing. Whatever they'd given her, whatever they'd done to her, besides going an astonishing way toward healing her, had also left her feeling strange and restless. Her skin tingled. Her breasts felt tight, sensitive. Her lips stung.

She closed her eyes, trying to concentrate on the odd sensations, and hateful erotic images danced through her mind. Bodies entwined, hands touching, mouths tasting, hair flowing, strength and a slow, sensual burn that threatened to engulf her in flames.

She heard a muffled noise of protest, and she knew it had come from her own raw throat. Her memory was spotty, disturbing, edgy, and she tried to force something solid to materialize from the gray mist.

Nothing was clear. Just hints and wisps of sensation that made her entire body ache in fear and protest.

What in God's name had he done to her?

Luke closed the door behind him, sealing the room away from prying eyes, and turned to look at the wall of security monitors. All was as it should be to the untrained eye. The current crop of followers were partway through their two-month stay, and they were going about their appointed tasks with docile obedience.

Rachel Connery looked far from docile. She sat on her narrow bed, staring sightlessly into space, one hand brushing her mouth. Her nails were short, bitten to the quick. It didn't surprise him.

She touched her mouth with an absent curiosity that immediately made him hard. She didn't know what he'd done with her mouth. What he had every intention of doing again, next time with her cooperation . . . or at least her full awareness.

She stretched out on the narrow bed and he groaned. She was too damned distracting. He reached over and turned off the monitor, glancing at the others surrounding it.

A handful of the Grandfathers were gathered in one of the smaller meditation rooms. Bobby Ray was with them as well. Odd, Luke thought, peering closer. Wishing he'd had the sense to install listening devices as well.

They looked calm, peaceful, decisive as they made their plans for the future of the Foundation.

Surely he had nothing to worry about?

6

Calvin Leigh was the very last person Rachel expected would show up at her room later that day. She would have slammed the door in his face without a word when she noticed what he was carrying. A thermos and two empty mugs.

"A peace offering," he said in his soft voice. "Made with freshly ground Sumatran beans."

For a moment she didn't move. "It's probably poisoned."

"I brought two mugs. We'd die together."

"This is a cult, isn't it? I wouldn't put it past you guys."

"It's not a cult, and it's supposed to be poisoned Kool-Aid, not coffee. May I come in?"

"Coffee is one of the few things I'd consider risking my life for," Rachel said, opening the door and allowing him into the shadowy room.

He didn't say a word as he busied himself at the small table, pouring two cups of wonderful-smelling coffee and handing her one. He didn't come equipped with milk and sugar, but then, she drank her coffee black. Luke and his minions probably knew that.

If there was poison in the coffee she couldn't taste it, and wouldn't have cared if she did. She took a seat on the narrow bed, crossing her legs underneath her, and surveyed the deceptively sweet little man.

He took his time, arranging the one straight-backed chair the room boasted, climbing up into it and sitting, perched like a naughty child ready for his punishment. He had small hands, with short, stubby fingers, and he pushed one through his curly black hair in a childlike gesture.

"I suppose you're here to apologize for what happened yesterday?" she said when half her mug of coffee was gone and he had yet to say a word. "You want to tell me that it wasn't your fault I was nearly killed, you warned me about Angel but I didn't listen, and that perhaps you shouldn't have started me out in such a demanding location."

He raised his head and looked at her. His eyes were very dark and completely free of emotion. "No," he said, quite calmly. "I set you up."

She slopped some of the precious coffee onto

her jeans in shock. Not that he'd done it, but that he'd confess it so easily.

"You did what?"

"Luke has told me I must confess my sins to you and ask for forgiveness."

"He told me he didn't believe in sin," Rachel drawled, blotting at the coffee stain.

"Oh, he believes in sin all right. How could he not, given his background and the life he's lived?" Calvin said. "He just doesn't choose to define it for the people who follow his teachings."

"He defined it for you."

Calvin stared at her with opaque calm. "My crime was to wish you harm, and to manipulate circumstances so that you would bring that harm upon yourself. Which you did, with only minimal hesitation."

"You knew I'd let Angel out."

"Of course. It was clear you were a trouble-making young woman, determined to find some way to hurt Luke. Despite the fact that Angel's paranoid delusions were ridiculous, I figured you'd fall for it. And you did." His solicitous smile didn't reach his dark, dark eyes. "How are you feeling, by the way? Fully recovered?"

"Surprisingly well, thank you," she said stiffly.

"Luke had the best healers working on you, praying for you throughout the night. And he used his own ... exceptional powers to aid in your healing."

It danced across her mind, like bat wings fluttering, the touch of his hands on her flesh, and then it was gone. Leaving a troublesome shadow behind. "How kind," she said faintly.

"So I am here to ask your forgiveness. I thought you were an unreasoning threat to Luke and I wanted to protect him. I should have remembered that Luke needs no protection. He is a law unto himself, and no one can hurt him."

"Were you afraid I was going to find out the truth about what's going on here?" she asked bluntly.

He didn't react. "You wouldn't like the truth. It wouldn't be acceptable to you, or understandable."

"And what is the truth?"

"Love. Love for all creation," Calvin said with simple, compelling sweetness. If only his eyes weren't so dark. If only he hadn't been responsible for her near-death, she might have been tempted to believe him. Except that she had never been much of a believer in love.

"Love for Angel?" she said cynically. "How is she, by the way? Is she still thinking I'm the spawn of the devil, or has she decided that Luke is a messiah after all and I'm just his sweet handmaiden?"

"Oh, Angel has left us," Calvin said, slipping down off the chair. He started toward the door.

The afternoon light had faded, plunging the room into eerie shadows, but Rachel made no move to light the oil lamp by the bed.

"Where did she go?"

Calvin paused in the open doorway, his ageless face without expression. "She died," he said. And closed the door behind him.

The chill that swept over Rachel's body was immediate and powerful. She sat motionless in the darkened room. Angel had been a strong, physically healthy woman—Rachel had the bruises and aches to prove it. Whatever had killed her couldn't have come from natural causes. Had she committed suicide after Rachel had so stupidly let her out?

Or had someone killed her? Punished her for hurting Rachel? Or for failing to hurt her enough?

God, she was getting as demented as poor Angel had been. Crazy thoughts, crazy fears. What in hell was going on in this place? Death lurked beyond that vast sea of smiling, happy faces, and she had no idea who she could trust. Who had lured her here with that letter hinting of murder? If that letter had come from Angel herself, if Rachel had fallen prey to some lunatic's paranoid delusions, then she had wasted her time and her emotions in coming here, seeking revenge. And she had put herself in the worst danger she had ever known.

Not the danger from a jealous misfit like Calvin. The danger was from Luke Bardell.

She shivered again, still cold in the temperate room. There was nothing to be afraid of, she reminded herself. He couldn't hurt her. He couldn't make her believe his crackpot religion—that was for blissed-out yuppies sick of Wall Street. He couldn't take her mother and her money from her—he'd already done that, and she'd survived. In a rage, granted, but survived all the same.

And he could have no effect whatsoever on her body. He was celibate, she was frigid. Together they made a perfect pair, she thought wryly.

Just a little while longer. She would give herself a few more days to find whoever wrote her that letter. If in that time all she encountered were the happy, shining faces of Luke's People, then she'd give up, as she probably should have done long ago. Give up the fight, give up her rightful inheritance. Give up the mother she'd never really had.

She glanced at her watch. It was five o'clock, and she was supposed to be on day two of her course of instruction in the ways of Luke's People. She was already a day behind, though she couldn't rid herself of the feeling that she'd had far too much of an indoctrination in Luke's ways yesterday, lying in that huge, smoky room with the sound of flutes and chanting in the distance. And Luke himself, far too close. If only she could remember details.

She could always ask him. He probably wouldn't

answer, he'd just smile that beatific smile that made her want to smash her fist in his teeth. She had never hit another living soul in her life. It would require touching, a risk that wasn't worth taking.

But if they were alone he might say more than he should. His manner with her was at odds with the distant serenity he bestowed on his flock, and she had every intention of exploiting that difference. Of making him take one step too far. And she'd be waiting to push him the rest of the way.

The refectory was empty except for the yellow-clad workers at the far end. They looked up at her, murmuring the required "blessings," but Rachel pretended not to hear them, closing the door swiftly.

The halls were deserted. She knew there had to be at least a hundred people in residence—the refectory had been filled when she was there before. But for some reason they were never around when she escaped her cell.

Escape. An odd, but emotionally accurate way to put it. She wanted to escape, and it wouldn't take much to get her to leave. She hated it here.

Just a few more days, she reminded herself. And if she hadn't come up with any proof, any answers by then, then she'd let it go. There was little she possessed in this world but her pride and her self-respect. If she ran away, as some part of her desperately wanted to, she'd end up losing even more than she already had.

She was about to head back to her room and await a summons to dinner when something stopped her. The high windows along the hallway let in a fitful light and the faint sound of birds. There was a door set deep into the stucco wall, and on impulse she pushed it open and stepped outside. Into the twilight coolness, the smell of the desert surrounding her.

The garden was austere, formal, Zen-like, with carefully sculpted pathways through the scrubby little pines. She let the door shut behind her, taking a deep breath of the fresh air, filling her lungs with it. It seemed as if she hadn't been outside in days, and yet she wasn't a woman who was particularly attuned to nature.

But right now she needed it, craved it, the stillness of the early evening, the peace of the desert, the calm solitude that was filling her soul with strength and renewal.

She found she could laugh at herself, a rare occurrence. She'd already been here too long; in a little more than forty-eight hours she was thinking like a new age flake. In another minute she'd be in the lotus position, chanting "om" and channeling some ten-thousand-year-old Chinese mystic.

She could do with some ten-thousand-year-old

Chinese wisdom at the moment. Something to make sense of everything here. The closest she could come would be Luke Bardell, and it would be a cold day in Shanghai before she'd turn to him for answers and expect the truth.

Deliberately she put him out of her mind. She'd spent too much time thinking about him, worrying about him. She would take the next half hour for herself, alone in the perfect stillness of the garden. One half hour when she didn't have to worry, didn't have to be angry, didn't have to fight.

When she stepped back inside the retreat center she could arm herself once more.

She thought she could hear the faint, familiar sound of the flute borne on the desert breeze. She recognized it now—Native American music, eerie and melodic, with a rhythmic underlay of drums, thrumming quietly in time with her heartbeat.

She shoved a restless hand through her short-cropped hair as she stepped forward into the garden. Had her mother walked in this garden? It seemed unlikely—Stella had been even less interested in nature than her daughter.

It didn't matter. Stella and her money didn't matter, at least for the time being. The quiet night was all around, and as the shadows lengthened Rachel moved farther away from the main building, until she came to a small, still pool.

She sat down on a huge rock and drew her legs up to her body, resting her chin on her knees as she stared into the blackness. In daylight the water would be a clear, innocent blue. Tonight it was black and bottomless, holding unfathomable secrets.

She was still sitting there, staring at the water, when Luke found her.

He moved very quietly along the stone path, with a grace that annoyed her. He made no effort to sneak up on her, but if she hadn't happened to look up she wouldn't have known he was approaching. Sundown cast strange shadows on his face, and even the loose white cotton clothes seemed dark and subdued in the half light.

"Did you come looking for me?" she asked, lifting her head to give him her best dispassionate gaze. One that matched his.

"No. I thought you were still in your room, nursing your wounds."

"I'm quite amazingly recovered," she said. "I don't suppose you'd care to tell me how you managed to achieve such a miracle?"

"Magic?" he suggested.

"I don't believe in magic."

"You didn't have to tell me that," he said, his voice wry. "I already figured that much out. Maybe it was the powerful drugs the healers gave you."

"What drugs?"

His faint smile made it clear she'd risen to the bait he'd tossed before her. "Or maybe it was just the healing power of many people."

"Magic again," she said with a sniff.

"Life is a lot more fun if you believe in magic," he said.

"Life isn't supposed to be fun. And I don't think I'm going to take lessons in philosophy from a convicted murderer."

He didn't even blink. "It was manslaughter. And I thought that was exactly why you were here."

She bit her lip. She wasn't going to find out what she wanted to know from him, how to catch him at his own game, if she couldn't get close to him, and the only way to get close to him was to take his supposed instruction.

She managed a conciliatory smile, glad the gathering darkness would hide the dishonesty in her eyes. "I want to learn," she said.

"And so you shall. Anything you want to know, my child. Ask me anything, and I'll answer."

She absolutely despised being called "my child." She was no longer anyone's child, and in all her twenty-nine years she'd never really felt like one. She certainly didn't see this new age Elmer Gantry as a father figure.

"Anything?" she echoed in a deceptively sweet voice. "Tell me what happened to Angel."

It didn't faze him. "I thought that Calvin told you. She died."

She waited, but he wasn't about to volunteer any more information. *Bastard*, she thought.

"How—did—she—die?" She spoke very slowly and carefully, as if to an idiot.

His response was less than satisfactory. "At peace," he said.

He was baiting her again, all with that soulful innocence. She jumped down off the rock and advanced on him, forgetting her own danger. "Who," she said, "or what killed her?"

"It was her time."

"One more evasive answer and I'm going to shove you in that pool," she said, her frustration boiling over.

"I would have thought your experience with Angel would have taught you the consequences of physical violence," Luke murmured.

"You said you'd answer my questions. What happened to Angel?"

He cocked his head to one side, surveying her out of half-closed eyes. "Such anger, Rachel," he chided. "You won't begin to heal until you release your anger."

"Then stop pissing me off."

"Angel died of a broken neck. She fell off the

roof of the hospital building and died instantly. Does that answer your question?"

"Fell? Or was she pushed?"

"Actually she jumped. She'd been locked away for her own protection as well as others, but once you let her out she headed straight for the roof. I wanted to spare you that information but you have a habit of pushing."

"Why should you spare me?"

"You're already dealing with enough guilt," he said in a soft voice.

"I have no guilt."

"Then you're unique."

"And you're annoying."

His smile widened. His mouth was surprisingly sensual in the darkness. Not that sensuality was an attribute she spent much time in noticing, but in Luke's case it was hard to ignore. Part of his stock in trade, she supposed dryly. It left her totally unmoved, a small blessing.

"Part of my job description," he said. "Spiritual leaders are supposed to be saintly and know the answers. Or at least the right questions."

"So tell me something else, O Great Spiritual Leader." She mocked him. "What are you going to do with the twelve million dollars that should have been mine?"

He shook his head, making an exaggerated clucking noise. "Stella wanted us to have it," he said patiently. "And Stella died believing her wishes would be honored. I can't betray that."

She wanted to hit him. Never in her life had she hit someone, but she promised herself then and there that before she left Santa Dolores she would haul off and clobber him. Preferably with something large and heavy.

But she plastered a calm expression on her face, hoping he wouldn't see the fury in her eyes. "Of course you couldn't. And I wouldn't want her dying wishes betrayed either," she added, lying through her teeth. "So why don't you tell me about the kind of peace Stella found here, that was so wonderful it took the place of her only child?" The bitterness was starting to creep back, just slightly, so she added an innocent smile to blunt its effect.

He took a step toward her in the darkness, and she held her ground, just barely. He was too close, and she hated it. She could feel the warmth of his body through the loose cotton clothing, smell the scent of his skin. He was so close she could practically taste him, and the thought terrified her.

She could feel her heart racing in sudden panic, feel the breath catching in her throat. At least he wouldn't reach out and touch her—she was safe as far as that was concerned. He never touched his followers. But then, she wasn't a follower.

And she didn't really believe that he didn't touch. Luke Bardell did whatever he wanted. He just did so discreetly.

She took a step backward, but it was too late. He caught her shoulders, and she could see the tattoo of thorns beneath the sleeve of his tunic. She tried to jerk away, but he was holding her too tightly, and she could feel the panic rise in her throat, strangling her. She couldn't breathe, but she couldn't let him know that, or he'd continue to hold her, closer, tighter, until her breathing stopped completely and her heart exploded and she was dead, dead like her mother, dead like Angel, dead, dying, lost . . .

He shook her, a short hard snap of her body, and when she lifted her head to glare at him he had already released her. "You wouldn't recognize it if I showed you."

"Recognize what?" Her voice was husky, her mind muddled.

"The peace that I could give you. You aren't ready for it."

It took every ounce of her strength to pull herself together, to stare at him with icy politeness. "Be sure to let me know when you consider me ripe," she said.

"Trust me, Rachel," he said, his voice a soft whisper on the night air. "You'll know."

7

She walked five paces behind him, like an obedient Muslim wife, but Luke wasn't fooled. She was neither obedient nor wifelike, and if his instincts weren't so well honed he might be expecting a knife between his shoulder blades.

Rachel wasn't that obvious, or that direct. He'd grown up in a society where resentments and differences were handled with fists and weapons, and the weaker the opponent the more damage you could inflict.

He wondered if things had been different, just what he would have been like. His mother got knocked up when she was eighteen, falling for the raven-haired, blue-eyed traveling evangelist who got strong men down on their knees and strong women down on their backs. He wouldn't have even known, if Jackson Bardell hadn't delighted in telling him he was no kin. He was just some bastard his mother had been too stubborn or too stupid to get rid of.

He'd followed in his daddy's footsteps—the father he'd never met. Hell, he didn't even know the man's name, just that he was killed a few years later by someone's jealous husband. It was when his mother had heard the news that she had finally agreed to marry Jackson Bardell. The worst mistake of her life.

She found that out soon enough. And she paid for her mistakes, ten times over, before she finally put a stop to it with a rope in the old barn. And then there'd been no one to stand between Luke and Jackson Bardell's drunken fists.

He used to think that anyplace in the world had to be better than southern Alabama. He had been wrong. The people of Coffin's Grove were close kin to those in the slums of Chicago, and not that far off from the exalted rich who had surrounded Stella and Rachel Connery. Wanton Stella and her cold-blooded daughter. He'd never seen two women more unlike in nature. Stella got what she wanted through trickery and deceit, using her charm, her body, her money. Rachel fought for what she thought she deserved. She was going to lose this time. He wondered how often she lost. How much.

He took her around the back way, to the

eastern entrance of the meditation room that led off his private quarters, and he stopped by the doorway, looking at her. It was almost pitch-black—there was no moon that night, and the clouds scudded across the starry sky like angry ravens.

"Did anyone see you come outside?" he asked. "Does anyone know where you are?"

She shook her head. "Not a soul," she said. "Your followers seem to keep to themselves—I never see them unless they're looking for me."

"They have their own duties."

"Well, you can murder me and dispose of my body and no one will be the wiser," she said matter-of-factly.

He leaned against the outer door, watching her. "Why would I want to do that?"

"Because I'm an inconvenience."

"Not nearly as inconvenient as you want to be," he said, knowing it would infuriate her. "We're very tolerant here—we make room for all sorts of awkward situations."

"I guess that about sums me up. An awkward situation." There was a note in her voice that caught his attention. Faintly bitter, it had little to do with her current circumstances. "I'm afraid it's a lifelong habit of mine—to be where I'm not wanted, causing trouble."

"Are you here to cause trouble?"

"Definitely. Does that surprise you?"

"No," he said, pushing away from the door, and she backed up, skittish. "And who says you're not wanted?"

He let his voice be deliberately, faintly provocative. Not enough that she could be certain of any innuendo, just enough to unsettle her. He liked seeing her nervous.

Besides, there might be someone close enough to overhear him. He didn't want to be too obvious, at least not to the others. The effect he had on people, the sheer power of his charisma, was his stock in trade. He could elicit just about any response he wanted, with varying degrees of intensity, from most of the people he came in contact with.

Rachel was less easy to play. She was unwillingly fascinated by him, he recognized that with no false modesty. She also hated and distrusted him, which was perfectly acceptable. As long as her feelings were intense and unavoidable, he didn't care how negative they were.

But what would prove her weakness, her final undoing, was the fear she had of him. She fought against it, but it was very strong, and sooner or later it would conquer her. That fear was entirely sexual, and he briefly wondered what had happened in her life to make her so frightened.

And then he dismissed it. He didn't care why she was frightened of sex, and of him. It only mattered that she was, and how he could use it to his best advantage.

"I should go back to my room," she said. There was no discernible stammer in her voice, but he knew that was only by rigid self-control.

"Why? You aren't going to change your clothes, are you?" She was wearing jeans and a T-shirt again, in direct defiance of him. It would be a simple enough matter to make her change—the clothes she was wearing fitted her body much more closely than the uniforms everyone else wore. He could see the soft swell of her breasts, the curve of her hips. She thought her own clothes were part of her defense against him. He could show her just how vulnerable they made her.

Except that he liked looking at her tight ass in jeans. It had been too long since he'd been able to indulge that particular sin, and for the time being he had every intention of enjoying it. Until he got her to take them off.

"I . . . uh . . ." She was stammering now, a major coup on his part. "I just thought I could . . . freshen up . . ."

"You mean you have to use the bathroom?"

"No," she snapped, pulling herself together. "If I had to pee I'd tell you. I just wanted a few moments of peace and quiet, some time to myself."

"Peace and quiet we have in abundance here at

the center. If you want time to yourself I'll take you someplace where you won't be disturbed."

"Where?"

"My private quarters."

From her expression you would have thought he'd said Alcatraz. "I don't think so."

"Afraid?" he taunted softly.

Her reaction was gratifyingly immediate. "Not of you."

"Why should you be?" he countered. "And yet you seem edgy whenever you're around me. I wonder why?"

"That's not fear, that's simple dislike," she shot back.

He grinned. Maybe it was a mistake, but he couldn't help it. She amused him, with her fuck-you attitude and her nervous mouth. He'd never known anyone who'd fascinated him more.

Which just went to prove he was overripe for a change. If he was going to become fixated on an angry young woman who was no more than passably pretty, then he better have a damned good reason for it. As far as he could tell, his only reason was boredom.

"Ah, I forgot," he murmured. "But then, you're here to give me a chance to change your mind, aren't you? You want to learn to trust me, don't you?"

He didn't have to read minds to guess at her

response. *Over my dead body*, her eyes said. But her mouth was still vulnerable beneath the angry edge.

"I want to keep an open mind," she temporized.

Her mind was more tightly closed than her legs, and they were locked together tighter than the entrance to Fort Knox, but Luke didn't mind. The challenge was half the charm.

"Of course you do. I'll arrange for them to bring supper in to us so we won't be disturbed. And we'll start on helping you learn to let go of your fears. Learn to reach out."

This time she didn't try to avoid the truth. "I don't want to reach out," she said.

"And you don't want to let go of your fears either. Why not?"

"Don't you have any fears?"

She was surprisingly disingenuous when she asked that question, and he almost gave her a truthful answer. That his fears were all inside him. That he'd killed, and he was terrified he'd learned the taste for it. That he'd find a reason to kill again. And again. And again. Till he couldn't stop.

Joliet Prison could warp a man's brain, if it wasn't twisted inside out already. He'd lived most of his life on the edge of society, accepting the unspeakable as everyday occurrences, but nothing had prepared him for the mind of Mallo Gilmer.

Mallo came to him sometimes in the night,

when he couldn't sleep, empty holes where his eyes once were, his teeth bared in a skeletal grin. That's all Mallo was now—a skeleton, buried in the yard at Joliet. No one wanted to claim his body. No one wanted to claim kinship with an aberration like Mallo. A man who'd taken pleasure in killing, a true sadist, an artist of painful, prolonged death.

In the books about serial killers Mallo's name always came up, listing the twelve men and women he'd killed, entirely at random, going into detail on some of the more grisly murders. But Mallo often used to moan that he'd never come close to the great ones in the annals of sin. Like Albert Fish, who killed and ate scores of children during the Depression. Or Ted Bundy, whose charm and intelligence drew people into his deadly web.

Mallo had no charm, and not so much intelligence as a certain evil cunning. He also wasn't particularly interested in killing children—he preferred to choose more easily disposable victims. Hitchhiking students, hookers, street people. It was only when he got greedy and gutted a yuppie's wife that anyone started making a concerted effort to stop him.

Once they began looking it was only a matter of time, and Mallo, knowing he was going to be put someplace where he could no longer practice his avocation, became wildly, gruesomely creative, crossing some invisible line that he could never go back on.

Everyone at Joliet was terrified of him, and rightly so. He looked like a balding Santa Claus—round-faced and jovial, with dark, merry eyes and soft hands. Calvin had belonged to him when Luke was first sent up, and since Mallo's last three boys had been found dead in the shower room it seemed likely that Calvin wasn't long for this world. Particularly since prison wasn't a place that embraced diversity, and Calvin was about as diverse as they came.

Luke never knew why he'd decided to interfere. Some errant strand of human feeling, probably, one he hadn't been able to eradicate entirely. Unfortunately rescuing Calvin from the thugs who were trying to kill him and wresting him away from his dangerous protector put him squarely in Mallo's path.

It would have been simple enough if he'd slept with him—he'd done worse things to survive in his lifetime and he was hardly likely to waste time with self-loathing. But there was something about Mallo that filled Luke with an almost superstitious horror. And Mallo knew it.

Card-carrying sadist that he was, Mallo found a new outlet for his hobby. Luke was too pretty, too powerful, too smart. Mallo knew just what he needed.

It had been subtle at first, but Luke had been preternaturally alert. Sly hints, faintly whispered suggestions, about the erotic lure of violence and death, and Luke would listen, unmoved, a faintly supercilious smile on his face.

Ah, but Mallo knew human nature too well. The doubts that spread through Luke's soul were like poisonous vines, weaving their way into his heart. It would have been kinder if Mallo had simply raped and killed him.

But Mallo's pleasure came from destruction. And his wounding of Luke's spirit was far more devastating than any wounding of his body could have been.

Even now, years later, he could hear his voice, softly whispering. "You haven't lived until you've tasted blood, boy. And you will. Sooner or later, no matter how hard you fight against it. You're a born killer, I can see it in your eyes. You know it too."

Mallo had known, without asking. Guessed that there was more in Luke's past than self-defense in a bar fight. He'd never asked.

Maybe it was a matter of time. Maybe Luke's gift, his talent for calling people to him, was simply a way of luring victims. He hadn't killed

Mallo, though he knew that was what Mallo had most wanted.

But at night Mallo would come back to him, and his soft, lisping voice spoke of death and blood. And he was afraid it would happen again, and this time he wouldn't stop. He'd killed Jimmy Brown in a bar fight over a botched robbery, a game of pool, and a blonde. He'd killed . . .

"You do."

He'd forgotten where he was. He'd forgotten she was the enemy, looking up at him. His amusement was stripped down to annoyance. "Do what?"

"Have fears," Rachel said. "I can see it in your face. The great messiah is frightened of something. Fancy that."

Her pleasure was so obvious it blunted his anger. "But it's up to you to find out what it is," he said. "And the only way you'll do that is to get close to me."

Her happiness vanished instantly. "You're too easy," he added, pushing open the door. "As long as you're afraid of me, you'll never destroy me. And that's why you're here, isn't it?"

She started past him through the door, but he dropped his arms, imprisoning her. She couldn't go forward or back without touching him. She stood motionless, and he was reminded of a white rabbit, facing certain death. She lifted her head to glare at him, exposing her soft, vulnerable neck. If he were a wolf he could tear her throat out.

"That's why I'm here," she said, defiant despite her fears. "If you knew that, why did you invite me?"

But she was no rabbit, and he had no interest in her throat, her life's blood. He smiled down at her, oh, so gently, and he felt her shiver. "Maybe I was bored," he said. "Maybe I wanted to see if I could get you off my back. Maybe I wanted to see if I could get you on yours."

He wanted to kiss her. He wanted to put his mouth against hers and see what she'd do. She'd panic, of course. Especially when he used his tongue. It would be worth it, just to taste her shock, just to risk being seen by some of his blind-eyed followers. He leaned toward her, hungry. Like a wolf.

"Luke?" Bobby Ray Shatney's voice was soft and respectful and faintly slurred from the Thorazine, and for a moment Luke didn't turn his head, still concentrating on his victim. She was looking up at him with a lovely combination of surprise and anger, and if Bobby Ray hadn't chosen to interfere she would have learned just what she had to be afraid of. He let the moment linger, then released her, turning to the newcomer. Rachel scuttled through the doorway like a startled crab, barreling into Bobby Ray.

"Blessings," Luke said softly. "What is it?"

"Catherine sent me to find you. It's time for the commitment."

He'd forgotten. Angel McGuiness's smashed body needed to be buried with all the new age pomp and circumstance befitting a lost member of the flock. He wondered for a moment whether Rachel felt any remorse, whether he should force her to come with him and see what her curiosity and thirst for vengeance had wrought. If she hadn't been so determined to bring him down, Angel would still be safely locked away. She wouldn't have had to take a swan dive off the fourth-story roof of the healing center onto a cement walkway.

But Rachel wasn't a woman who spent much time considering her own shortcomings, her own guilt. She was too caught up in blaming others. Which was just fine by him—it only made her more vulnerable. And in the end, her guilt would overtake her, destroying her.

But not before he had her.

"Of course," he murmured. "Why don't you escort Rachel to my rooms while I take care of this? She wanted some moments of peace and quiet."

He could see that she wanted to protest, but

Bobby Ray had already put a courteous hand under her elbow and was leading her away. Luke watched them go with a faint note of foreboding. Alfred made sure that Bobby Ray was drugged into docility, and he believed firmly in Luke's divinity. There was no way he could prove a danger to anyone in the compound, even if he wanted to. Rachel was entirely safe with him.

Nevertheless, Luke decided that Angel didn't need much more than a cursory service, committing her crushed body to the sun-baked earth of Santa Dolores. Our Lady of Sorrows.

Suddenly she could breathe again. Rachel glanced at the young man who led her down the corridor, doubtful, but he seemed the soul of sweetness. He was probably the youngest person she'd seen there, maybe in his late teens. Another lost innocent led astray by the master con man, she thought grimly, shaking off the oppressive feeling he always left her with.

She felt mauled, and yet he hadn't touched her. Her entire body felt bruised, sensitized, aching, as if he'd put his hands on her.

But he hadn't touched her. And he wouldn't. He wouldn't dare.

"Where did Luke go?" she asked the boy. On closer inspection he wasn't that much younger than she was—maybe in his early twenties, but there was something curiously unformed, childish about him. With his angelic face and tousled shock of dark hair he seemed like an overgrown Tom Sawyer, all ingenuous charm and awkwardness.

"To bury Angel," he replied in his sweet, quiet voice.

She shouldn't have asked. It wasn't her fault that Angel had died. They should have known better than to leave a newcomer with that kind of responsibility. Besides, Calvin had been behind it all. If anyone was responsible for Angel's death it was the jealous little man who'd confessed to it. There was no reason for her to feel a speck of guilt, and she refused to acknowledge it.

"Don't you want to be there?" she asked Bobby Ray in a curious voice.

He shook his head. "I never liked Angel," he said evenly. "She was crazy." He smiled at her with liquid innocence.

"I would have thought Luke would expect compassion for the afflicted," she said.

"Luke doesn't expect anything of us. We simply learn to exist, in our own way. That's the power of the Foundation of Being."

He seemed so earnest she wasn't about to dispute it. The room he led her into seemed similar to the others, if a little larger and a little emptier. White adobe walls, plank flooring, a few cushions on the floor. Hardly conducive to comfort, she thought wryly. She would have rather had an overstuffed sofa and a large-screen TV.

However, at least Luke wasn't anywhere around, which was the best thing that could be said about anyplace at Santa Dolores. She rubbed her arms, feeling suddenly chilled. There was a fireplace in one corner, and the smell of burning piñon pine was crisp and resiny in the stillness. She half expected Bobby Ray to leave her, fading away like most of the ghostly creatures who called themselves Luke's People, but he was still there, watching her, as she warmed herself by the fire. Luke's private quarters, she thought. A perfect place to start searching, if only she were left alone.

"You really don't need to stay with me," she said. "I just wanted someplace where I could be by myself, and Luke suggested his rooms." She glanced around the empty space. There were no other doors but the one through which they'd entered. "Where does he sleep?"

You would have thought she'd asked where he kept the bodies, the way Bobby Ray reacted. "Luke is celibate," he said repressively.

"So am I," she shot back. "I didn't say I wanted to sleep with him, I just asked where he slept."

"Here."

The thin pallet in the corner didn't look much more comfortable than a bed of nails. And yet Luke didn't strike her as the self-denying type.

"Why?"

"It's all he needs," Bobby Ray said simply.

"Humph," Rachel muttered. "You must think he's some kind of god."

Bobby Ray moved closer, his placid face oddly shadowed, his eyes so dilated they looked almost black. "Not exactly," he said.

For a moment she felt a little shiver of doubt. It was no wonder she was spooked—this entire place reeked of death. She'd been there less than twenty-four hours when someone had tried to kill her, someone who killed herself immediately afterward. It wasn't surprising that she was looking for monsters beneath the most innocent of faces.

"What do you mean, not exactly?"

He wasn't a physical threat, the way Luke was, even though he came up to her and took her hand. She let hers lie in his cold one, waiting.

"I wrote you the letter, Rachel. I'm the one who knows the truth about your mother's death. About all the deaths here at Santa Dolores."

And he put his hand over hers, trapping her.

8

Rachel should have felt elation. She should have felt joy and triumph, knowing that revenge was moving closer. Instead she looked into the innocent face of Bobby Ray Shatney and wondered why she suddenly didn't trust him.

"You knew my mother?" she asked warily. "You were here when she was?"

"I've been with Luke since I was eighteen. I've known everyone who's ever been here. Those who are still here. Those who left of their own free will. And the people who just disappeared without a trace."

"Have there been many of them?"

"The ones who disappear? A few. They were the unbelievers, the ones who wanted to destroy Luke. It could happen to you."

"It's not going to," she said firmly. "Not with you to help me."

Bobby Ray looked so incredibly young, with his soft cheeks, his faintly dazed expression. "I don't know if I can," he muttered.

"You said you were the one who wrote me. You said they murdered my mother, you said she never had cancer and that she knew what was happening to her!" Her voice was shrill, but there was no way she could calm herself. "You have to tell me what you know."

"I'm not sure," Bobby Ray said. "I'm not sure of anything anymore. They give me these drugs, and they confuse me." His eyes were strange—unfocused and yet oddly watchful. "I loved Stella, you know. She was like a mother to me. My own mother died when I was young, and Stella had such a soothing touch."

Rachel just looked at him. He was older than some of the young men Stella had slept with, and she'd never had a soothing, maternal bone in her body. But he looked so sad, so lost, that she didn't want to doubt it. "I'm sorry about your mother," she murmured gently.

For a moment she couldn't read the expression on his face. "I've got to get out of here. Luke will be coming back soon. He trusts me, but he doesn't trust you."

He was already backing away from her, heading

toward the door. "But we need to talk!" she protested. "Come to my room later and we can . . ."

He shook his head. "Your room isn't safe. He'll be watching. Listening."

"How?" she asked bluntly.

"Luke knows everything."

"He's not some kind of tin god. He's only human, for heaven's sake."

Bobby Ray shook his head pityingly. "Don't underestimate him. He's not like other people."

"That's for sure," Rachel muttered.

"I don't know how I can help you. Things are so confusing to me now. Stella said she wasn't sick, and I believe her. She told me she didn't think anyone had really been sick, that they were killing her for her money. She wanted me to get in touch with you, to try to help her before it was too late. But I wasn't in time."

"She wanted me? She wanted my help?" Rachel heard the longing in her own voice and hated it.

Bobby Ray nodded. "She said you were the only one who could help her."

"And I didn't. I didn't come in time."

Bobby Ray shook his head. "It's too late now. Leave this place. Luke's too strong, too powerful. Get out while you still can."

"But . . ."

He was gone before she could scream at him. Before she could tell him she couldn't give it up, she couldn't let go, couldn't just forget that her mother might have been murdered.

It could all have been one of Stella's ornate fantasies, of course. Stella loved to be the center of melodrama, and dying of breast cancer might have been too mundane for her. She would have been entirely capable of turning the whole thing into a giant conspiracy, just to get more attention. And she'd drag everyone into that fantasy with her—Bobby Ray and Rachel and any other gullible fool.

There was no way she could find out. They hadn't done an autopsy, and her remains had been cremated and scattered in the New Mexico desert. Any trace of Stella had been washed away by acid rain months ago.

She sank down in front of the fire, staring into the glittering orange depths. She'd been an unwilling audience to Stella's histrionics all her life. She'd been told to be patient, to be quiet, not to interfere, not to get in anyone's way, from the time she was old enough to obey. She'd seldom seen Stella during her early years, and Rachel had never decided whether that was a blessing or a curse. The caretakers she'd hired had been efficient, responsible, and far from loving, and Rachel had been a skinny, sallow-faced child, prickly, full of anger at the world. As a child she'd read voraciously: books were her comfort, her parents, and her friends, and early on she'd identified with Mary Lennox in *The Secret Garden*. The thin, sour, unwanted child who'd been transformed by the magic of a garden and love.

But there were no secret gardens for Rachel Connery. Only the eager, fumbling hands of her third stepfather.

It was Stella's longest marriage, a testament to the cruelty of fate, Rachel always thought. The touching had started when she was nine years old, culminating in rape when she was twelve.

She could barely remember what happened when she told her mother. Stella wouldn't have listened. Those years were hazy now, thankfully so. Rachel had withdrawn into a dark, private place where no one could hurt her and by the time she slowly, cautiously emerged, Husband Number Three with his filthy habits was long gone, and Stella had embarked on her series of boy-toys.

And Rachel had been patient. Waiting for a sign of love or affection from her preoccupied mother. Waiting for the ice that had locked around her to melt. Waiting for miracles.

The time for patience was gone. She was suddenly chilled, and she wrapped her arms around her body, wishing she had a sweater. Wishing something could warm her, melt the ice inside her.

At least Luke didn't know anything about her.

Didn't know about old vulnerabilities, new pain. There was no way he could reach her, hurt her. Not if she didn't give him that power.

And she wouldn't. Not for twelve million dollars, not for that mindless peace the others seemed to be enjoying. She would never let him get to her.

She heard the door open behind her, and she stiffened her shoulders, prepared to do battle once more. The light cast the elongated shadow across the room, but she knew at once that it wasn't Luke. She seemed to have developed an unnatural instinct about him, which she could only hope would help her in the long run.

"I brought you some food," Calvin said. The tray he carried was almost as big as he was, and there was no enticing smell of coffee this time. Rachel accepted its absence with a fatalistic shrug. The lack of caffeine was only adding to her edge.

He set it down on the floor in front of the fire, looking at her expectantly. There were two bowls of some lentil-veggie mash and a loaf of fresh baked bread. No butter, but Rachel was beyond caring. "Who's the other plate for?" she asked, reaching for the bread.

"Luke's eating in the refectory with his people. He said I was to keep you company. If you were willing."

She gestured toward the other plate. "Help

yourself," she said. "And while we're eating you can answer some questions for me."

"He said you would ask." Calvin sat down across from her, the firelight casting strange shadows on his odd, ugly face.

"And what did he tell you to say?" She managed to choke down a few bits of the lentil mash. She couldn't remember the last time she'd eaten, and she made herself swallow another bite. Food had always been low on her list of priorities, but it had been too long since she'd eaten, and her body was beginning to assert its need.

"He said to tell the truth, of course," Calvin replied. "Anything you want to know."

She didn't believe him, of course. But that didn't keep her from trying. "You're his helper, aren't you? His partner in crime?"

"What makes you say that?"

"Just a guess."

"I know Luke better than anyone else does," Calvin said. "I look after his best interests."

"Even when he doesn't recognize them?"

"Particularly then." Calvin's voice was affable. "Take, for instance, the problem of you. I think he underestimates just what kind of trouble you could start."

"And that's why you tried to kill me?" She took another spoonful of lentils, trying to savor it. It was a lost cause, and she set the spoon down again. "But how could I make trouble if you're all as saintly and innocent as Luke pretends to be? If this little cult really exists for the betterment of mankind and not the lining of Luke Bardell's pockets, then why should he have to worry?"

He didn't answer her question. "I didn't like Stella either. She was greedy. She wanted to monopolize Luke. She wanted everything, and she didn't want to share."

"That sounds like my mother," Rachel said wryly.

"She was too needy. Like you."

It took her by surprise. She wanted to scream at him. She wanted to take the nearly full bowl and shove it in his smug little face. Instead she set it down, very carefully. "I'm not like my mother," she said in a deceptively calm voice. "And I'm certainly not needy."

"That's not what Luke says." He continued to spoon away at his own dinner, not meeting her eyes. He didn't need to, Rachel thought bitterly. He knew exactly how his airy words were affecting her. "He says you're the neediest human being he's ever met. He's a sucker for the needy. Always has been. That's why he started the Foundation of Being."

"Is that why he keeps you with him?"

He looked up and grinned at that. "We all have

our needs," he said. "Luke needs me as much as I need him. Whether he admits it or not."

"You mean the great messiah wouldn't admit something?" Rachel said in mock amazement. "I thought he was perfect."

"Far from it. He's human, just like the rest of us, searching for some kind of peace and helping other people to find it as well." He rattled it off as if by rote.

"You don't believe that."

"You don't care what I believe. You're like the rest of them. Like your mother. You're only interested in Luke." It didn't seem to distress him.

"Yes," she said, for once completely honest. "I'm only interested in Luke." *And how I can destroy him.*

"It won't do you any good," Calvin whispered. "You can't hurt him, no matter how much you want to. I look out for him, and there are others as well. No one would let you hurt him."

"Who says I don't want to learn from him?"

"The only thing you want to learn is how to bring him down. But it won't work. He's got a gift, Luke has. For drawing people to him. He'll get you as well, see if he doesn't. No matter how much you think you hate him, he'll have you eating out of his hand before long. You'll be just as helpless as everyone else is, desperate for a

word, a smile, even a glance. I can see it now."
His glee was appalling.

"I'd kill myself first," Rachel said flatly.

"There are those who have done that. And
there are those who have tried to kill Luke. No
one ever wins. Only Luke triumphs in the end."

"Over the bodies of the vanquished?" Her voice
was sharp.

"And over the fortunes of the deluded," Calvin
added smugly. "You finished with your dinner?"

Somewhere along the way she'd lost her appetite. She shoved the tray away from her. "Why
aren't you busy trying to convince me of his saintliness? I would think you'd want me to doubt my
paranoia. Instead you're feeding it."

Calvin rose, hoisting the tray up. "I don't think
I could say anything that would make you trust
Luke. And I have my own reasons."

"And what are they?"

He was already at the door when he turned to
look at her out of his small, dark eyes. "Maybe I'm
trying to scare you away," he said. "You're nothing
but trouble here. Go someplace and forget about
Luke. Forget about this place. Forget about your
mother. Trust me, you could lose a lot more than
twelve million dollars."

And then he was gone.

She didn't waste any time. She searched the barren room with a determined thoroughness, trying

to blot out Calvin's words. It took her exactly five minutes. There was nothing in the cavernous chamber but the thin pallet that was purportedly Luke's bed, a few cushions, and the fireplace. No place to hide papers, or contraband.

She stared in frustration at the blank walls. Surely he couldn't spend all his private moments in such ascetic surroundings? For all his vaunted abstinence, he didn't strike her as a man who ignored the call of his senses. There must be some hidden life, or room, like Bluebeard's chamber. Maybe filled with the corpses of the women who'd tried to destroy him.

Now she was getting crazy, and it was all Calvin's fault. He was setting her up once more, but she couldn't figure out why. Her distrust of Luke Bardell was already overpowering—she didn't need anyone feeding it. Bobby Ray had already done enough.

She was tired of waiting for him in this empty room, waiting for him to grace her with his presence, to string her along with another pack of lies. She was tired of being passive. Bobby Ray Shatney had to be somewhere nearby—none of the followers seemed to leave this place, and he said he'd been with Luke since he was a teenager. Odd, when there were no other children around. Not that Bobby Ray was a child, but he had been when he first came here.

For some reason his name, his eyes, seemed familiar, though she couldn't imagine where she might have seen him before. Particularly if he'd been cloistered with Luke's People for so long.

What kind of life was that for a young boy? What kind of life was it for anyone?

Maybe she could force him to remember something specific. Something that would help her decide whether he'd just been one of Stella's pawns, or if there really was more to her mother's death than she suspected.

She had her hand on the door when it opened, and she let out a tiny shriek, startled, as Luke stepped into the room.

It would help, she thought nervously, if he weren't so damned tall, even with bare feet. He towered over her, and it took her a moment to realize his ridiculously long hair was wet.

Water glistened on his skin, and his tunic was untied, hanging loosely about his body. Rachel held still, panicked, waiting for him to touch her. Instead he moved past her, into the room, heading for the small fire that had been built to offset the late-summer chill of the New Mexico Mountains. Expecting her to follow.

He'd closed the door, but it would be easy enough to open it, to escape. And God, she wanted to escape. As much as she hated the thought, she was feeling unaccountably vulnerable, and she was wise enough to want to avoid the enemy when her defenses were compromised.

"Running away?" he murmured, staring into the fire, his long hair a wet swathe down his back.

Fear was one thing. Pride was another.

"No," she said. Moving after him, still keeping her distance.

"Just as well," he murmured, squatting in front of the fire. "I locked the door."

She'd just managed to calm some of her nerves when they began screaming again. "Why?"

"So no one would interrupt us."

She swallowed, grateful that the shadowy room would hide her sudden blush. "I thought you said there were no locked doors at Santa Dolores?"

His grin was far from saintlike. "Except for mine. So, did Calvin tell you all my dark secrets?"

"No."

He sank down in front of the fire, cross-legged. "Why not? Didn't you ask him? He could have told you how we met in prison. He could have told you about my childhood."

"I don't give a damn about your childhood."

"No? You don't want to hear about the poor, abused, motherless child who grew up with his old man beating on him every time he had too much to drink? Except that he wasn't really my old man, which was part of the problem." He looked at her expectantly.

"You don't sound particularly traumatized," she said.

"Some of us move past our deprived child-hood," he murmured, and there was no missing his meaning.

"You think I had a deprived childhood?" He was luring her closer, she knew it, but she couldn't help herself. The glow of the firelight against his skin was pagan, mysterious, but it drew her, despite the danger.

"I think so, yes," he said. "Or at least you're convinced of it, no matter how much money you had at your fingertips, no matter that your life was never in danger. You're feeling put upon and resentful that life has handed you a few hard knocks, and you want to make me pay for it." His enigmatic smile was far from reassuring. "Are you going to come here and sit down or are you going to try to break down the door?"

She had no real choice. She knelt down beside the fire, well out of his reach. "What would happen if I screamed for help?"

"A dozen people would come running. Though I don't know why you should. I'm not keeping you here. You came to Santa Dolores of your own free will. You're here with me because you wanted to be. If you want to leave, ask me, and I'll open the door for you."

"I'll stay," she said, wary. "If you promise not to touch me."

"Why are you afraid of being touched?"

"I'm not," she said. A bald-faced lie.

"Not afraid of being touched? Then that means you're afraid of me."

"No."

"No?" His voice was soft, musical, a weapon of desperate power. "Then come here."

He was closer than she realized, so close she could see the droplets of water on his eyelashes. He had long eyelashes, dark, almost hiding his eyes. "No," she said.

"Answer my question." His voice was low and insistent. "Why are you afraid of being touched?"

"I'm not afraid. I just don't like it."

"Anyone's touch? Or just mine?"

"Don't flatter yourself," she said with a bitter laugh. "I don't like anyone touching me. Putting their hands on me, trying to make me do things, pretending to care about me . . ." She let her voice trail off, knowing she'd already revealed too much. She went on the attack. "And why don't you like being touched?"

He didn't flinch. "What makes you think I don't?"

"Catherine told me no one was allowed to

touch you. Your celibacy extends beyond sexual matters, you keep yourself aloof from any human intimacy. No hugs, no touching, no handshakes even."

"No caresses, no kisses," he added, his voice soft and wickedly seductive. "It's my choice."

"Why?"

The smile that twisted his mouth was a far cry from Luke's usual saintly beauty. "Because I like power. The more I withhold from the people here, the more they crave. The more they're willing to follow me, sacrifice everything for me. Because I'm untouchable, everyone wants to touch me. It obsesses them."

She stared at him in shock. "You admit that?"

"Of course," he said. "What harm will it do? Everyone knows you're here to try to hurt me. No one would believe you if you told them the truth."

"And what is the truth? Are you some new age messiah or are you just a phenomenally accomplished con man?"

"The very fact that you still have doubts is reassuring. You think it's possible I'm really a spiritual leader?"

"No," she said flatly. "You've already admitted you aren't."

"I haven't admitted a thing. That's the problem, Rachel. You don't understand the basic tenets beneath the Foundation of Being. No one is supposed to be a saint. We all have our failings, our weaknesses, our character defects."

"Your sins," she said flatly.

"There's that word again," he murmured. "You don't have any sins? It must be nice to be perfect in an imperfect world."

"Your followers think you're perfect. They think you're some sort of god."

"And what do you think, Rachel?"

She hadn't realized how close they were. She scrambled to her feet, desperate to put some distance between them. "I think you're a menace."

"Only to those who are vulnerable. Are you vulnerable?" He rose, a fluid motion, and there was no escape. "Do you think I can hurt you?"

"No," she said, her voice stubborn. It would be useless to run for the door. It was locked, he'd told her.

"Yes," he said.

And he moved closer.

9

He wasn't that close to her, she told herself. Not close enough to touch, not close enough to feel his breath stirring her hair. And yet he was there, all around her, a seductive menace, intruding, snatching away her safety.

"Poor little rich girl," he murmured, his voice lightly mocking. "You're so damned angry you want to hit something. You want to hit me, don't you?"

Rachel's back was pressed up against the wall. She could feel her heart thudding wildly in her chest, she couldn't breathe, all she could do was stare up into his watchful, enigmatic eyes.

"What are you afraid of? What do you think I can do to you? Do you think I've got supernatural powers, the ability to cloud people's minds and make them my slaves?"

"You seem to have a certain amount of success doing just that," she said in a shaky voice.

"Do I?"

"You know you do." She was trying desperately to muster her defiance. "You can have anyone you want eating out of your hand."

"I can't have you."

He was too close. The words were almost a whisper in that hypnotic voice of his.

She forced herself to look up at him, searching for dispassion in her angry, frightened soul. He was quite astonishingly beautiful, if one were to be swayed by surface impressions. His gray-blue eyes were deep and mesmerizing, his mouth oddly unsettling as it hovered much too close to hers. "You don't want me," she said flatly. "You just want to . . . want to . . ."

"To what? Conquer you? Destroy you? Seduce you?"

The last possibility was the most frightening, enough so that she fought back. "You're like all men, you want to prove your superiority. Well, I concede the point. You're very gifted at demoralizing people."

"Am I demoralizing you? Stripping away all those prudish inhibitions you wear around your body like an iron corset?"

"How has this gotten to be about sex?" she snapped at him, still fighting.

"Oh, Rachel," he murmured in his low, seductive voice, "it's always been about sex." He pressed his forehead against hers, and that touch alone paralyzed her. "Didn't you know that? It's why you're so terrified."

"I'm not—" she began, but he cut her off.

"Close your eyes," he whispered, and his voice sank into her bones. "Stop fighting, just for a little while. It won't hurt, I promise. Just lean back against the wall and let go."

She was tempted. Oh, God, she was so tempted. She closed her eyes, her fierce will helpless against the siren lure of his voice.

"There's peace here, Rachel. No more battles. Life has been a battle for you, but you don't have to fight any longer. You can just let go. Surrender. You can't win all the battles. You can't slay all the dragons. Let someone else do it for you. Just this once."

The tone of his voice was even more evocative than his words, and she felt herself slipping, against her will, her skin tingling with longing and awareness.

"You can have it, Rachel. No more fear. No more anger. You can just let go. Can you feel it? The peace flowing through your body? Melting the hurt, washing it away, so that you're floating, free. Can you feel the healing begin? The wholeness spreading through your body?"

She couldn't open her eyes. She was helpless beneath the spell of his voice. She couldn't speak, couldn't move, trapped in some wicked, sensual web that she didn't want to escape.

"Do I have you yet, Rachel? Do I own you, body and soul?"

She wanted to say yes. More than anything she'd ever wanted in her life, she wanted to say yes. But her voice wouldn't work, wouldn't say the damning words. She forced her eyes to open, to look into his startlingly cynical ones.

"Bullshit," she said, and the mood was shattered.

His mouth curved in a wry smile, but he didn't back away. She was still trapped between the wall and his lean, graceful body. "You're a challenge, Rachel," he murmured.

"Is this how you get your followers?" she demanded in a shaky voice. "By trying to hypnotize them?"

"Only the stubborn ones. And you'll be pleased to know you're my first failure. Though for a while I almost had you."

"I'm immune to you," she said.

It was a mistake. They both knew that she wasn't. "Should I make you eat your words? I could, you know. Quite easily."

This time she was smart enough to keep quiet. If he was disappointed that she wouldn't rise to his bait, he didn't show it.

He leaned closer, and his lips brushed the side of her face as he whispered in her ear. "Run away."

She couldn't move. She realized she was so tense with fear she felt paralyzed, and a strange aching stirred in the pit of her stomach. She closed her eyes, and she could feel the cool dampness of his cheek against hers.

"The door's not locked, Rachel. Run away."

Easier said than done, and he knew it, she thought bitterly. To escape, she'd have to touch him. She'd have to put her hands on him, willingly, and shove him away. That in itself was almost beyond her capabilities.

"Back off," she said in a fierce voice, her eyes still tightly shut.

She could sense the sudden stillness in his body. Sense his amusement as well as he stepped away from her, freeing her.

She could breathe again. She opened her eyes to glare at him. "I don't like touching people," she said. "I don't like being touched. I don't like kissing, I don't like hugging, I don't like men, and I don't like sex. And I certainly don't like you."

There was an odd gravity in his face as he digested her angry words. "I could teach you to," he said simply.

She looked at him, at this man she hated

enough to kill, and knew it was the truth. And that was the most terrifying thing of all.

"I'm leaving," she said.

He nodded, as if expecting it.

"Nor just your august company. I'm leaving Santa Dolores."

That managed to get a reaction out of him. "I didn't realize it would be so easy," he murmured. "I thought you were a more worthy adversary."

It was a battle between pride and fear, and fear won. "She who fights and runs away lives to fight another day," she said with mock flippancy.

"Then I haven't won?"

"Not by a long shot," she said. "This is just a tiny skirmish."

His smile was devastating. Rachel stared at him in stunned disbelief. It was no wonder people were lining up to hand their fortunes over to him. For the sake of that glorious smile she might almost be tempted herself.

Except that he already had her fortune. And the last thing to tempt her was a man's smile. Particularly this man.

"Most people aren't allowed back at Santa Dolores if they leave too soon," he said idly.

She paused at the door, turning to look at him. "But you'll let me come back," she said.

He smoothly covered what she thought might have been surprise. "Of course."

He paused. "And then I'll seduce your mind and soul until you're completely helpless. And then I'll fuck your body and your heart until all you can do is cry for more. I'll make you like it, Rachel. I'll make you *need* it."

She slammed the door behind her as she ran down the deserted hallway, half expecting to hear his laughter following her. She was covered in a cold sweat by the time she reached her room, and she barely made it to the bathroom in time before she was thoroughly sick.

When she was finished she collapsed on the cool tile floor, shivering in reaction. It hadn't been that bad in a long time. It had never been that bad. And unwanted, the memories came flooding back.

Some children were lucky enough to blot it all out. Create a nice, safe blank spot in their minds, forget anything ever happened. Forget the shame and the guilt, forget the disgust and the anger. The feel of those soft, plump hands, touching her, stroking her. The sound of his voice, calling her a good little girl, his precious baby girl.

Damn his soul to hell! And damn Stella too, for not believing her, for ignoring her third husband's miserable looks as she slapped Rachel across the face and called her a liar. That much lingered in her nightmares.

The names Stella had called her hadn't made much sense then. A lying little tramp was one of the milder epithets, all the while Garrison protested that she was being too harsh on the poor girl.

But Rachel preferred Stella's slaps to Garrison's surreptitious caresses. And exile to Miss Elvin's School for Girls was safety, at least for a while. Until Stella had moved on to husband number four.

She'd tried sex once, with the brother of a college friend, and hated it. She never wanted to try it again. Even now, the memory of Larry's slightly drunken instructions made her stomach knot in dread.

And now here was Luke Bardell. Liar, thief, murderer, looking at her, taunting her, threatening her with just what terrified her the most.

She pulled herself up to a sitting position, leaning against the open doorway. Someone had lit a small oil lamp, leaving it on her dresser, and she could see the spartan confines of her cell. The narrow bed with its plain white sheets. White cotton, like the loose clothes that Luke wore. She could see him lying in that narrow bed, covered only by the sheets. She could see herself there as well, trapped beneath him, helpless to escape.

The low, wailing sound startled her, until she realized it came from her own throat. She pushed herself up, holding on to the sink for a moment as she pulled herself together. She brushed her teeth and splashed water on her face, trying to calm the shakiness that was tearing her apart.

It took her five minutes to throw all her clothes into her suitcase. She had no idea what time it was, and she didn't care. The hell with waiting— she wasn't going to spend one more night under that roof. He was getting too close, he knew her weaknesses and her fears too well.

By the time she returned she'd be ready to nail him. Her defenses would be back in place like a suit of armor. Her main mistake had been to underestimate him in the first place. She thought she was immune to his seductive beauty—she'd been immune to everyone else she'd met in her life.

But she hadn't counted on Luke's particular gift. No ordinary man would be capable of drawing hundreds and thousands of followers, both those at the center and those suckered in across the country. Charisma, she thought coldly. A simple trick of nature she didn't know how to combat. For now, she had no choice but to run.

Luke pushed the button on the cellular phone, severing the connection. She would be allowed to leave. They would have a taxi waiting for her by the time she emerged from her room, and he knew she'd head straight for the airport.

She was running, scared shitless, a fact that amused him. He hadn't realized that beneath all that spoiled anger how very frightened she was. He hadn't suspected she was frigid either, despite Stella's mocking comments.

It would make his triumph all the more delicious. He no longer had any doubts about whether he'd take her to bed. He wanted her, it was that simple, and he was tired of ignoring his basic urges just for the sake of the power he accumulated.

And the challenge, already powerful, had now become irresistible. A frigid, angry, spoiled young woman, lying in his bed purring with helpless pleasure.

There was only one problem with it. He wasn't sure he was prepared to wait patiently for her return. He'd spent too damned long as a saint, and serenity was a highly overrated commodity. He wanted her, and he wanted her now. On her back, on her knees. Any way he could take her.

Where would she go? According to Stella, she had no other relatives except a handful of ex-stepfathers, and none of them had been particularly paternal. Would she go back to New York, find another job, try to forget about her brief sojourn in New Mexico?

If she had any sense of self-preservation she would. But she didn't strike Luke as the self-preserving type. She wouldn't let go of her anger, admit defeat, and get on with her life.

She'd be looking for new ways to beat him.

He wondered how long it would take her to find Coffin's Grove.

"Bobby Ray tells me that Rachel is gone, Alfred," Catherine said, patting her wispy gray hair.

Alfred looked up from his paperwork, his troubled face a perfect match for his dove-gray clothing. "I'm not sure that solves our problem."

Catherine smiled serenely. "You need to have faith, Alfred. If I know our Luke, and I know him well, he'll spend the next week or so on retreat. If, when he emerges, we still get the sense that things are dissolving, then we can make our move. We already have our plan, and our tool in place. It should be quite simple to implement things if need be. In the meantime, remember that the Infinite is on our side. We are the forces of right, and that will guide us."

For a brief moment doubt clouded Alfred's steely eyes. "Are we, Catherine? Are you sure?"

Catherine put her arms around Alfred, holding his head against her breast as she stroked his hair. "Have faith, Alfred," she said again in her warm, maternal voice. "And all will be well."

Bobby Ray Shatney did what he was told to do, and he needed to be content. But that was easier said than done. They were weaning him off the drugs now, and too often he felt the rage begin to fill him. The killing rage. They thought he would do what they told him, but they were wrong.

Luke was letting her leave. The Grandfathers were making no move to stop her, and they seldom let anyone return if they left before their two-month stint. He might never see her again.

No, that was unthinkable. There was unfinished business with Rachel Connery. He knew what Stella would have wanted him to do, and he intended to do it.

If Rachel didn't return to the Foundation of Being of her own accord, then Bobby Ray had no choice but to go after her. She couldn't be allowed to live. He knew that now.

What would Catherine think? At that moment he didn't care. Catherine would probably send him after her with a blessing, but if she didn't . . .

He could feel the blood lust curling at the base of his brain. He needed to find release.

Catherine would do.

PART TWO

COFFIN'S GROVE, ALABAMA

10

When Rachel made her escape from the retreat center she was conscious of nothing but her need for safety. Safety and solitude. She sat up in the Albuquerque airport for hours, waiting for the first plane out, and it didn't matter that it was a tiny little prop jet heading for California when she desperately wanted to be back in her apartment in New York. The sooner she got out of the state, away from him, the better.

It was more than twelve hours later when she finally stumbled into her stuffy New York apartment, collapsing on her bed and pulling the pillow over her head. Only to find that she couldn't sleep.

His voice still echoed in the back of her mind. She could see his eyes, watching her, that faint mocking streak that none of his deluded followers noticed. She could hear the sexual promise in his voice, a promise that was more a threat to someone like Rachel. She could feel his hands on her body. Feel his breath against her cheek. Feel the heat and dampness of his mouth as it skimmed over her body . . .

She sat upright suddenly, shoving the pillows away from her. Her mind was playing tricks on her, making things seem even more terrifying than they were.

There was a thick file on her desk, full of clippings and photocopies of articles on Luke Bardell and the Foundation of Being. She knew everything the public knew, which wasn't much beyond PR-spun stories, and now she knew far too much about his private persona. She picked up the file, wanting nothing more than to burn it, burn him, out of her life, out of her consciousness. She dumped it in the wastebasket, only to have a piece of paper flutter onto the floor, facedown.

She stared at it. She could tell by the paper that it was something she'd printed out from the Internet. There was no way it could lead her in any useful direction. She should just ignore it, not even look at it, dump it in the trash with the other stuff and carry it straight out to the incinerator. She needed to make a symbolic gesture, to admit not defeat, but her willingness to let go. If she wanted to survive.

But the piece of paper lay on her smoke-gray

carpet, and she knew its contents would determine the path her life would take.

"Ridiculous," she said out loud, her voice sounding strange and distorted in the empty apartment. "You've been with those new age flakes for too long. Pick the damned piece of paper up and throw it out."

She picked the paper up, turned it over, and read it, knowing she was sealing her doom.

It was a simple chronology of Luke Bardell's known life. Born December 8, 1960, in Coffin's Grove, Alabama. Mother died when he was eight, father committed suicide when he was sixteen. Moved to Chicago in 1976, convicted of manslaughter in 1980, served four years in Joliet Prison.

Coffin's Grove. The name stuck in her head like a message. A message she was at a loss to understand.

Just simple facts. With so many questions behind them. How had his mother died? What had made his father commit suicide eight years later? Had Luke been the one to find him?

Rachel had been relentless in her quest for information. She'd read the court transcripts of his trial, every single piece of public record. But she'd never thought about his past. Or anything about a little town in Alabama named Coffin's Grove. Not until an act of clumsiness brought it back.

She pulled the file out of the wastebasket and

dumped it on her desk. She shoved her hair out of her face—it was getting too long, she needed it trimmed, but she didn't have time to bother with such mundane irritations. She had to find out everything she could about Coffin's Grove, if she was going to do battle with the devil himself.

It was hot, miserably steaming hot when Rachel stepped off the airplane in Mobile one week later. She was used to the humidity of a New York summer, but it was nothing compared to the liquid air that surrounded her, filling her lungs and clamping a tight fist around her heart.

It took too damned long to get the anonymous white rental car, too long to orient herself. She hadn't been able to touch the airline food, and the various greasy restaurants at the airport hadn't looked any more promising.

She was losing weight, something she couldn't afford to do. She didn't want to be rail-thin—too many men found skinniness attractive. She was feeling light-headed, from the heat, from lack of food, from tension, but she didn't want to stop long enough to do anything about it.

She wanted to make Coffin's Grove by nightfall.

The road atlas offered only minimal help as she sped along the heat-baked highways, the narrow, secondary roads, back into the overgrown forests that looked like they belonged in swamp country.

The air conditioner was blasting cold air against her face, and she switched on the radio, hoping for distraction.

"The devil came down to Georgia," sang a rough voice, and Rachel almost drove off the road in her haste to turn the damned thing off. She was spooked enough as it was.

She was in Alabama, not Georgia, she reminded herself. And Luke Bardell wasn't the devil, even if he seemed almost otherworldly in his power. Besides, he didn't go down to Georgia, he came up from Alabama.

She shook her head with self-disgust. The last week had taken her obsession and deepened it, until she wasn't sensible. She wasn't eating, or sleeping, driven with her need to destroy the man who had taken everything from her.

For some reason she no longer thought about the money he'd conned out of her mother. She didn't even think about Stella, lost to her decades ago. Never hers to begin with.

Luke Bardell had possessed her mind. If she could destroy him, expose him as the charlatan and manipulative con man that he was, then she could finally find peace.

Couldn't she?

The roads turned to gravel, the trees loomed higher and darker overhead, and she couldn't rid herself of the notion that she was traveling to some dark, disenchanted place, like a twisted Brigadoon. A town of Spanish moss and rotting houses, wasted lives and poverty.

The reality of it was enough to force a bitter laugh from her. The sign was freshly painted, with neat black lettering. COFFIN'S GROVE, FOUNDED 1822. POPULATION 730. HOME OF LUKE BARDELL. She couldn't believe it. He hardly seemed to qualify as a hometown hero.

The town was picture perfect. Neat white houses, neat trimmed lawns. Pretty little gardens, white picket fences, everything polite and prosperous. There were no blowsy roses or luscious peonies, only small, tightly budded flowers in pale, subdued colors. Life here was restrained and well bred, Rachel thought, pulling the car up in front of the Village Cafe.

It was no illusion that she was being watched. Coffin's Grove wasn't a mecca for visitors, and the customers in the tiny little coffee shop stared at her as if she were a Martian who'd just landed.

She ordered coffee and toast. She needed the caffeine, and she thought toast would be one thing she could manage to keep down. The middle-aged waitress who'd taken her order wasn't the one who brought her food. Rachel watched with interest as an older man intercepted her, taking the tray and heading for her table.

"Mind if I join you?" he said pleasantly enough.

Rachel studied him. He was in his sixties, a friendly, slightly pompous-looking man who was, she decided, absolutely harmless. If she had to make a guess, she'd peg him as some sort of town official. The mayor, perhaps, or the chief of police.

"All right," she said, managing to sound gracious.

"You're not from around here," he said, lowering his impressive bulk into the protesting chair across from her. "I know, because I've lived here all my life, and my daddy and my granddaddy before me, all the way back to the War of Insurrection. My name's Leroy Peltner, and I'm the mayor of Coffin's Grove."

"Do you personally welcome all your visitors, Mr. Peltner?" Rachel murmured, sipping at her coffee. It was weak and oily, a nasty combination, but she drank it anyway, eyeing the plate of butter-drenched white bread with distaste.

"Call me Leroy. I'd tell you my daddy was Mr. Peltner, but no one called him that either. We're a neighborly town, Miss . . ." He waited for her to supply her name.

"Rachel Connery," she said dutifully.

He blinked. The reaction was so slight she might have been imagining it. After all, there was no reason for her name to mean anything to this pompous old man.

"We're a neighborly town, Rachel," he said again. "We like to welcome everyone who comes by. Besides, we're not exactly a tourist center. Our only claim to fame is long gone."

That easy, she thought. Or was it too easy?

"What's your claim to fame?" She couldn't bring herself to call him Leroy.

"Didn't you see our sign? Luke Bardell comes from these parts."

"Who's Luke Bardell?" She was a good liar, but she didn't think she fooled him. He'd reacted to her name, though why he should have was beyond her.

"Heck, I thought everyone knew who Luke Bardell was. Don't you ever read *People* magazine?"

"Not if I can help it," she muttered.

"He's founded some newfangled kind of religion, kind of like Scientology without the movie stars. Has some fancy place out in the Southwest, but he was born right here in Coffin's Grove, and his momma and grandma before him."

"What about his father?"

Leroy Peltner hadn't been elected mayor on the basis of his poker face or his diplomatic abilities. He was two seconds too late in hiding his reaction.

"Well, him too," he said, taking out a handkerchief and mopping his brow. The cafe was air-conditioned to the point of chilliness, but Leroy Peltner was sweating up a storm. "Course, what with the tragedy we don't like to talk about Jackson Bardell. Hell, it's water over the dam, excuse my French, and we like to concentrate on happier things around here."

"Tragedy?"

He ignored her question. "What brings you to Coffin's Grove, Miss Connery? Or is it Mrs.?"

"It's Ms.," she said, knowing it was what he expected from a nosy Yankee bitch.

"And you know perfectly well who Luke Bardell is, don't you, honey?" He leaned across the table, too close, and put his hand on hers.

She snatched it away so quickly she knocked over a glass of water. "What makes you think that?"

"Because no one ever comes to this godforsaken burg unless they're curious. So let's just cut the horseshit, lady. What exactly are you, a reporter or a cop?"

She watched the water pool on the gold-flecked Formica and start a path toward the edge of the table. "Why should I be either one?"

"Don't toy with me, honey. If you want my help, if you want to know about Luke Bardell, you just come right out and ask. We don't have any secrets around here." He looked over his shoulder at the group of people huddled by the counter, and raised his voice. "Do we, boys?"

"No, sirree." "Nope." "Not a one." They were like a Greek chorus.

Rachel plastered a smile on her face. She could manage a certain amount of charm if the situation called for it. Leroy Peltner knew her name, but he didn't know why she was here, of that she was reasonably certain.

"Actually," she said, "I'm writing a book about the Foundation of Being."

"No shit?" Leroy's Southern gentleman politeness had vanished. "You gonna try to dig up some dirt on old Luke?"

"Is there any to dig up?"

He eyed her speculatively. "There's always dirt, sugar. What's it worth to you?"

"That depends on the quality of your dirt."

Leroy leaned across the table, his voice low and insinuating. "Honey, I got the finest dirt around."

"Leroy!" The voice was sharp and clear, and poor Leroy jumped a mile, sweat beading up on his wrinkled red forehead.

"Sheriff Coltrane," he said, his nervous stammer almost indiscernible. "I was just welcoming this young lady to our fair town. She's writing a book on our Luke."

Sheriff Coltrane wasn't much of an improvement over Leroy Peltner. He had to be somewhere in his mid-fifties, a weathered face hidden by dark glasses and the hat he had pulled low, and his bulky compact body looked to be made of pure, ornery muscle. Something told Rachel he wasn't going to be as easy to play as Leroy.

"You go back to work, Leroy. Eva Lou has some papers you need to sign."

"Hell, Coltrane, I don't need . . ." His whine tapered off as the sheriff turned his sunglassed eyes to him. "Pleasure meetin' you, Ms. Connery. I hope we get a chance to talk real soon."

Leroy practically scurried from the cafe, and the other patrons were now studiously ignoring the newcomer. Apparently Sheriff Coltrane put the fear of God into just about everyone.

"Don't count on it," he said.

Rachel blinked. "Don't count on what?"

"On seeing Leroy anytime in the near future. The old fool shoots off his mouth—it makes him feel important, but you can't believe a word he says. Just last month he was doing his damnedest to get some TV crew down here looking for the Goatsucker. Two years ago it was flying saucers. Leroy's got a hell of an imagination and a need to be the center of attention."

"Then why is he the mayor?"

Sheriff Coltrane's smile was tight and cold. "No one else would take the job. And we're loyal around here. 'Cept for Leroy when he gets carried away by a pretty face. No one's got anything to tell you about Luke Bardell that you don't already know. If I were you I'd get back in that rental car and head on out of town before it gets dark."

"It's still summer, Sheriff. It doesn't get dark all that early."

"No one's gonna help you," he said again.

"Are you trying to interfere with the freedom of the press, Sheriff?"

"Don't give me that ACLU crap. And you aren't the press. You're just some woman who claims to be a writer. You got any credentials on you?"

"No."

His smile was downright nasty. "Now I don't know what you've heard about small Southern towns and their sheriffs, but we follow the letter of the law. I can suggest you leave town, but I'm not about to make you go. I'm just warning you that you're wasting your time."

"It's my time to waste."

"So it is. But the nearest motel is twenty-seven miles away in Gaithersburg, and these roads are mighty dark at night."

"I saw a sign for a bed and breakfast when I drove in."

He had tobacco-stained teeth that showed when he grinned. "That's run by Esther Blessing, and I don't think she's gonna take you in."

"Why not?"

"Because she's Jackson Bardell's mama. And she's never forgiven Luke."

"Forgiven him for what?"

"Who knows? This is a small town, Miss Connery. I expect she's already heard that you're here, and why. If you walk up her front steps you might get a blast of buckshot."

"Cut it out, Sheriff!" The weary-looking waitress seemed to be the only person in the cafe brave enough to stand up to him. "Esther's more interested in money than revenge, and besides, there's nothing she'd like better than to fill this young lady's head with lies about Luke."

"Who says they'd be lies?" someone piped up.

"You shut up, Horace Wildeen, or I'll shut you up," Sheriff Coltrane said without looking back at him. He continued to stare at Rachel through those mirrored sunglasses, and she was just as glad she couldn't see his eyes. She knew just what they'd look like—cold and flat like a reptile's. "It's up to you, miss," he said. "I'm not about to mess with your civil rights." He said the phrase as if it was an obscenity. "It'll be your funeral."

And without another word he stalked from the cafe, leaving the place in a nervous silence.

"Well," Rachel said after a moment, "this sure is a friendly little town."

"Luke's a controversial subject, honey," the waitress said, refilling her coffee cup. "People around here either think he's Jesus Christ risen from the dead or the devil himself. And the two sides aren't ever going to agree."

"And what do you think?"

Her name, Lureen, was embroidered across her shallow chest. "I think he's a little bit of both, sugar," she said in a low voice. "A little bit of both."

"She's here."

" 'Bout time she showed up. I thought she was more impatient than that."

"You probably scared the hell out of her."

"I tried. She doesn't scare easy."

"I noticed that," Coltrane said. "Lureen's doing her part, but Leroy almost blew it."

"Leroy's an idiot."

"Tell me something I don't know," Coltrane said. "You coming out here, or do you want me to handle it? I can take care of her if you want me to."

"Watch her."

"She's going after your granny."

"Not my granny," Luke said. "Jackson's mother. If I know Esther, she'll fill Rachel's head so full of horror stories she won't know which way's up."

"What if she calls the cops?"

"You're the cops, Coltrane. You've got connections."

"Yeah. But you told me not to hurt her."

Luke lit a match, watching the flame flare up

before he lit the end of his cigarette. He took a deep, appreciative drag on it, reveling in the forbidden pleasure. "Just watch her," he said.

"You still in New Mexico? I thought you were going to come back here and take care of things?"

"Relax, Coltrane. I've got everything well in hand."

"Where the hell are you, Bardell?"

"Close," Luke murmured. "Closer than you think." He pushed the button on the cell phone, severing the connection. He could just picture Jimmy Coltrane's peeved expression.

Jimmy Coltrane was fifteen years older than Luke. He'd been a bully in his teens, a mean cop in his twenties. He was the one who'd found Jackson Bardell with half his head blown away; he was the one who'd taken one look at Luke, taken the gun from his nerveless hand, and calmly wiped the fingerprints clean. He then placed it in Jackson's dead hand.

It wouldn't have fooled anybody—there were paraffin tests and forensic reports, but Coltrane saw to it that no one bothered making any of those tests. Everyone knew Jackson Bardell was a sadistic drunk. No one missed him except his mama, and Esther was always crabbing about something. At least this time she'd have a reason.

Luke had never been sure why Coltrane had done it. Maybe just because he'd always hated

Jackson Bardell. Maybe because he knew that sooner or later the tide would turn and Luke would be in a position to repay him. Or maybe he just liked the feeling of power it gave him.

Luke didn't give a shit. Jackson Bardell's body had been cremated, the files had been destroyed in a fire that had swept through the town building, and there was nothing anyone could do but listen to Esther's ravings about that son of the devil who'd killed her boy.

She was as mean and ornery as her only child had been. She used to hurt him when he was too young to fight back, and then he'd taken off.

But now he was back again. And before he left he was going to pay a little visit to Esther Blessing.

And tell her just how her son died.

11

Sheriff Coltrane wasn't as smart as he thought. Esther Blessing didn't even blink an eye when Rachel showed up at the tall, white-painted Victorian house with the green sign hanging outside.

She didn't look like Luke. That was Rachel's first thought, and she ignored the odd strain of relief that swept through her. Esther Blessing looked older than sin and twice as mean. She was a tiny woman, wiry, with mean dark eyes and grizzled white hair that stood up all around her head. Her mouth was small and unpleasant, and she and her entire house smelled of day-old cigarettes.

She looked Rachel up and down with a disparaging glance, but it seemed as if it were the response she showed to the entire world. "We don't get many visitors in these parts," she said, unconsciously echoing Leroy Peltner.

Rachel had had enough time to consider her options. If the woman pulled out a shotgun, Rachel was ready to run. "I'm here doing research on Luke Bardell."

The little old lady froze, and if anything her expression grew more sour. "Why?"

"I'm writing a book about him."

Esther Blessing snorted. "You think he's some kind of saint, girly?"

It was a gamble, but the last few weeks had taught Rachel that she had nothing to lose. She looked Esther straight in her mean little eyes. "I don't think so, Mrs. Blessing. I think he's a crook, and a charlatan, and a liar."

"What about murderer, girly? Did you think about that?"

For some reason Esther's avid interest made Rachel uncomfortable. She ignored the feeling, ignored her strange urge to defend her enemy. "I thought it was manslaughter."

"I ain't talking about the Polack he killed in a bar," Esther said. "I'm talking about my son. Jackson Bardell. Murdered in cold blood by that little bastard."

Shock turned Rachel cold. "He killed his own father?"

"Aren't you listening to me, girl? He was a bastard. Marijo MacDonald was already knocked up when she tricked my boy into marrying her. She spread her legs for that traveling preacher man, and when he abandoned her with a bun in the oven she turned to my boy. Hell, it was no wonder. That boy was the prettiest thing you'd ever seen, and he could talk just about anyone into anything."

"Luke?"

"No, his real pa. He went from town to town, preaching the Gospel, healing the sick, and sleeping with the pretty girls. Till someone kilt him, which served him right. That didn't do Marijo much good, though." Esther cackled.

"It sounds like he takes after his real father."

"Never trust no preacher man's son, girly. Especially if they're bastards. Jackson tried to teach the two of them about repentance, Marijo and that bastard son of hers. Didn't do no good, though. And look what happened."

The smell of cigarettes warred with old sweat and some kind of overpowering air freshener, and Rachel knew if she tried to vomit all she'd manage to bring up would be coffee. She bit her lip, concentrating on the turkey-red carpet beneath her feet.

"What did happen?"

"You know how his mother died. The fool girl killed herself, she did, when her guilt got too much. She always was a silly fool, no match for my Jackson. He hated her, and the boy too."

"Why didn't he divorce her?"

"We don't have divorce in this family," Esther said flatly. "It ain't godly."

"What makes you think Luke killed your son?" Rachel persisted. "Why haven't you told anyone?"

Esther's coarse laugh was like chalk on a blackboard. "Honey, everyone already knows. They drove him out of town back then, when they couldn't prove nothing, but now that he's got buckets of money they're falling all over him, trying to kiss his ass. You better watch your step, girly. They don't want anyone tarnishing their local saint, even if he is the spawn of the devil. He means money for this town. The first industry we've ever had."

"How do you feel about that, Mrs. Blessing?" Rachel asked faintly.

Esther Blessing leaned forward and her breath was fetid on Rachel's face, whiskey and cigarettes and decades-old venom. It was all Rachel could do to stop her instinctive recoil.

"I'm gonna kill him, girly," the old woman said with a soulless cackle. "He can't get away with murdering my boy. Sooner or later, I'm gonna kill him."

The bedroom Esther Blessing allotted her had to be the fussiest, ugliest room Rachel had ever been in. The walls were covered with a lime-green-flocked wallpaper; there were ruffles and knick-knacks everywhere. There wasn't a clear space of room atop the dresser or the small table, but neither was there a speck of dust in the place. With all those porcelain bunny rabbits and kissing kinder it must have been a full-time job for her landlady.

She didn't want to be there. She should be used to the feeling—it could hardly feel less hospitable than the austere cell in Santa Dolores.

But this felt different. For all the fuss and frills, for all the ruthless cleanliness, there was a sense of sickness and decay in the tall white house. A sweating evil that seeped into her pores and covered her with a slimy film of decadence that nothing could wash away.

She laughed at herself as she stood beneath the lukewarm shower. She was becoming melodramatic in her old age, when she'd always prided herself on coolheaded practicality. She'd always avoided grandstanding, since her mother had been so very good at it. But now that Stella was dead she found she was falling into the trap after all. The curse of inescapable heredity.

When she was a child she used to dream she was adopted. That Stella had swept down on some orphanage with her money and her jewels and picked out the infant who most resembled her. She'd grown tired of her new toy, of course, but somewhere in the world Rachel's real, loving parents were looking for her.

By the age of nine she knew that was bullshit. Stella had popped her forth all right—she still complained about the fourteen-hour labor when she'd had enough martinis. And the physical resemblance was undeniable—they had the same eyes, the same elegant bone structure, and beneath Stella's constant dye jobs, the same mousy brown-blond hair.

She'd met her father only once. He didn't want her, Stella had told her brutally when she was three. He was more interested in young men than a family. It had taken far too long for Rachel to understand, and the one time she'd run into him he'd been very drunk. So drunk that he'd simply looked up at her blearily, not realizing who she was.

He was dead now. So was the stepfather who'd molested her, so was her mother. And for one brief, furious moment she had one more thing to resent Luke Bardell for. He'd done what she'd always longed to do. Killed his tormentors.

The moment she stepped outside Esther's house the humidity settled back down around her like a shroud. It was late afternoon, and the bugs were out, their incessant whine a distant drone in the back of her head. Fortunately mosquitoes never found her particularly appetizing, though this bunch were bigger and meaner than anything she'd ever run into. She headed toward the rental car, planning to close the windows and turn the air conditioner on full blast, when Esther Blessing stuck her head out the front door and screeched across the short, short grass.

"Dinner's at seven-thirty, and if you're late don't be expecting kitchen privileges." She paused, peering at her. "Where are you going, girly?"

"I'll take care of my own food."

Esther's snort carried all the way out to the sidewalk. "If you're the one who's been responsible for it so far then you've done a piss poor job. You look like a stiff wind would carry you off."

"Lucky there's no wind, then," she said, unlocking her car.

"Suit yourself, girly. Just don't get caught on a back road after dark. Leroy Peltner says he's seen the Goatsucker around here."

"I can think of worse things," she muttered to herself.

"What's that you say?" Esther screeched.

"I said I'll be careful."

Esther didn't look particularly gratified as she let the screen door slam shut once more, disappearing into her dark, tobacco-laden house, and for a moment Rachel regretted leaving her suitcase up in that fussy, stifling room. The afternoon air was so thick she could hardly breathe, and the town made her nervous. It was as if someone was watching her, staring at her, spying on her.

But she wasn't going to do that, wasn't going to run. She'd already run from Santa Dolores, and she couldn't go back until she had more to fight him with. And she was on the right track, she knew it. How would his blissed-out followers feel if they knew he'd killed his father, if not by blood, by upbringing? When had that dangerous charm emerged? He was a man who was followed by death. Did he summon it?

She didn't like it here in this steamy little town. It was too claustrophobic, and despite the fresh white paint on many of the buildings, there still seemed to be an air of decay about the place. As if those coats of paint covered up rotted siding and rotted souls.

She didn't know who was going to help her, and she wasn't going to ask. Lureen at the Cafe had already given her grudging directions on how to get to the graveyard, but she balked at telling her where to find Jackson Bardell's old house. It was deserted, she said. Had been since Jackson killed himself. By now the swamp would have taken over.

The graveyard wasn't beside the old church, one of the few buildings in town without a fresh coat of paint. It was on the edge of town, heading toward the deep, swampy forest, and Rachel couldn't shake off her uneasiness as she drove in that direction, air conditioner blasting full force. This wasn't what she'd expected to find when she'd come down to Alabama. She'd expected antebellum charm and small-town friendliness. This sense of mordant decay was playing havoc with her mind.

But then, that's what Luke Bardell seemed to specialize in, whether she was in his unsettling presence or thousands of miles away. It was her greatest danger. He made her feel vulnerable, imaginative, two things she'd fought against for most of her life. And she wasn't going back to Santa Dolores until she'd managed to wipe such weaknesses from her life.

The grass in the graveyard was neatly trimmed, the granite markers clean and symmetrical. She wandered haphazardly, reading names and dates, the casualties of every war since the 1850s, the usual number of children taken during times of fever. There were Peltners and Coltranes and Bardells, but nowhere could she find Luke's parents.

Again that eerie feeling of being watched, of eyes staring into the middle of her back. Was there a gun trained at that vulnerable point as well? She could see Esther Blessing holding a shotgun—it suited her dark, angry eyes and her dark, angry soul. What about the others, Coltrane and Peltner and even Lureen? Did they want to hurt her? Something strange was going on in this town, which shouldn't surprise her. Any town that spawned the likes of Luke Bardell had to be twisted.

She stopped in the middle of the graveyard and gave herself a brisk shake. She could probably blame her flaming paranoia on Luke Bardell as well, except that she'd always had a faintly paranoid streak. It came from having no one to trust.

But there was no reason why the citizens of Coffin's Grove would wish her any harm. And if she thought about it, allowed herself the dangerous luxury of examining these imaginary feelings, she could sense no danger from those watching eyes. No physical danger.

The place was creeping her out. She turned, ready to give up, when she found what had been eluding her. Jackson Bardell's gaudy monolith.

It was absurd of her to have missed it before. It was taller than the other gravestones, with a dog carved in granite at the foot. Surrounding it were bunches of plastic flowers in various unlikely shades of purple and yellow, mud-splashed and sun-faded. And a telltale pile of cigarette butts of varying vintages. Two different brands. Two people stood over his grave. Did they both mourn?

She looked at the deeply etched words. JACKSON

BARDELL, DEVOTED SON, EXPERT HUNTER, DUTIFUL HUSBAND. CUT DOWN IN HIS PRIME. 1930–1976.

No mention of his own son. Cut down in his prime was Esther's doing, to announce to the world that she knew he'd been murdered. She said she was going to kill Luke when she got the chance. It was only surprising she'd waited so long.

She headed toward the gate, almost tripping over the small, marble plaque set in the ground, far away from Bardell's ornate tombstone. MARIJO MACDONALD. 1940–1968.

No Bardell added to her name. But a fresh handful of wildflowers lay beside the marble stone, not yet wilting from the heat.

Someone had been here before her. Recently. Someone who'd cared about Marijo MacDonald, when her own husband hadn't seen fit to put her name on her tombstone. Rachel looked up, suddenly alert, staring around her. There was no sign of anyone. Whoever had been here, whoever had visited Marijo's grave and then stayed to watch her, was gone.

She wanted to run to her car, slam the door, and drive the hell out of town. But she'd come too far to run away. Again.

There were little patches of small white wildflowers growing along the edge of the fence where the mower's blade had missed them. Rachel didn't even think about what she was doing, she moved purely by instinct. She picked a small handful of the delicate white blooms and lay them carefully beside the others on Marijo's grave.

She looked back at Jackson Bardell's ostentatious display and a sour grin twisted her face. Let him keep the plastic tributes, she thought. He deserved them.

There'd been other MacDonalds in the graveyard, presumably Marijo's family, but she rested nowhere near them. She was off alone, probably because she was a suicide.

But so, ostensibly, was Jackson Bardell.

Luke Bardell had taken her mother. But there was no denying that he'd lost his own as well. It made no difference in the long run.

But it lingered in her mind as she started up the rental car once more.

Luke stepped out of the darkness of the thick growth of trees, taking his time, listening as the sound of her tinny little car disappeared into the afternoon air. The car suited the kind of person she thought she was. White and anonymous, automatic transmission and lots of air-conditioning.

He didn't see her that way. He could see her naked, on leather. And he would, sooner or later.

He didn't bother going anywhere near Jackson Bardell's grave. He'd put the old man behind him, out of his life, his conscience. Instead he went to Marijo's grave, staring down at the pale pink flowers he'd left earlier, the white ones lying beside them.

He squatted, touching one, turning it over. Marijo had been the opposite of Rachel Connery. Sweet-natured, helpless, almost simple in her needs and her loves. But something told him she would have liked Rachel. She would have folded Rachel in her warm arms and stroked her hair; she would have murmured all the safe, loving things that a child like Rachel needed to hear.

As she had with him.

He glanced back at Jackson's massive headstone, testing himself, waiting for the flood of rage that could sweep over him at unexpected moments. Right now it was gone, squashed down in a tight dark place that never saw the light. At least not if he could help it.

It still lay there, though. He knew it, and there was nothing he could do to exorcise that fierce demon of murderous hatred. It was his cross to bear as he smiled benevolently on the troubled people who dumped their substantial incomes in the capable hands of the Grandfathers. It made him one of them.

He knew Esther's house too well—years hadn't been able to erase the memories from his mind. He knew which window didn't latch, he knew which step creaked, he knew how much codeine cough syrup the old lady sucked down every night as she smoked and watched TV from her airless bedroom. Old Doc Carpenter always kept her well supplied, and he doubted she'd changed her ways. The packs of cigarettes she went through every day was enough to produce an impressive cough that the codeine couldn't stop. It could only send her into a drugged-out bliss.

It had always pleased his baser sentiments to know that the old bitch was addicted to something that would make her constipated as hell.

He wondered how lightly Rachel would sleep in that breathless mausoleum. Would she hear him as he opened the back window? Walked up the stairs? Opened her door?

Would she feel it as he pulled the covers from her body and stared down at her? What would she sleep in? The summer was hot, and Esther didn't believe in air-conditioning or open windows. If she had any sense she'd sleep butt naked.

But she hadn't shown much sense so far. Courage, but stupidity. She'd probably be wrapped up in a flannel nightgown, sweating, dreaming nightmares that he'd pop up and ravish her.

She had no idea who the real enemy was. The real danger to her pristine body and her ice-cold soul. Her real enemy lived inside that skinny, angry body she protected so fiercely.

Why the hell had Stella ever had a child? And what had she done to make such a mess of it? Even a helpless soul like Marijo, with no money and no education, had managed a halfway decent job until she'd ended up hanging herself from one of the rafters in Jackson's barn. There were dried tears on her swollen face, and Luke had forgiven her.

But Jackson never did.

Damn! He hated being back here. He hated this town, the people, the memories that could creep beneath his skin and itch like crazy. He preferred keeping his distance, buying up just enough property to make sure he owned the town, and the people in it. Leroy knew it, so did Coltrane. So did most everybody but Esther Blessing.

She'd shoot him if she saw him, he had no doubt whatsoever. If Doc Carpenter had cut her back on the codeine, or if old age had turned her into a light sleeper, she might hear him coming up those stairs. And she'd blast a hole through his head bigger than the one that killed her precious son.

So be it. Life had been a cocoon out in New Mexico. He could just see the tabloids now, and a faint smile twisted his face.

Not before he had sex with Rachel Connery. He wasn't going to leave this world with unfinished business.

* * *

Esther was a meat-and-potatoes cook. She fed Rachel pot roast and boiled potatoes, swimming in greasy gravy, and Rachel simply stared down at her plate in numb dismay. She couldn't make herself eat, and she knew she had to. She couldn't make herself leave, and she knew she had to.

The windows in her room were painted shut, and the air was stifling. Esther had grudgingly given her a small electric fan, but all it did was stir the sluggish air around the big room.

Rachel had stripped down to a tank top and panties and sat in front of the fan, searching for relief. In the distance she could hear the noise from Esther's television, blaring between the closed doors. It was already past eleven—how late would the old lady play that thing?

She took a nail file and managed to pry open one of the windows, but the damp, lifeless air was no improvement. Even the low-wattage electric light seemed to add to the ovenlike atmosphere, and Rachel shut it off, lying down on the narrow, lumpy bed and staring upward in the darkness.

She could practically feel Luke's presence in that house, in that very room. Logic told her he would have spent a fair amount of time here, and yet she couldn't see a child being comfortable in such a dead, dank place.

She rolled over on her stomach, listening to the sound of her breathing beneath the rumble of the television. Canned laughter echoed through the upstairs, and she had the eerie feeling that all those people laughing at some late-night comedian were really laughing at her.

She'd leave tomorrow, she promised herself. The town records were gone, the graveyard told her exactly nothing, and no one seemed inclined to talk about the saint who had emerged from their midst. She'd find what was left of the house where Luke grew up and then she'd drive the hell out of there, as fast as she could go. She had a strong suspicion Sheriff Coltrane wasn't about to stop her for speeding.

She closed her eyes. She could almost feel him there, watching her. His eyes skimming over her body, her long legs, her hips, her back. The nape of her neck. She felt safer lying on her stomach. Less exposed.

God, she needed to sleep. She couldn't remember when she'd had more than a couple of hours of straight sleep. She was exhausted, and her stomach was a knot of tension inside her.

She needed sleep, she needed safety and comfort.

But she couldn't rest until she found the answers she was looking for. About Stella. About Luke Bardell.

Surely Esther would approve of her mission to destroy Luke. And yet Rachel was loath to ask for the old woman's help.

She didn't want anyone's help. She wanted to see Luke's destruction on her own terms. She wanted him in the mud, groveling for forgiveness. She wanted him vanquished, out of her life.

And then maybe she'd be able to sleep again, she thought. Ignoring the fact that she hadn't slept well since she was eleven years old.

12

Rachel was slowly suffocating.

The bed was too soft, but it cushioned her, wrapping her in a dangerous comfort that she could no longer fight. She drifted, deeper and deeper into sleep, kicking the covers away from her body and burrowing down in the too soft mattress. The night was pitch-dark, a cocoon of heat and blackness sucking her into a world that was part dream, part nightmare.

She could feel him in her room, smell him. But she couldn't open her eyes. Some distant, dancing part of her mind argued—if she opened her eyes it would prove he could scare her, convince her that anything was possible, that he'd left his monastic existence and followed her into this sweating, swamp-filled nightmare. If she kept them shut, allowed her body to stay in this half-world, then she would prove he couldn't frighten her.

The noises were muffled, odd. Esther's television set was still on, reassuring Rachel of the normalcy of things. She could hear an undercurrent of cheeping noise from the swamp on the edge of town. And the distant rumble of thunder, issuing a warning.

She shifted restlessly, telling herself it was all right for her eyes to blink open, to reassure herself. But her eyelids were too heavy, and she sank in deeper.

The memory was there, inescapable, but this time she willingly tried to dredge it up. The old man coming to her bed while she slept, touching her, whispering to her. She fought for that sense of horror and sickness, but this was a different time, a different man, and her body knew it.

Fingertips lightly grazed her body, so softly it was a feathery caress. Hands slid down between her legs, touching her there, and she shifted uneasily, restlessly. *Wake up*, she told herself. But she could only hear the thunder and feel the darkness cover her.

He wasn't there, because she couldn't feel him. Only the touch of his hands, the perfect erotic fantasy. Disembodied, caressing her, with no purpose but to serve her. He wouldn't hurt her, this creature of the night. She knew that now, and she slid farther down on the mattress, letting her body receive the attention it craved.

His mouth was there as well. Lips pressed against the side of her throat. Tongue licking. She shivered in the heat, keeping her hands beside her on the mattress as his head moved down. There was no heavy fall of hair brushing her, so she told herself those rich, wondrous lips weren't Luke's, as his mouth covered her breast beneath the thin tank top and drew it deep.

There was a sound then. A deep sound of utter longing that couldn't have possibly come from her. She longed for nothing, she had no desire to have a man's mouth at her breast. She had no desire.

When he released her breast it was full, aching, damp, and he covered it with long, sensitive fingers as he moved to the other breast, sucking it deeply. She moaned again, arching her back, and she wanted his hand between her legs again, this time beneath the thin cotton of her panties, she wanted him to climb onto the bed.

And then he wasn't touching her. She waited, for the sound of rustling clothing, for anything to promise her that he wasn't finished, when a bright flash of lightning turned the room into daylight, and her eyes flew open. For that brief, shocked second she saw him, and then the room was plunged into darkness again, followed by a crash of thunder.

She dived across the bed for the lamp, switching it on, a furious scream bubbling in her throat. Only to find the room deserted. The door was still locked, the chair firmly in front of it. The window she'd managed to crack open wasn't wide enough for a man. How in God's name could she have thought she'd seen Luke Bardell in her bedroom?

She leaned back against the pillows, forcing herself to take deep, calming breaths. It was nothing. Nothing at all. She'd had erotic dreams before, whether she wanted to admit it or not. In the past she'd woken up with a start, her body spasming. This was the same thing, only the lightning had woken her earlier, before her body had claimed the release her conscious mind denied her.

There was no way Luke Bardell could even be in Alabama, much less be in the house of his worst enemy. It had all been a dream.

And then she looked down and saw the damp circle of cloth covering each breast.

Luke Bardell moved through the night like a shadow. He was hard as a rock, but he had no intention of doing anything about it just now. There was something about this particular affliction that amused him. If Rachel Connery knew just how hard she made him she'd probably freak.

Or run into the bathroom and throw up, as she had at Santa Dolores.

Ah, but when she was asleep, or drugged, it was another matter. She purred like a kitten under his touch, arching her back and offering that cool, pristine body that he found he'd become obsessed with.

He wasn't sure why. She wasn't stunningly beautiful, and she was too nervous to be any good in bed. None of that seemed to matter. He'd told himself it was the challenge, but he knew better. He'd seduced virgins and lesbians, women who thought they were ugly, women who thought they were frigid. He'd slept with women who hated him and women who loved him. There was no new ground to be gained with making Rachel Connery come.

But he wanted to. He couldn't stop thinking about it. And oddly enough, it wasn't the thought of her body that made him needy. It was that haunted look she got in her eyes, when she thought no one was looking.

Hell, he'd been in the desert too long. He knew it, and his body was reminding him of that fact. He was going to be out of there by fall, with a nice little nest egg to keep him in style for, oh, say, fifty years. He was going to disappear, make a new life for himself. No more Luke Bardell of Coffin's Grove, Alabama. No more Luke Bardell of the Foundation of Being. No more bad boy, no more messiah. He was going to spend the rest of his life as a man. Nothing more. Nothing less.

He paused in the darkness to light a cigarette, drawing the smoke deep into his lungs. The smell of Esther's house had his nicotine craving going full force, and he was going to indulge himself for the next few days. While Luke Bardell was on a spiritual retreat, replenishing his soul in solitude and meditation, the bad boy of Coffin's Grove was on the prowl. And his quarry was getting restless.

He glanced up at Esther's house. She'd kept the light on, probably spooked as hell. He couldn't believe how heavily she'd slept, and he couldn't resist putting his hands, his mouth on her, seeing how far he could go before she woke up screaming. If it hadn't been for that damned bolt of lightning he probably would have gotten her panties off her.

Coltrane would be somewhere around, probably looking for him. He'd shit if he knew Luke had gone into Esther's house. It wouldn't serve anybody's best interests if Esther blew a hole in him as she so wanted to do. Except, maybe, Rachel Connery.

He slipped into the darkness, whistling softly. "The Devil Came Down to Georgia" was going through his mind, he wasn't quite sure why. He didn't care. In the night he was invisible, no one knew where he was, and he was free. For a short, sweet time he was free.

"You don't look like you slept too well, girly." Esther Blessing dumped a plate of grease in front of her. Rachel's stomach recoiled in horror at the sight of the bright yellow eggs, the sausage, the pile of white detritus that could only be grits.

"The storm kept me awake," she said faintly, reaching for her coffee in a vain effort to keep herself alert. She'd been awake the rest of the night, lying on the bed, staring into every corner of the fussy bedroom, waiting for her ghost to reappear. The more she looked, the more she had known that he couldn't have been there. In a room that crammed with knickknacks he couldn't have entered, or escaped, without knocking something over.

"Nothing could interfere with my beauty sleep," Esther said with a smirk. "Maybe it's the result of living with a clear conscience."

Rachel looked at the smug old woman and sincerely doubted it. "I think I'll be leaving today," she said, making an effort to stir the food around on her plate. She'd managed to swallow a piece of toast, but that was about as far as her recalcitrant appetite could take her.

"You already found out what you need to know? You're a fast worker."

"I get the feeling I'm not wanted in this town."

Esther cackled. "You got that right. This town makes a living off'n that spawn of Satan. They don't want you interfering."

"What about you? I would have thought you'd leap at the chance of my exposing your grandson for what he is."

"Not my grandson!" Esther snapped. "No kin to me at all, thank the Lord, I already told you that. Anyway, I figure my time will come. I don't need your help to see justice done. I've waited twenty years since my Jackson was killed, I can wait a few more." She made a rough, hacking sound in the back of her throat and reached for her pack of cigarettes.

Rachel kept herself from voicing the obvious. It might be a neck-and-neck race, who would die first, Esther from her cancer sticks or Luke from long overdue justice.

"If you say so. I don't suppose you have any old pictures of Luke, any stories from his childhood that you'd want to share?" It was highly unlikely, but she couldn't leave without asking.

To her surprise Esther pulled out a chair and sat down. "There weren't many pictures, and I burned 'em all," she said. "As for stories, I could tell you things that would make your skin crawl. The way he used to stare at me, out of those crazy eyes of his, like I was the evil one and not him.

He never made a sound when I whupped him, neither. Not even when he was four years old and I took his daddy's belt to him. That boy was so black and blue he could barely walk, but he never said a word. It weren't natural."

Rachel's stomach lurched. "Four years old?" she echoed faintly.

"Yeah, he was a wicked child from the very beginning. Nothing could change him, not beatings, not locking him up in the closet for a night. Nothing would make him show any weakness. The only time I ever saw him cry was when they buried his mama, and he was to blame for that as well."

"Why? Do you think he killed her?"

Esther shot her a glance of withering scorn. "His mama was the only thing he cared about. She was a silly little tramp, with no more sense than a baby. Even when Luke was four years old he seemed smarter."

"So why was he to blame?"

"His existence, girly! He never should have been born. If Marijo had been the good girl she was supposed to be, then my boy would have respected her. But she gave him a bastard and he never forgave her. He tried to beat the badness out of both of them, but it never did any good. So finally Marijo did the only thing she could do to make things right. She hung herself out in Jackson's barn."

"So she should have had an abortion and never told Jackson she was pregnant, is that it?"

"Abortion is a sin. I don't hold with harming an unborn child," Esther said righteously. "She shoulda kept herself pure until Jackson was ready for her."

"Foolish Marijo," Rachel said lightly.

"She learned her lesson in the end, I guess. She's roasting in hell now."

"Why do you say that?"

"She killed herself. You think that's going to put her into heaven? Mealy-mouthed little creature, always looking like she was scared to death of me and my boy. God knows neither of us would hurt a fly."

Rachel looked at Esther's strong, gnarled hands, the hands that had whipped a four-year-old till he couldn't walk, and she shuddered.

"He found her, you know," Esther continued in a chatty vein. "It was Thanksgiving, she'd put the food on the table and just walked out. Jackson made Luke sit and eat his meal, and he didn't find her until four hours later. Too late to do anything about it. Sure put a damper on the holidays that year, let me tell you."

"I can imagine," Rachel said faintly.

"That was when he changed. He was always a

quiet little boy before that, downright eerie. After he found his ma and cut her down he got even stranger. Defiant, sly. The teachers were afraid of him. Hell, even I was afraid of him, an eight-year-old. But I didn't know how much wickedness truly resided in his heart. Jackson tried to beat it out of him, but it was no use. Jackson had been a father to the little bastard, even though he had no responsibility to him once Marijo died, and what did that boy do? Took his father's gun and blew his head off."

"I thought the police said it was another suicide."

"My boy thought too highly of hisself to end his life. Besides, I brought him up to believe it was a sin. And he sure as hell didn't want to spend eternity at Marijo's side—their six years of marriage was suffering enough."

"I thought you said Luke was eight when she died?"

"He was. Jackson married Marijo when Luke was two."

The woman's logic was appalling. "So what happened to this spawn of the devil after your son died?"

"After Luke murdered him? The boy just took off, and good riddance. He knew that Jackson had a lot of friends around here, and not one of them had been partial to that scrawny little changeling except a few bleeding-heart teachers. And why they bothered, when he never showed up for school, was beyond me. But Luke lit out from here after the inquest. Didn't even stop by to see me."

"What would you have done if he had?"

"Kilt him," Esther said flatly. "He must have figgered that out."

"Must have," Rachel echoed. "And you never heard from him again?"

"Nope. Not until I read about him in one of those newspapers they have by the checkout counter at the Piggly Wiggly. Heard he'd killed another man, and ended up in jail for it. Which is where he belonged. But now he's got thousands of fool people handing him their money, thinking he's Jesus Christ or something. For the sin of blasphemy he oughtta be destroyed, if not for all his other sins."

Esther looked like the woman to do it.

Even the coffee was churning in Rachel's stomach. She plastered her best social smile on her face, the one Stella had taught her to present to the world, no matter what. "I'm sure he'll meet his just rewards," she said in a soothing tone.

"Is that what you are, missy? Are you going to right the wrong that was done to my son so many years ago?"

Rachel just looked at her. "I think I'll leave that up to you," she said.

Esther cackled. "You may think so, girly, but my money's on you. I think you're going to be the death of him, whether you want to be or not."

"I don't want to be the death of anyone," she said in a faint voice.

"You don't always get what you want," Esther said. "You'll end up killing him. Destroying him. One way or another."

Rachel never thought she would be grateful for the sweltering, smothering heat that folded around her when she stepped from Esther's house. It felt as if Spanish moss was growing in her lungs, but she didn't care. Being away from the fetid air that wicked old woman breathed was relief enough.

She didn't really want to be anyone's destruction after all, not even Luke Bardell's. He'd had a tough, tortured childhood. So what? Most of the people she knew had miserable families. So he'd killed, maybe more than once.

Maybe he killed Stella, she reminded herself. Maybe he learned the taste for it and couldn't let go.

She couldn't let go herself. Much as she wanted to drive out of Coffin's Grove, away from Luke Bardell's childhood and any pity she might have felt, she wasn't ready to do it. Even knowing he was far beyond the need for pity, and that he wouldn't thank her for it.

Besides, she tended to reserve any stray pity for herself, she thought with a grim smile. Poor, pitiful Rachel.

She didn't want to drive back through the town and risk running into any of Luke's protectors or detractors. She shouldn't have come here in the first place—it only made her doubt her determination.

There must be a roundabout way back to the highway. There was a pale gray line on the map, signaling a gravel road. She'd go that way, and circle back around the outskirts of the town.

Esther was nowhere in sight when she left the house. Without thinking, Rachel stole a handful of tightly budded white roses, pricking her fingers as she did so, and dumped them on the front seat of the car. The streets were still, hot, and deserted as she drove away, and she took a deep breath of the artificially chilled air inside her car, hoping for the smell of roses to fill the air. Esther's flowers had no scent.

She had never been terribly good at following maps—Stella had always told her she was geographically dyslexic—and she hadn't realized she'd be on the same road that ran by the graveyard. On instinct she stopped, scooping up the thorny flowers and taking them with her.

She made it to Marijo's headstone when she looked down at the flowers in her arms. They were crawling with tiny worms, eating their way through the pristine, satiny flesh of the scentless roses.

She threw them away from her with a cry of disgust, away from the sweet simple wildflowers that adorned the plaque. Fresh flowers. Someone had visited the grave since last night.

She looked around, at the dark, swampy woods that lay beyond the neat little graveyard. There was no one to be seen, no one was watching her. She would be driving through that swampy forest, assuming she'd read the road map right. Maybe she'd find the ghost of whatever had haunted her last night.

She climbed back in the car and locked all the doors. She turned the air-conditioning on max, turned up the radio, and started to drive. It was some Christian rock station, with someone howling about the devil getting you in his clutches, and she snapped it off again with a shudder. She didn't believe in the devil, or in God either, she supposed. She believed in evil, and evil lay in Coffin's Grove, in the house of Esther Blessing. And it lived in Luke Bardell's damaged soul.

It was dark midday with the pine forest looming up around her. She could smell the dampness of the swamp, the sickness and decay, even through the air-conditioning. The road narrowed, and she could see stagnant pools of standing water glistening behind the trees. She wondered if they had alligators in there.

Maybe she should turn back. Stella had been right, at least in that one area—Rachel had a lousy sense of direction. Maybe this narrow road was a dead end that would stop in a bog, and the car would sink down, taking her with it, disappearing without a trace.

"Idiot," she said out loud, slowing her speed to a crawl as she drove deeper into the thick forest.

The trees were ancient, towering, turning the swamp into a dark, gloom-infested place, so different from the bright clean light of New Mexico. She couldn't imagine two more disparate places. And that might be the key to Luke Bardell's enigmatic nature. He had a swamp soul in a desert climate.

She would have missed the house if she'd been driving any faster, if she hadn't been considering finding a place to turn around and head back. It was very old, and the forest had already begun to take the land back. Vines crawled up the siding, Spanish moss hung like a curtain from the huge trees surrounding the place. It might have had paint, once, but now it was long gone, and all the windows were shattered by some vandal's target practice.

It was just a house, an abandoned house in the midst of a swampy forest. And yet she found herself pulling to a stop at the edge of the weed-tangled property.

She turned off the car, and the icy air-conditioning died with a weary shudder. When she opened the door the damp heat blasted around her, wrapping her in a blanket of humidity. She was crazy to stop, but she couldn't help herself.

She knew whose house this was. She knew who had been found hanging in the tumbled-down barn by her eight-year-old son; she knew who had died inside. Despite Esther's accusations, she didn't know who killed him.

She approached the house slowly, warily, picking her way through the tangled undergrowth. Her jeans felt clammy against her skin, and even the loose T-shirt clung to her body. It was hot, and yet she felt shivery, cold, frightened. And still she kept coming.

The front door was long gone. It looked as if someone had beaten it down, years ago. Maybe the police, when they came out to check on another suicide. Maybe Jackson Bardell himself, looking for the traveling preacher's bastard child he'd been left with.

Inside the house it was as still as death, dark and smelling of mold and rotting vegetation. Even in the best of times this house must have been dark and depressing, but now it was like a living creature, swallowing everything.

It was a house of many small rooms, most of them empty of everything but trash. The largest room lay at the end of the narrow hallway, and a dim light from a glassless window cast a pool of illumination onto the stained floor.

She stood over that spot, staring down. There was no mistaking what that stain was, whose life's blood had flooded over these worn floorboards. Jackson Bardell had died there, either by his own hand or that of the bastard child who lived with him.

It wasn't a noise that alerted her. Just a sixth sense that prickled along her arms, chilling her. She looked up, and he was standing there, as if he'd materialized out of thin air. As he had last night, in her claustrophobic bedroom.

"Hey, Rachel," Luke Bardell said softly. And he came toward her, stepping onto the ancient pool of blood.

13

He looked strange, different, somehow more menacing with his face in the shadows. Gone was the loose white clothing he wore in New Mexico. Now he was dressed entirely in black, black jeans, cowboy boots, a black T-shirt. He looked strong, dangerously so. The messiah in the desert was threat enough—this man, with his sultry eyes and his lean, wiry body, flat out terrified her.

"What are you doing here?" Her voice was harsh. She didn't move—it wouldn't have done her any good. Either he'd let her go or not, and trying to run for it would be undignified. He knew how much she hated him and everything about him. He couldn't know for certain just how much he frightened her.

"I was born here." His voice was different too,

with the barest trace of a seductive drawl. She hated Southern accents. "Not in this house, of course. But I spent most of my childhood right here."

He seemed oblivious to the decades-old bloodstain beneath his boots. He glanced around him, and she saw his hair was tied back with a black leather thong. "The question is, Rachel, what are you doing here? And don't tell me you're on vacation—Coffin's Grove isn't the tourist center of the world. As a matter of fact, their only claim to fame is me. Local bad boy turned spiritual leader."

"Cult leader."

"Whatever you choose to call it, Rachel." He took another step toward her, out of the ancient stain, and she felt an irrational thread of relief. "You came here looking for me, didn't you?" Again that low, erotic drawl.

"Don't flatter yourself. I thought you never left your inner sanctum. If I thought you were going to be here it would have been the last place I would have come."

"Your mistake," he murmured. "As far as everyone knows I'm still back there, shut up in my meditation chamber, fasting and praying."

"Not everyone."

He tilted his head to one side, surveying her. Her stomach felt like it was caving in—the gnawing anxiety was knotting it. His faint smile made it worse. He was a different man outside the retreat. Even more dangerous.

"I'll have to do something about that, now won't I?" He came closer still. He'd never struck her as a particularly well-built man, but the tight black T-shirt defined muscle and sinew to a degree that made Rachel's mouth go dry.

She did take a step back then. "Are you going to kill me?"

"Why should I do that?" His voice was lazy. His eyes weren't.

"Because I could tell the truth about you." She must be half-crazy, she thought. Giving him a reason for killing her.

"I told you," he came closer, "that no one would believe you. You have no proof."

"If I told the right people they could find the proof," she persisted.

He shook his head. "I don't leave a trace when I travel." He moved suddenly, his hand catching her neck as she came up hard against the rough wall, his thumb stroking her sensitive skin. "I could cut your throat and be back in Santa Dolores by dinnertime, and no one would ever know I was here."

"What about when they found my body?" she asked hoarsely.

"They wouldn't." He leaned closer, so close she could feel his breath on her face. Taste the cigarettes he'd smoked. "There are swamps all over here. I know where the deepest holes are. You could drive a semi into some of them and it'd never be seen again."

She wouldn't let her knees buckle. She didn't know what the worse danger was, the threat of death or the slow, sensual caress of his thumb across her throat. "Why didn't you do that with your father?"

She thought it would make him back off. It didn't. "You've been listening to Esther, haven't you?" he murmured. "You should know better than that. She's a crazy old lady; anybody could tell you that."

"Then you didn't kill your father?" She didn't blink. She didn't dare.

His smile was cool. He glanced back at the rusty stain that seemed darker than ever. "There was too much blood," he said, ignoring her question. "Getting rid of a body is one thing, covering up the evidence is another. There were brains and bits of bone and skin all over the place."

Rachel's stomach lurched once more. "Did you kill your father?" she persisted, refusing to back down.

"If I cut your throat," he continued in that calm, musing voice, "it would make a mess as well. I suppose I could strangle you, though I have more experience with a knife." His smile was mocking, wolfish.

"Did you?" Her voice was sounding a little ragged, but she wasn't willing to let it go.

For a moment his expression was blank. "I'll tell you one thing for certain. I swear to you, I didn't kill my father," he said, his voice absolutely clear. And she found, to her amazement, that she believed him. A man she considered incapable of telling the truth, and she believed him.

And then he smiled. Leaned closer, so that his lips brushed her ear as he whispered, "Of course, Jackson Bardell wasn't my father."

That moment of trust shattered as quickly as it had appeared. She shoved at him in fury, another mistake. He was too close, and too strong. He caught her hands in one of his, jerking her away from the wall, toward him, her body smack up against him. "Don't ask me if I killed Jackson Bardell, Rachel," he whispered. "You might not like the answer."

She was shaking. He knew it, had to feel the tremors racking her body, but there wasn't a damned thing she could do about it.

He wrapped his other arm around her shoulders, holding her close against him while he kept her hands captive. "Why are you so scared of me, Rachel?" he murmured. "What do you think I'm going to do to you? You don't really think

I'm going to kill you, do you?" He waited patiently for an answer, and finally she shook her head.

"And you're not worried I'll rip you off. I already have your money. You haven't given up the fight, but you must have a pretty good idea that you can't win. So what is it? You think I'm going to rape you? Every time I get too close you start acting like a trembling virgin sacrifice. I don't rape, Rachel. It's no fun, and it's too easy."

"It wouldn't be easy with me," she said flatly.

His smile was slow in starting, full of mocking disbelief, and if she had a hand free she would have slapped him. But she didn't.

And he was holding her much too close. His long legs were pressed up against hers, and the feel of them was disturbing. Almost as disturbing as his hips.

"Then what are you afraid of?" he asked again, his voice low-pitched and sultry. "Afraid I'll seduce you away from your Judeo-Christian beliefs and you'll end up a fool like the rest of the people who believe in me?"

"Is that what you think of them?"

"They'd have to be fools, wouldn't they, to believe in a con artist and liar like me? Tell me what you're afraid of, and I'll let you go."

She stared up at him, mesmerized, unable to break free from his hands, his body, the seductive power of his voice. He was waiting, with deceptive patience, for her answer, and she knew he wasn't going to release her until she told him something. Something close to the truth.

"All right," she said. "I'll tell you."

He waited, not releasing her. It had been a small hope, and she took a deep breath, then regretted it. Her intake of breath brought their bodies closer. "I'm afraid of being touched."

"Bullshit. You don't like it, but you're not afraid of it. You're afraid of *me* touching you. Why? Afraid you might learn to like it?"

She jerked away in rage, but he just kept her held tight against him. "Don't flatter yourself."

"Oh, I don't." Somehow she'd gotten pushed up against the wall, his arm around her, holding her tight as he leaned against her. "But I have this gift. Or curse, you might prefer to call it. I can draw people to me. I can make them do things they'd never think of doing. I can make them my willing slaves. Is that what you're afraid of, Rachel? Afraid you'll be my slave?"

"That's not going to happen."

"What if I gave you your choice?" His voice was so low it rumbled in his chest. Against her trapped hands. "You can drop all your efforts against me. We can declare a truce, you can go back to your normal life, and maybe I'll see about getting the Grandfathers to release some of Stella's money. I can tell them Stella wasn't compos mentis when she made that final will, that the pain and the drugs she was taking confused her."

"Will they listen?"

"Of course. I thought you knew, I can make anyone do anything if I'm determined."

"Was she out of her mind with pain and drugs? Did you make her write that will?" She could hear her neediness, and there was no way she could cover it up.

There was something unfathomable in his eyes. "I could tell you anything and you'd believe it. I could tell you what you desperately need to hear; I could give you back your mother when you'd thought you'd lost her. It would be so easy."

"Did you make her write the will? Did she know what she was doing, or was she too sick to realize?"

He looked at her for a long moment. "She wrote the will six months before she died. She knew exactly what she was doing. She didn't care about you, Rachel. She never did, and now she never will."

Everything suddenly became very still. "What if I refuse to believe you?" she said in a dead voice, knowing she already believed. "What if I fight you?"

"Then I'll destroy you. I'll take away your last

and only defense, the one strength you hold on to. I'll make you want me, Rachel. I'll make you need me so badly that nothing else will matter."

She summoned a twisted smile. "You can't do it. You can't brainwash me into becoming one of your mindless followers."

"Maybe not," he agreed softly. "But I can make your body need me."

She found she could laugh. "No, you can't! Haven't you been listening? I'll spell it out for you. I'm frigid. I hate sex, I hate men, and I hate you."

"You're halfway there already, you're just so busy fighting it that you don't know what's going on," he whispered. "That's what you're afraid of, Rachel, whether you admit it or not. Deep down inside you're afraid I'm right. And that you want me just as much as I want you."

She shoved, and this time he released her. He didn't step back, though, and she was trapped between his body and the wall, even if he wasn't touching her. "I don't want you, I don't want anyone," she said fiercely.

"It's what's making you crazy, isn't it? Here you thought nothing could ever make you want sex. Need it. And now you find that the person you hate most in the world is the only person you want to fuck."

She gathered her strength for one last assault.

She looked up at him with clear intent. "If you ever touch me in a sexual way I'll kill you."

His grin was lopsided. "Too late, Rachel. I've already done it, and more. And you're not going to kill me. You need me." He moved his head down toward her.

"Don't!" She couldn't keep the raw panic from her voice and she no longer cared what he thought.

"Are you a virgin? Afraid to try?" he taunted.

"I've tried it. I hate it."

He nuzzled the side of her face, gently, and there was no way she could escape him. His skin was warm, slightly rough where his afternoon beard was coming in, and he smelled like tobacco and coffee. The flaming hypocrite.

"Try it again," he said. He caught her chin in his hand and tilted her desperate, defiant face up to his. "We can start with a kiss." And he set his mouth against hers.

She froze in disgust. It had been years since a man had come close enough to try to kiss her, and she knew there was no escape from him. She held herself still, waiting for the wet, horrible assault.

It didn't come. His lips brushed against hers, lightly, a feathery caress that made her shiver. He lifted his head a fraction of an inch. "That wasn't so terrible, now was it?"

"Do anything more and I'll bite your tongue off," she said furiously.

He laughed, damn him. "Try it and I'll beat you." He kissed her again, just as lightly, then drew away.

"Why are you doing this? There's no earthly reason why you'd want to kiss me."

"Isn't there? Maybe I just want to torture you," he suggested calmly.

"It isn't torture. I can stand it. I've put up with worse." She reveled in the grimness of her voice.

He was hardly appreciative of the compliment. The mockery in his eyes was almost as infuriating as his hand still keeping her face captive. "Let's see if I can up the ante," he murmured. And this time when he put his mouth on hers it was damp and open.

Whatever tiny portion of calm and sanity she had left vanished. She'd been kissed before, and survived the experience. She'd had consensual sex without making a scene. But Luke Bardell's mouth against hers was terrifying. He was like a giant bird of prey, pressing, devouring, sucking away her breath and life and destroying her. She beat at him in panic, but he ignored her struggles, one arm around her, keeping her prisoner, the other holding her face still so he could assault her mouth.

She hated it, and she hated him. She hated the treacherous gentleness, the slow, devastating eroticism that was making her bones shake. She hated his long fingers stroking the side of her face even as he held her. She hated the fact that she wasn't fighting him, she was simply standing rigid in his arms as his mouth raped hers.

It wasn't rape. It was seduction, slow, determined, demonic, and he was sucking her will from her with his clever mouth. She leaned back against the wall, his body pressed against hers, and she was trapped, helpless. She had no choice but to let her mind float, away from this place, away from what he was doing.

She closed her eyes, but there was no safety there either. The danger was even more intense— her breasts were burning, tingling, her hips were restless, and she told herself it was disgust building inside of her. But she was horribly afraid he was right, that he could see right through to her well-guarded heart. That all the defenses and anger couldn't keep him away when he was so determined to destroy her.

Because it would be destruction. She would have nothing left if she stopped fighting. He would devour her whole and then spit her back out into the dust.

He lifted his head to stare down at her in amusement. If he was the slightest bit moved by the kiss he showed no sign of it. "What do you want to do next?" he whispered.

"What are my choices?"

He took her hand and drew it down his body, and her struggles were absolutely useless against his strength. He placed her hand over his zipper and held it there, forced it there, so that she could feel the size of him. He was unquestionably hard, and she shivered in reaction. A reaction she told herself was revulsion. But she wasn't quite certain if it was that simple.

"Well," he said in a meditative voice as he leaned his forehead against hers, all the while he forced her hand against his erection, "you could always run away, screaming for help. You could beg and plead and promise never to bother me again and maybe, just maybe, I might show you some pity."

"I don't want your pity," she said in a tight voice.

"Or you could get down on your knees and take me in your mouth."

She tried to jerk her hand away, but his grip was like iron, for all the seeming gentleness in his voice. "Why don't you just kill me then?" she said. "I think I'd prefer it."

"A fate worse than death?" he murmured, and the thread of laughter made her hate him all the more. "I don't think so, Rachel. I'm going to take you to bed. And what's worse, you're going to like it." He brushed his lips against hers, just briefly. "Aren't you?"

She brought her knee up, swift and hard, but he was too fast for her, spinning out of her way before she could connect with his testicles. She'd taken him off guard, but even then he was too alert.

"Don't you listen?" she snapped. "I don't want you, I don't want anyone, and there's no need to prove your manhood by making the frigid little girl enjoy sex. Save it for someone else. Save it for one of your panting followers." Her rage was fierce and genuine, and it covered up the tremor in her voice. "You offered me a bargain; all right, I accept. I'll make no more claims on Stella's money. I'll let you run your little cult in peace, fleecing the unsuspecting. I will disappear from your life." Her mouth twisted in a grimace. "I'll even accept your pity, okay? Just don't come near me again."

"I didn't exactly offer you that. I said it was a possibility, if you begged and pleaded. A few tears would help matters, I think."

"Nothing makes me cry."

"I could."

"Go to hell." She'd had enough. She stalked past him, half expecting his arm to strike out and capture her, but he just leaned against the wall, watching her out of hooded eyes.

She forced herself to walk slowly through the empty house, retracing her steps to the front. She had no idea whether he was following her or not, but for some reason he was giving her a chance to escape, and she had every intention of taking it. He was standing in the room beyond, a shadowy figure, when she left the house and headed for her car.

It wasn't there. She'd parked in front of the tangled old ruin when she'd made the very dire mistake of investigating, and while she'd been battling with Luke, someone had taken it.

"What did you do with my car?" Her voice was fierce as she stared out into the overgrown forest.

He was closer than she'd realized. "Not a thing. I was with you, remember?"

She could still feel his mouth pressing against hers. "I can find my way out on foot. There's a road I can follow."

"There are alligators. Water moccasins, all kinds of nasty critters. This isn't the friendliest part of the world, Rachel. Especially for a city girl like you."

She turned to face him. "Where is it?"

"Sheriff Coltrane must have done something about it. It's a habit he has. Lots of teenagers come out here to make out and to scare each other. They say Jackson Bardell's ghost walks these woods, his head half blown off, looking for the other half."

"Don't!" she said with a shudder.

"Or they come out here to screw on the wooden

floor where their parents won't catch them. Didn't you ever do that, Rachel? Didn't you ever sneak out to have sex with your boyfriend? Or did you wait until you were in your twenties to find out you don't like it?"

She'd been pushed far enough for one day. She could still feel him against her hand, the pulsing strength of him. She could still taste his mouth. His voice was low, insinuating, sneaking into her blood until she wanted to scream.

She turned to look at him. "I learned I didn't like sex when I was twelve years old and my stepfather raped me," she said with deliberate calm. "And nothing's about to change my mind."

He didn't even blink. "Don't you think it's time you tried it with a man instead of a pervert?"

"I'm not sure you qualify."

He threw back his head and laughed. "Rachel," he said, "I suspect you'll be the death of me."

"I can only hope so."

14

He'd made a mistake with Rachel Connery, a mistake he seldom made. He'd underestimated her. Her dislike of men and sex went a lot deeper than the game he was playing with her.

Stella had said something about it, but Stella's take on the world had been a grand drama where everything revolved around her. She blamed Rachel's lies for the failure of her third marriage. She hadn't been able to come up with a scapegoat for marriages one, two, four, and five, but if pushed she probably could have blamed them on her daughter as well.

Luke looked down at Rachel, momentarily abstracted. She was miserable, a woman who never cried. She needed years of therapy, she needed a mother's caring, she needed a tender, patient lover who'd let her evolve at her own pace, learning to trust her body and his.

Tough luck that she ended up with him.

"I'll give you a ride back to town," he said abruptly.

"Why?" At least she had the sense not to trust him. Beneath all that pain and rage she was still damned smart.

He managed a convincing shrug. "Maybe I feel guilty."

"I doubt it."

He ignored her snort of disbelief. "The least I can do is take you to your car."

"Where is it?"

"I expect Coltrane left it at Esther's."

"You're going to drive me to Esther's?" Her voice was rich with disbelief.

"I didn't say I was going to walk you to the front door," he drawled. "There's a limit to that Southern gentleman bullshit."

"There's a lot to be said for a martyred messiah," she shot back.

It was a throwaway line, one of the barbs she flung out at random in an attempt to protect herself, but oddly enough, this one hit its mark. She had no idea how close she was coming to the truth. Even he wasn't sure.

"I'm not in the mood to be martyred," he said. "Not today."

"Maybe some other time," she said sweetly.

"You want a ride into town, or would you rather walk for miles in this heat?" He added just the right touch of impatience to his voice. She'd be more likely to agree if she thought he was irritated.

She just looked at him. She really had extraordinary eyes, he thought, keeping his own face expressionless, slightly bored. It was those eyes of hers that were his downfall. He could resist her anger, he could resist her body and her sarcastic tongue. But those deep brown eyes, so full of pain and fury, need and defiance, did him in.

"I guess you owe me one," she said grudgingly.

He'd forgotten what they were talking about. "One what?"

"A ride. You can drop me off a block or two away from Esther's."

He reached past her to touch her arm, and she jumped back as if he were a water moccasin. "We'll go out the back way. Unlike you, I have more sense than to leave my vehicle out in plain sight of passersby."

The word vehicle should have tipped her off, but she was still too unnerved by his touch. It was too damned easy to throw her for a loop. She'd just about started babbling when he'd kissed her. And the damnable thing was, he wanted to kiss her again, and to hell with her panic.

Nice guy, he mocked himself, leading the way

through the tumbled-down ruin that had seen the worst years of his life. Joliet Prison had been a summer camp compared to the emotional and physical havoc of life with Jackson Bardell. At least in Joliet he hadn't had to worry about protecting his mother.

The back part of the house had already been claimed by the swamp. The barn where he'd found his mother hanging was long gone, and soon the rest of the house would go as well, collapsing into the ooze and muck. But there was still a patch of solid ground beyond where he'd managed to park.

"There it is."

She spun around, starting back into the house, but he put his arm out, catching her across the waist, keeping her from escaping.

"I'm not riding in that thing."

"Look at it this way, it's not a Harley."

She glared up at him. He could feel the faint tremor in her skin where his arm touched her waist, but she wouldn't give in to her fear. "At least on a motorcycle I'd be safe."

"If Esther didn't see me first. It's hard to steer those things with a bullet in your brain."

She looked back at the aging black converted van in disbelief. "You're not the type for a Winnebago."

"It's not a Winnebago. Just think of it as an oversized hearse."

She glared at him, definitely not amused. "Is this where you've been sleeping?"

"I couldn't very well get a decent rest when the ghost of my victim was wandering around, now could I?" He paused. "How come you never say my name?"

"I don't like it."

"Luke? The apostle, the physician, the healer?" He shook his head in mock disapproval. "How unbiblical of you."

"The charlatan, the cheat, the extortionist . . ."

"I don't need to extort money. People hand it over quite willingly. And you forgot murderer in your litany of compliments."

"You're admitting you killed Jackson Bardell?"

"I'm admitting that I was convicted of killing a man in a bar fight," he said smoothly. "And that's as far as my confessions go. For now." She hadn't moved away from his hold, which was a good sign. He had to get her used to his touch, and he wasn't in the mood to be terribly patient about the process. "Are you going to get in the van?"

She suddenly realized he was still holding her. She backed away nervously, glancing around her for possible escape. The only place she could go was his van. "You'll drive me straight into town?"

"Straight into town," he said. "Cross my heart and hope to die."

And she was fool enough to believe him.

* * *

He was right—it looked more like a hearse than a Winnebago, Rachel had to admit as she climbed up into the front seat. It wasn't made for life on the open road, for middle-class comfort and RV campgrounds. It was more like a boat, everything neat, compact, shipshape.

He climbed in beside her, making no move to start the engine. Instead he leaned back and looked at her, and it was all she could do not to jump out and take off into the swamp.

"I thought you were going to drive me to Esther's," she said. "I don't see you starting this thing."

"All in good time. It's early."

She glanced out into the tree-shrouded afternoon. She couldn't see the sky through the towering pines, but the light was gray, ominous, unnaturally dark for that time of day.

"It's going to storm," she said.

"You've been in Alabama for twenty-four hours and you think you can read the weather?"

"Then why is it so dark?"

"It's going to storm."

She wanted to hit him. "Then I'd appreciate getting to my car before it hits. I don't like thunderstorms."

"No, I imagine you don't," he said softly. "That's

just something else you're afraid of. Sex, men, thunderstorms, being poor. Me. Anything else?"

"Yeah," she said. "I'm afraid of alligators and poisonous snakes, or otherwise I wouldn't be here in this hearse with you."

"They have some amazing thunderstorms in New Mexico," he said, ignoring her remark. "The whole sky lights up, and the thunder echoes from canyon to canyon till you think the ground is shaking."

"I can skip that," she said with a shudder.

"Maybe."

She jerked her head to glare at him. "Why would I go back to Santa Dolores?"

"Why did you come to Coffin's Grove?"

She couldn't think of an answer, not when she was no longer sure. Her confrontation with Luke Bardell had moved past the point where she could handle herself. In the meditation center there was a certain amount of safety, a certain amount of control. Out here, in this steaming swamp, there was nothing she could use for self-defense. It was just the two of them, and she knew that she was far outclassed. He could destroy her.

He smiled, that faint, infuriating smile. "I'll tell you why, Rachel, even if you don't want to admit it. You can't let go. You can't let go of anything. You can't let go of the stupid dream you have of a loving mother, a fantasy of something that never existed in your life. You can't let go of the pain, you can't let go of the money you think you're owed, and you can't let go of me. Whether it's hatred or fascination or a little of both, you're just incapable of turning your back on me and getting on with your life."

"Watch me."

"It would be a pleasure. But you're not going to do it." A distant rumble of thunder matched the deepness of his voice, and in the gathering darkness his eyes were almost incandescent.

The electricity in the air must be from the gathering storm, she thought, trying to breathe. Her skin felt hot, prickly, her blood thick and throbbing through her veins, pooling in strange places. He had his hands draped loosely on the steering wheel, even though he was making no effort to start the van, and she could see the wreath of thorns around each wrist with shocking clarity. He had elegant wrists. Beautiful hands. A strong, sinuous body. It was no wonder his followers were blinded by his undeniable beauty. It was only lucky that her hatred kept her immune.

The storm was coming nearer, and the wind had begun to pick up, tossing the moss-laden branches back and forth like skeletal arms waving their tattered grave clothes. She reached for the door handle, fighting the panic, the inevitability that was crowding down around her, half expecting him to stop her.

"I may bite, but I'm not lethal," he murmured without moving.

She didn't release the door handle. "I'm not sure of that."

The rain started then, spitting at the windshield. It was getting dark in the front of the van, but he made no effort to turn on the motor. "We get hellacious storms down here," he said in that infuriatingly gentle voice. "Flash floods that could carry you off before you knew it. Hailstones the size of golf balls. Leroy Peltner's brother was killed by one of them. Then there's the wind. It can whip through the place, uprooting trees and bringing them crashing down on houses and cars, flattening them."

"Then don't you think we ought to get the hell out of here, considering we're surrounded by trees?" She was aiming for asperity in her voice, instead she got an annoying quaver.

"In a really bad storm there's no place safe," he said. "You've just got to trust your luck. And whether the devil's on your side or not."

"What about God?"

"You don't believe in God, Rachel. You don't believe in goodness or love or mercy, do you?"

"I haven't seen enough to form an opinion."

"But you believe in the devil?"

"When I'm sitting in a car with him, yes," she said.

He laughed, a quiet, disturbing sound. "I think it's time you sold me your soul, Rachel."

"It's not for sale."

"Everything's for sale. Your soul in exchange for whatever I can pry out of the Grandfathers. I expect I can get at least half a million for a settlement."

"In return for my soul? That's paltry."

"Maybe." He had a dreamy expression on his face in the eerie light of the storm. "There's a bed in the back . . . Why don't you unfasten that seat belt that's not doing you a lick of good and climb back there?"

She was cold. Suddenly, desperately cold. "I thought you wanted my soul, not my body?"

"With you they come as a package deal."

"Let me get this straight," she said, her teeth chattering. "You're offering me five hundred thousand dollars to sleep with you? That must make me the highest-priced whore in the world."

The smile on his face was faint as he leaned over and unfastened her seat belt. "You might make the *Guinness Book of World Records*. Get in the back."

She stared at him, so dangerously close. And she knew she was going to do it. She hated him more than any human being on this earth; she feared him and his inexplicable power over her.

The more she fought, the more she ran, the deeper the fear went. The only way she could exorcise it was to call his bluff.

"All right," she said.

She was hoping to shock him with her acquiescence. She should have known he wouldn't give her that much—he was too adept at guarding his reactions. "All right," he echoed, faintly mocking.

She glanced into the back of the van. It was pitch black, and outside the storm howled around them. "I can't see back there."

"You'll find your way," he said.

He wasn't going to make it any easier for her, a small consolation. If he'd swept her in his arms, murmured loving things, she would have run. Instead she climbed out of the black leather seat and made her way into the cocoonlike darkness. She almost tripped over the bed. It lay across the back of the van, big, the covers rumpled. He wasn't following her, he was still lounging in the front seat, and she wondered if there was a side door. And she wondered if she felt like diving out into the storm and risking the fury of nature.

He knew her too well. "Don't make me chase you in the storm." His dry voice floated from the front seat.

"Why would you bother?"

"I wouldn't want to waste you on an alligator."

She sat down on the bed. There was room for

her to sit up, but not stand. She pulled her T-shirt over her head and began to fold it with absurd precision. She kicked off her running shoes and skinnied out of her jeans, folding them with the same care. The darkness in itself was reassuring. She reached behind her to unfasten her bra, then stopped. "Do you need me to take all my clothes off, or just from the waist down?"

"This isn't a visit to the gynecologist, Rachel. Everything must go." His voice was lightly mocking.

She stripped off the rest of her clothes, silently, efficiently, and then lay down on the bed, her hands at her sides, waiting for him, her eyes shut in the thick darkness as she listened to the storm surrounding the metal box that enclosed them.

She knew what would happen, she told herself. He would cover her with his naked body, he would force wet, slobbering kisses on her mouth. He would make her touch his . . . his thing, and then he would put it inside her. It would be too tight, it would hurt, and he would hunch and sweat and groan on top of her, he would pinch her breasts and buttocks, he would mutter obscenities before he collapsed on top of her in exhaustion. She'd survived that much and more in the past—she'd survive it this time.

And when he finished she would look at him out of her cold eyes and know she was invulnerable after all. That nothing could touch her, not even the cleverest of con men. The man who tricked and seduced her mother wouldn't be able to touch her.

She heard the faint snick of a cigarette lighter, and the flare of light in the back of the camper blinded her. He was holding it above her, looking down at her, and she couldn't see his face beyond the mesmerizing flame.

"Very nice," he murmured, and there was no missing the irony in his voice. "A virgin sacrifice, nicely staked out. Do you want me to tie your hands and wrists to the bed? It might help you get in the mood to be martyred."

He was goading her, but she was beyond reacting. All she had to do was keep herself in one piece. Let him touch her body all he wanted to—it didn't really matter. As long as she could keep her mind, her emotions, inviolate.

"The Foundation of Being doesn't go in much for human sacrifice," he said lazily, flicking the lighter closed, plunging the van into blackness once more. "But I'm beginning to think the practice has been underused."

She could hear the rustle of his clothing, the slither of his belt, the thump as he kicked off his boots. She scooted over on the mattress, unable to control that start of panic, then once again lying still as he stretched out beside her. It took her a moment to realize he was still wearing his jeans, though nothing else, and some of her panic subsided.

She could feel his fingertips lightly brush her face, her short tangle of hair, her tightly closed mouth. She shut her eyes as well—she couldn't see anything in the darkness, and it was one more defense she could close down around her. He let his fingertips dance lightly over her mouth, and she considered biting him, hard.

"Tell me, Rachel," he murmured, his voice seductive. "Is there anything you find particularly revolting, or is it the entire act?"

She had to open her mouth to speak. "Why? So you can make sure my degradation is complete?"

"No. Your surrender."

"I have. Surrendered, that is. Haven't you noticed I'm not fighting you anymore? You can do your worst."

"Such an optimistic point of view. And you're still fighting me, for all that you're lying naked in my bed. I imagine you'll fight me with your last dying breath."

She froze. "You're going to kill me?"

His laughter was both a relief and an annoyance. "No. I have better, more pleasurable ways to destroy you." And to prove it, he let his hand trail down the side of her neck, a soft, sweet caress that burned like acid on her skin.

Doubt hit her hard. "What if I just give up?"

she said suddenly. "Declare you the victor? Will you let me go?"

She opened her eyes, gradually growing accustomed to the dark. She could see him as he lifted his head to watch her, though there was no way she could read his expression. Except that she knew what he would look like. Determined. Triumphant. Dangerously erotic.

"No," he said. "Too late."

"Will you let me leave?"

"No."

She tried to sit up, but his arm snaked around her waist, bare skin against bare skin, muscle against softness, pushing her back so that she lay against the mattress, staring up into darkness. Staring up into Luke Bardell's twisted soul.

"Please," she said, begging for mercy as she'd swore she would never do.

"No," he said again. And he kissed her.

15

She was hating this, Luke thought, working at her mouth. She was despising this, and him, and if he had a speck of decency left, he'd let her pull on her clothes, get in the passenger seat, and he'd drive her back to her car. He could have the Grandfathers send her a check—hell, he could get money to her from his own private stash. It would shut her up, get her out of his life, and it would be a kind, generous thing to do.

Of course, he didn't have any decency in him, and hadn't for years. The sight of her pale, slender body shouldn't have been cause to send his libido into overload, but then, he'd never been particularly sensible where Rachel Connery was concerned. Which was a warning in itself.

But he was tired of being sensible. Careful. If Calvin wasn't able to cover up for him, if the

Grandfathers discovered he wasn't on some spiritual retreat, praying and fasting, he'd live with the consequences. He had a huge amount of money stashed away in various places, all instantly accessible. Unfortunately he had a pretty good idea how fast money could disappear, and he'd wanted to wait until he had at least twice that much before he decamped.

But being a holy man was wearing on his nerves. He wanted to be bad again. He wanted to be selfish and sinful and shimmering with lust. As he was right now, and reveling in it.

She had jaws of iron, and she kept them tightly shut against his mouth. He didn't mind. He wasn't in the mood to force her. Outside the storm raged, battering the ancient camper. Inside it was dark and warm. It smelled of rain and wet earth, it smelled of her and him and sex, and he had every intention of taking his time.

He nibbled softly on her lower lip. "You're too skinny, you know," he murmured against her mouth.

It was enough to get her to open it. "If you think criticizing my body is supposed to arouse me, then you're way out of practice."

He touched her mouth with the sensitive tips of his fingers, gently, so as not to panic her. "Trust me, if you tell most women they're too skinny they'll be your slave for life."

"Is that what you want from me?" Her voice was caustic. She was still fighting. Good.

"A slave for the night will do." Her lips were surprisingly soft. She usually had them clamped together in a firm line, but in the darkness, naked, she was more vulnerable.

He feathered a kiss against those lips, so briefly she didn't have time to react. He kissed her eyelids, feeling them flutter beneath his mouth; he kissed the soft skin of her temple. He could feel the powerful tension rippling through her body, and inwardly he smiled. This was going to be a challenge and a pleasure. And very nice indeed.

He moved his mouth down the side of her face, kissing her on the soft skin beneath her jaw. "I thought I was going to have to pry you out of your clothes," he murmured against the scented sweetness of her skin. "How come you decided to make it easy for me?"

"I want this over with as quickly as possible," she said grimly.

He wondered if she could feel his smile against her skin. "I'm a Southern boy at heart, sugar," he murmured. "I take my time."

Another shiver rippled her skin, and he recognized her fear. He kissed the hollow of her throat, tasting her pulse. "Don't worry," he said. "You'll like it. Or is that what you're afraid of?"

"I'm not afraid of you."

"That's a change. Five minutes ago you said you were."

"Are you going to fuck me or argue with me?"

The word sat strangely on her tongue. He doubted she'd ever used it in its literal context before. But then, he doubted she'd fucked much before.

He leaned over her, his body hovering above hers. "Oh, I'm going to fuck you," he said with a breath of laughter. "Slowly, deliciously, and most royally. Now why don't you open your mouth to do something more than fight with me?"

She struggled for a moment when he kissed her, then stopped herself, sinking back on the rumpled bed, letting her mouth go slack. The virgin sacrifice again, he thought, sliding one hand beneath her short-cropped hair and tipping her face up to his.

He'd kissed her before, when she was drugged and semicomatose, and she'd been more responsive. Now she lay there beneath his kiss, determined to show him he couldn't move her.

She didn't realize she was sparring with the king of determination.

He caught her lower lip between his and bit, gently. He wondered briefly whether she was turned on by pain. He hoped not—he wasn't in the mood for that particular kink. If the only way he could get her turned on was to hurt her he might change his mind about the whole project.

"Don't," she said, her voice a quiet, desperate plea.

"Then kiss me back."

She did. Or at least she tried. She met his mouth with inexpert force, banging against him, and she ground her teeth against her lips in a furious effort.

"Not that way," he said. "This." And he kissed her lightly, tantalizing, nibbling on her mouth until she began to mimic him, her lips reaching for his, clinging for a brief, tantalizing moment.

He could tell the instant that it changed. That the slow, insidious warmth began to sneak beneath her defenses. He doubted she recognized it, she was too busy concentrating on kissing him back to recognize the telltale shimmer that danced across her skin, the odd, hesitant catch in her breathing.

She was a fast learner. With him, at least. A sudden gust of wind hit the trailer, buffeting it, and she let out a frightened cry, her arms coming off the mattress, around his neck in unexpected panic. The feel of his hot, damp skin must have been just as terrifying, for no sooner did she touch him than her arms fell away, back on the mattress again, and she turned her head from his mouth.

He didn't mind. He'd already coaxed the first response from her. He could wait for more.

"You know," he murmured, letting his hand trace delicate, random patterns up her arm, "maybe I should just get you drunk. Then you'd forget that you hate sex."

"It's already been tried." Her voice was flat and uncompromising in the darkness, and he might have thought he'd imagined that brief shimmer of response. Except he wasn't a man to imagine such things.

"Really?" His hand trailed up to her shoulder, then down again, a slow, gentle caress.

"Believe it or not, there have been other times, other men, that I've actually wanted to sleep with."

"Nice euphemism."

"Fuck you."

"That's what I was talking about." She was getting more and more pissed, but it was distracting her from her fear. When she was angry she forgot she was frigid.

"Does that mean that you want to sleep with me?" he added, moving his legs closer. He wished to hell he'd taken off his jeans, but he'd figured that would send her into hysterics.

"Not in this lifetime."

"Don't worry," he said, moving his mouth next to her ear. "You'll be too busy to sleep."

She was wearing tiny gold studs. Expensive, he thought, biting lightly. She shifted uneasily, her hands flat on the mattress, clutching the rumpled sheet.

"Can't you hurry this up?" she demanded in a strained voice.

"Why? You got a plane to catch or something?" She smelled good. More than good, she smelled delicious. Like soap and perfume and nervous womanhood. The scent of her mixed with the damp air, and he figured she was going to get her wish if he didn't take a deep breath and slow down.

"As soon as I can get to Mobile."

"Well, sugar," he whispered against her throat, "we're not going anywhere in this storm, so get used to it. Just lie back and think of England."

She made an odd sound. In someone else he might have thought it was a laugh, but as far as he could tell Rachel Connery had absolutely no sense of humor.

He could always see well in the dark, and even in the shadowy depths of the van he could see her martyred face clearly. Pale skin, trembling mouth, eyes tightly shut against the horrors she was about to endure. He was half-tempted to shove it in and get it over with.

If he didn't have an important agenda, that was

exactly what he'd do. But screwing Rachel Connery wasn't enough. He needed to subjugate her body and soul, and that was going to take a little more effort.

He put his hands on her small breasts, covering them, and she jerked nervously, then settled back again, gritting her teeth. He was right, she was too thin. If she got a little meat on her bones her breasts would swell and plump up. He'd like to see her that way. Fat and sassy. It seemed a far cry from the skinny, angry woman lying in his bed, but he could still imagine it.

He leaned over and whispered in her ear. "Roll over on your stomach."

He'd pushed her too far. She sat up quickly, shoving him away from her. "I've changed my mind," she said. "I'm getting out of here."

"You're staying." He pushed her back down on the bed, allowing himself the slight relief of a little enthusiastic force.

Anger was wiping out her fear. "If you don't let me leave it will be rape."

He slid his hands over her shoulders, pinning her to the mattress. "So sue me."

Outside the thunder rattled the old camper. Inside she looked up at him, her defiance vanished. "Please don't," she whispered.

"Sorry," he said, covering her body with his, holding her there. "It's too late to turn back."

* * *

She despised herself, almost as much as she despised him. She'd chickened out, she'd begged for mercy, and all he'd done was laugh at her. They said rape wasn't about sex, it was about anger. This horrible time in the cramped back of Luke Bardell's old camper wasn't about sex either, it was about intimidation and subjugation.

She could turn off her mind. He was heavy on top of her, though not quite as heavy as she expected. If she thought about it she could probably feel his erection beneath the jeans he still wore, but she had no intention of thinking about it. She wouldn't fight him anymore, since it did no good. She'd endure.

He was hot in the damp warmth of the camper, his body hard against hers. His chest pressed against her breasts, the hair against her skin, as his hands slid up her sides, slowly, tauntingly.

She shivered in the darkness, she wasn't sure why. He didn't kiss like anyone else. His kisses were damp, hot, strangely disturbing. They weren't the wet, slobbering kisses she'd had to endure before.

He covered her breasts with his big, hard hands again, and she held herself very still. Another unnerving sensation, one she had to get used to. Her skin felt hot and prickly, the sensitive flesh burning to the touch. She wanted to run naked in the rain, feel the cooling dampness soothe her. But she was lying pinned beneath a man who intended to have sex with her, and there was no escape.

She knew he would put his mouth on her breasts, and she told herself she was prepared for it. She wasn't.

He flicked his tongue across her nipple, like the snake in the garden of Eden, and she could feel it harden in his mouth. She kept her hands still on the mattress, determined not to fight him, when all she wanted to do was punch him when he moved to her other breast, biting this time, lightly, just enough to make her arch her hips in angry retaliation.

He probably didn't think it was anger. He moved down her torso, kissing her belly, cradling her hips with his hands, and she shut her eyes again. Enduring. Enduring.

He pulled her legs apart, and she let him, because she wanted him to get this over with, so that she could retreat safely back into her world. She waited for him to shuck off his pants, to push and probe and hurt her, and she braced herself, biting her lip in preparation for the assault.

He put his mouth on her. His mouth, and his tongue, and she screamed in rage, hitting at him. He ignored her, clamping her hips with his hands, holding her still as she struggled in fury.

She reached down and yanked at his long hair, but he paid no attention. "Stop it," she screamed, panting in fury. "Don't do that." She tried to kick him, but he had her legs imprisoned with his body, and there was no way she could escape. She could only buck and thrash, trying to stop him, trying to hurt him, trying to blank everything out of her mind and ignore what he was doing to her.

It was all part of the subjugation process, she tried to tell herself. He had absolutely no reason to want to do this to her, it would give him no physical pleasure. It was part of his plan to destroy her, and she wouldn't let him.

She couldn't seem to catch her breath. Her skin was on fire, her heart was racing, and all she wanted to do was get away from him. She bucked her hips, but it made no difference. Instead she felt him touch her, slide his fingers deep inside her as he used his mouth, and she wanted to scream.

For a brief moment her body convulsed, but she fought it off in terror, backing away from it. He lifted his head to look at her, and in the darkness she could see the glitter in his dark eyes, the dampness on his mouth. He wiped it against his shoulder, staring at her. "You just keep fighting," he murmured.

"I always will. Now get off me, or finish it," she

said fiercely, the anger in her voice covering the tremor.

He unzipped his jeans and pushed them down. She made herself look at him, to solidify her disgust. Even in the dark she could tell that he was tremendously aroused, bigger than anything she'd ever had to put up with. It would hurt even more, she thought with perverse satisfaction. She would hate it. And she would endure.

She closed her eyes, clutching the sheet again, and waited. He pulled her legs around his body, levering forward so that she felt him against her, hot, hard, probing. She wanted to tighten against him, but her body was weary of fighting. He was braced over her, teasing her, and she wanted to scream at him, to tell him to hurry up.

"You hate this, don't you?" he murmured, his fingers in her tangled hair.

"I hate this," she said.

"Brace yourself, sugar. I'm not finished with you yet." And he filled her with a deep, swift shove that slid in fully, damply.

She tried to catch her breath from the shock of his invasion. No pain. It wasn't fair—there was no pain. Just a sense of stretching, fullness, of being taken over. She clutched the sheets so tightly her fingernails dug into her palms.

She took a brief, shaking gulp of air. "Finish it," she said in a furious hiss.

He laughed, damn him. She could feel his amusement vibrate through his body and into hers. "Finish it?" he echoed. "I've only just begun."

Endure, she told herself as he pulled out of her, then slid back in, impossibly deeper. Her body was damp, lubricated, and she could only blame him. It wasn't her fault, she didn't want him, she was doing this because she had no choice.

Oddly enough, she felt it first in her chest. A tightness that spiraled out to her breasts, an ache that teased and tormented her. Her stomach felt strange, gnawing, and she knew it had nothing to do with food and everything to do with hunger. He was moving, pushing deep inside her, then sliding out again, in a slow, lazy rhythm, as if he might keep doing it all night long. She tried to open her eyes, to focus on him, to focus on how much she hated him, but she couldn't. He kissed her eyelids, thrusting deep, and she made a despairing little sound in the back of her throat.

That strange, frightening ripple began to stir within her again, and she tried to stop it once more. But it was like the alien thing inside her, growing, taking over her body that she'd once thought she controlled perfectly.

He shoved his hands under her butt, pulling her up tighter against him, pushing in deeper still. "I can keep this up all night long," he whispered dreamily. "If I come, I'll just get hard again.

You make me want to fuck, Rachel. I've been hard since the first time I saw you, and it's going to take some time to take care of the problem. You won't get anywhere by fighting it."

"I won't stop fighting you." She could barely recognize her voice.

"I'm not talking about me. Fight me all you want. It's your own body you're so busy battling. And you're going to lose."

"No."

"Hold on, sugar. This ride is going to change your life."

He pulled her legs around his waist, and she was shaking so hard she had no choice but to let go of the mattress beneath her, to put her arms around his sweat-sleek shoulders and hold on. It wasn't cold, it was hot, steamy, churning, and she couldn't stop trembling. She wanted to scream, or cry, she wanted to hurt him, and she did, digging her fingernails into his back, scratching him. She needed something with a desperation she couldn't recognize, she needed to get away from him, she needed to hide . . .

"Don't fight it, Rachel," he whispered again, and put his long fingers between them, touching her. "Give it to me, Rachel. Stop fighting. Now."

It hit her with the force of an explosion, and she screamed. He covered her mouth with his, drinking in her cries, but it wouldn't stop, wave after wave of something that caught her body and shattered it. She felt him come, deep inside her, and it set off another series of hot, fierce clenching, lashing her body, and all the fight had been whipped from her. She couldn't breathe, couldn't see, and she collapsed against the mattress, her entire body on fire.

He pulled out of her, moving away from her in the darkness, and for a moment the place was like a tomb. Still and quiet and breathless.

The lighter flared, illuminating his face as he lit a cigarette. She tried to focus on his expression, but her eyes weren't working. Small wonder. Nothing in her body was working. She tried to lift a hand, to brush her hair out of her face, but it was trembling so badly she had to let it fall back to the mattress.

She turned her head to look at him. He looked odd, distant, almost perplexed, as he stared at his cigarette as if it might have the answers to the questions of the universe.

"Not bad," he murmured reflectively. "If it's that good the first time, imagine what it would be like when we've had a little practice."

She wanted to cover herself with something, but she couldn't move. All she could do was lie there and shake.

Luke moved then. Draping a sheet over her,

tucking it around her shivering body with gentle hands. "It's not cold in here," he observed mildly.

She couldn't say anything, she was shivering too badly.

He stubbed out the cigarette abruptly. He got on the bed with her and pulled her body into his arms, sheet and all, holding her tightly against him, so tightly that she suddenly felt safe.

And she began to cry.

16

Arrogant asshole that he was, he'd told her she wouldn't be sleeping. He hadn't counted on any number of things, including the fact that once she started crying, she couldn't stop until she'd wept herself into a state of exhaustion.

She wasn't very good at crying. Obviously something else she hadn't had much practice at, something else she despised. She was noisy, choking and gasping as she wept, beating at him, beating at the bed, beating at herself. He ignored her struggles; he just wrapped himself around her and held her while she stormed and raged. She didn't say anything intelligible, which didn't surprise him. She was beyond words, lost in a high, lonely place of pain she'd been avoiding for too long.

She fell asleep crying. He didn't realize women could do that. Every now and then a stray sob would shake her body, and then she would sink back into boneless sleep. He tried to loosen his grip on her, but she cried out when he did, so he simply draped himself around her, one hand cradling her head, his thumb gently stroking her tear-damp face.

He'd done exactly what he set out to do. He'd gotten her in bed and he'd made her come. He brought her down to his level, the most basic, human level, and in doing so he'd destroyed every defense she had.

And all of sudden, he wasn't so sure it had been that good an idea.

For one thing, he was still horny. He'd gotten used to regulating his libido, and his access to willing, discreet women was limited in the New Mexico desert. He'd learned to wring the maximum of pleasure out of each coupling and have that suffice for months at a time.

It hadn't worked out that way. For one thing, he hadn't been able to focus entirely on his own pleasure. She'd been too distracting. When he was in bed with a woman he was used to thinking with his cock, not his brain, but Rachel Connery had a bad habit of engaging both organs. It was a damned good thing he didn't have a heart—she'd probably mess with that as well.

And demoralizing her might not have been the smartest move on his part. She was a complicated woman, too smart for her own good, too vulnerable for his. He didn't like women like her. He liked street-smart women, resilient, tough, sassy women who took what they wanted and left what they didn't. He liked sweet women as well, innocent and helpless, in need of nurturing.

Rachel was none of those things. And the more elaborate his plans to neutralize her, the more power she seemed to gain. Lying in his arms, exhausted from sex and tears, she had a tighter hold on him than she'd had before.

It would be worth Stella's money just to get her out of his life, out of his brain, out of his . . .

She shuddered in her sleep, burrowing her head against his shoulder. Outside the storm was still raging—he'd almost forgotten they were in the midst of a hellacious thunderstorm. For a brief moment he shut his eyes, envisioning a tornado scooping up the house, the camper, and sending them to eternity. Or maybe, if they were lucky, the land of Oz.

It wasn't going to happen. Life didn't come with easy solutions, and if they ended up in Oz Stella would be there as the wicked witch.

Another gust of wind buffeted the camper, shaking the bed. Rachel was too far gone to notice, lost in a deep sleep that may or may not have been dreamless. Poor little Dorothy, unable to find her way home.

As for him, he knew his own role perfectly well. Not the heartless Tin Man. He was the Wizard, the trickster, full of empty promises and gaudy lies. He wasn't the answer to Rachel's needs, he wasn't the answer to anyone's needs. And sooner or later he was going to disappear, unencumbered, to live off his ill-gotten gains.

The rain was slowing, now a gentle tapping on the metal shell of the camper instead of the drenching downpour. It would be steamy, misty outside, and he needed to get away from her, from her clinging arms and her long legs, from her muffled, sleepy sobs and her needs. Most of all he needed to get away from his own need. Of her.

This time when he pulled free she didn't wake. She tried to hold on to him, but he extricated himself before she could realize what he was doing, and she fell back among the rumpled sheets with a sigh, her face against the mattress.

He grabbed his pack of cigarettes, zipped up his jeans, and stepped out into the rain, shirtless, barefoot, not caring what swamp creatures he might run into. A hungry alligator would be less dangerous than Rachel Connery's arms.

The rain was fine, almost a mist. He was able to light a cigarette, cupping it with his hands, and then he started down the path, away from the camper that was half-hidden by the old house, away from the place he'd always hated.

To a place that was even worse.

The barn had collapsed more than a dozen years ago. He'd tried to knock it down himself, in a blind rage when he was thirteen and bleeding from the beating Jackson had given him. He hadn't been strong enough then, but wind and weather and the swamp had taken care of it. It was just a pile of rotting boards and beams. His mother had hanged herself from one of those beams, and he'd been the one to find her. He was eight years old, and that was when he knew he would kill Jackson Bardell.

That old bitch Esther used to say his mama would haunt the place, haunt the old barn. That she would never rest because she'd committed such a great sin. Luke had never been able to shove the words down the old lady's throat, and he no longer cared. Wherever his mother was, it wasn't haunting a rotting ruin. She was someplace fine, he knew it. There had to be some peace, some justice, for someone in his life.

He stared down at his cigarette in disgust, then tossed it on the pile of rotting wood. It sizzled, and went out. He'd lost the taste for cigarettes, which was just as well. He had a helluva time sneaking them in Santa Dolores.

He lost track of the time he stood staring at the old ruins. The rain picked up again, heavier, a warm curtain of water soaking his jeans, his hair.

He felt it running down his chest, his arms, and he wished that something, somewhere, could make him feel clean again.

The rain muffled the sound of his return to the van. The door was open, and for a moment he was afraid she'd run away. And then he saw her.

She didn't know he was watching her. She stood in the rain, naked, her face tipped back, letting the water stream over her cheekbones, her eyes, her mouth. She lifted her arms to the stormy skies, and as if answering her supplication, the clouds opened up and drenched her, drenched him as he watched her.

She turned then, and stared at him through the curtain of rain. There was knowledge and acceptance in her face. And need.

He crossed the clearing, caught her in his arms, and pushed her up against the side of the van, kissing her with such rough abandon that he didn't know if he hated her or loved her. She put her arms around his neck, and when he unfastened his jeans to free himself she was ready, wrapping her long legs around him as he pushed into her, impaling her on his rigid flesh, holding her against the cold wet siding of the van as the rain fell around them.

She came immediately, tightening around him with a hoarse cry of wonder and despair. This time he was past thinking. He only knew he needed her, with a blind, driving lust that wiped his mind and soul clean until there was nothing left but his body and hers, pumping, deep, feeling her all around him, her rain-soaked breasts pressed against his chest, her mouth caught with his, her legs tight around his hips as he drove into her. He didn't want it to end, ever. He didn't want to think or talk, he wanted to fuck her from the back, he wanted to come in her mouth, he wanted to take her every way he could think of and then do it all over again.

She cried out again against his mouth, as a second orgasm tore through her, and he was helpless to resist the pull of her body, the pull of her soul. He surrendered to it, coming inside the tight pulsing need of her, and his last conscious thought was that he had just made the worst mistake of his life.

She couldn't walk when he released her, and he had to brace her against the wet metal side of the van until she could pull herself together. He understood the feeling. His own legs were shaky, and it had nothing to do with physical exertion and everything to do with sex.

Rachel closed her eyes, leaning against the trailer, her face tipped up toward the rain. At least this time she didn't cry. She probably didn't have any tears left after that bout in the back of the van. He waited until it looked as if her knees wouldn't collapse under her, and then he pulled up his jeans and zipped them, ignoring the fact that he was already half-hard again just from watching her face.

"Get back in the van and get your clothes on," he said in a low, flat voice. "You'll catch your death out here."

She opened her eyes to look at him. "It's not cold."

"Get your goddamned clothes on," he said. "Or get on your hands and knees in the mud and we'll try it that way."

She slammed the door behind her. He reached for his cigarettes again, but they were squashed, and besides, he didn't really want them. He tossed them into the underbrush with a muttered curse, and rubbed his back. It was sore, and he could feel scratch marks. Claw marks. And he grinned a small, sour grin.

He gave her five minutes before opening the van door again. She was sitting in the front seat, her T-shirt and the bra she didn't need back in place, her jeans tightly fastened. He climbed in beside her, turning to roll down the window and let some of the steam out, when he heard her horrified gasp.

He glanced back at her out of hooded eyes. "What's wrong?"

"What happened to your back?"

He didn't think she could still be that naive. "You did, sugar."

"Oh," she said in a small, shocked voice.

"Don't worry about it," he said in a calm voice. "I like it." He reached down and started the old van. "So where am I taking you?"

"Do I have a choice?"

"You always have a choice," he said lazily. "I can take you back to your car. You can even run in and tell Esther what I did, and I bet she'd get me with a shotgun before I could get away. Course there'd be a big scandal, but apart from everyone knowing you had sex in a swamp with me I think you'd survive. I wouldn't, but that would suit you just fine, now wouldn't it?"

"It wouldn't get me my mother's money."

He grinned. "Good point. You got to keep your priorities straight. Money's more important than my head on a platter any old day."

"Maybe."

"Or I can take you up to Mobile and put you on a plane."

"You forgot my rental car. With my purse and my credit cards."

"Coltrane can see to that."

"I think I'd rather get there under my own steam."

"Then again, you can come with me."

"Where?"

"The next town over. Thirty miles away, with a big, fancy, discreet motel with big beds and dirty movies on the television. I could continue your sexual education." He glanced at her, half expecting her to start screaming at him.

He'd underestimated her. "No, thank you," she said, sounding like an aristocratic bitch, just like her horny mother. "I think I've learned enough for one day."

He shrugged. "It's up to you. Anytime you feel like experimenting . . ."

"I'll come right down to Santa Dolores and ask for you," she supplied sweetly.

"I bet you would." He muttered it, half to himself, rousing himself enough to be amused by the very notion. He could just imagine what the Grandfathers would do. Calvin would shit a brick.

The dirt road was a mass of rain-filled potholes. He drove carefully enough, when he really wanted to slam his foot down on the accelerator. Or the brake. In the misty post-storm light she looked pale and drained. The rain had washed the tears from her face, and she'd managed to finger-comb her short hair into some semblance of neatness. If it weren't for the spectacular love bite on the base of her throat you might never know what she'd just been doing.

She'd hate that hickey when she saw it. At the moment she was too worn out to hate him, but that would come back again as well. With luck he'd scared her away for good. But the way his luck had been running lately, he could expect more disaster to follow in her wake.

They were already at the edge of town, driving past the old graveyard. He glanced at his mother's grave automatically, then kept driving. "You put flowers on my mama's grave yesterday."

She didn't say anything, and he didn't expect her to. He didn't bother asking why she hadn't put any on Jackson's. She knew things without asking, without listening to whatever lie he felt like telling her.

"Let me off here," she said suddenly. They were a block away from Esther's old house, and even from that distance he could smell the dank, lifeless air in the polished hallways.

"Why?"

"I have an aversion to the sight of blood," she said.

"You don't want her to kill me?"

"I don't want to watch."

"Careful, Rachel. I might start thinking you had feelings for me."

She looked at him, her eyes still and calm, her mouth swollen from his. "Oh, I have feelings for you, all right, Luke Bardell."

"But you think cold-blooded murder is a sin?" he suggested.

She shook her head. "No," she said. "Just in poor taste."

She managed to surprise a laugh out of him. "Far be it from me to be déclassé enough to be murdered. Your mother would be horrified."

He didn't miss the sudden blankness in her face as he pulled the truck to a stop. "Maybe she wouldn't be that surprised," she said. And she slid out of the cab of the truck before he could stop her.

He was half-tempted to go after her, but Esther was already standing in her doorway, peering down the street with those nasty little eyes of hers. Good thing she was nearsighted and too damned vain to wear glasses. He probably could have walked Rachel to the front door after all.

What the hell had she meant by that? Stella had died of cancer spreading like wildfire through her body. He couldn't remember whether she was one of those who'd asked to be helped at the end. He doubted it—she hadn't been in much pain, and Stella had been nothing if not strong-willed. She wouldn't have shuffled off this mortal coil a moment before she had to.

Why did Rachel think there was more to it? Was it part of her bizarre need to destroy him, so that she'd think him capable of anything? Or had someone been filling her with doubts and lies, feeding her anger and distrust?

She wouldn't listen to Esther—she was too smart for that. And everyone at Santa Dolores worshiped him to a nauseating extent. Except, perhaps, Catherine Biddle. But even though she tempered her adoration with a refreshing cynicism, he had no doubt she was as devout a follower as anyone.

It must just be some sick fantasy on Rachel's part. Part of her need to reclaim her mother, and cast him as the villain. She was going to have an unsettling time in the next few days, coming to terms with the fact that he'd gotten her in bed and made her enjoy it. With any luck it might drive her away completely. It was what he'd hoped for, planned for. That by giving her the royal screwing she so richly deserved, he'd finally get her off his back and send her screaming back to her safe, celibate little world.

But something told him it wasn't going to work out that way. As he watched her walk down the neatly trimmed sidewalks of Coffin's Grove, he knew the battle was over. But the war was far from won.

The van was a little big for a U-turn on the narrow residential streets, but he didn't give a shit. He drove up over one curb, knocking a trash can into the gutter, and drove off like a bat out of hell. He didn't want to see Rachel and Esther together. He didn't want to see Rachel again.

Not until he made sense of his own tangled agenda.

Not until he didn't want her.

Not until hell froze over.

* * *

The old woman was peering at her from the front door. The car was parked at the end of the walkway, where she'd left it the night before. The keys were in it, her purse lay on the passenger seat, her suitcase on the back. It wasn't locked.

Esther wasn't the only one watching her. Heading down the highway with a rolling gait was Mayor Leroy Peltner in his rumpled white suit and impressive belly, and he was coming straight for her.

She wondered whether she'd have time to dive into the car and get the hell away from them. *Coward*, she berated herself. Just because she felt stripped raw, vulnerable, didn't mean she had to forget why she'd come.

"Afternoon, Miz Rachel," he said.

"Hello, Mr. Peltner," She kept her hand on the door handle, ready to move.

"Leroy," he corrected her, wiping his sweating brow with a crumpled white handkerchief. "Helluva storm we had a while ago. I was hoping you wouldn't get caught in it. Us natives are used to it, but a Northern gal like yourself might run into trouble."

That was exactly what she'd run into out at the old Bardell place. The worst trouble she'd ever met in her twenty-nine years. "I was fine."

"Coltrane said he found your car abandoned out at the Bardell place, with no sign of you."

"He didn't look very far."

"Hell, did you have to walk all the way back here?" He glanced at her wet hair, her dry clothes.

"I got a ride."

"Who from, sugar?"

She looked at him. "A nice man in a big black van."

"Now ain't that sweet. I was plumb worried about you."

He was lying, and she knew it. He knew where she'd been as well as Coltrane did. He probably knew what she was doing. Her face felt flushed, but she kept her expression calm and innocent. "You were going to tell me about Luke Bardell, Leroy," she reminded him, leaning against her rain-slick car. Even with the sun out the water still beaded heavily on the finish, soaking into her cotton clothes. She didn't care.

Leroy blinked. "I was? I can't imagine what I was gonna say, missy. We're proud of our native son. He's proof positive that there's redemption in all of us."

"What did he need to be redeemed from, Leroy?"

"We're all sinners, Rachel," he said serenely.

"What's going on out there?" Esther called, peering nearsightedly down the walkway.

"I've got a plane to catch," Rachel said, pulling

open the car door. "If you'll excuse me, Mayor, I need to get going."

He stared at her, obviously torn between delight and the dictates of proper social behavior. "You sure I can't talk you into staying a few more days?" He sounded less than eager.

"I think Luke's accomplished what he wanted," she said, climbing into the driver's seat. "Check with him if you don't think it's okay to let me leave."

"I don't know what you're talking about, sugar," he protested, sweating even more profusely.

"You don't really have any deep dark secrets to tell me, do you?" she said. "You're just trying to keep me distracted so I won't find out anything."

"There's nothing to find out. We're a clean-living, God-fearing town," Leroy said.

"Does Esther know that Luke's really your good buddy? She's a mean old lady—I bet she wouldn't think twice about taking a shotgun to you and Sheriff Coltrane if she thought you were in league with the devil."

Leroy looked like he wanted to vomit. "You've been out in the sun too long . . ."

"It's been raining," she said. "Think about your sins, Leroy. And watch out for Esther." And she took off into the late afternoon with a satisfying squeal of her tires.

17

It was late, and he should have been bone-tired. But all Luke could think of was Rachel. The way she looked, the way she smelled, the strange, choking noise she made when she cried. The way she screamed when she came, ripping into the skin on his back like a wild woman.

He was almost ready to get the hell out of Coffin's Grove, this time for good. He'd already taken care of Leroy and Coltrane. They were ready to forget they'd ever known him, hadn't seen him in over a dozen years. Which suited him just fine.

He supposed, when it came right down to it, he was a forgiving man. Maybe the messiah business was wearing off on him. He never used to be softhearted, to think about anyone but himself.

There were very few people in the town of

Coffin's Grove who'd ever given a rat's ass about him. Most of them had known about Jackson Bardell, but no one had done anything to help him. He'd been trash, a motherless child who sassed the adults, stole when no one was looking, and deserved every beating he ever got.

Coltrane had kept an eye out for him. So had sweet Lureen, who'd initiated him into the joys of sex at age fifteen. There were a few others who'd worried, who'd tried to do something, but mostly they'd just wrung their hands and let him hurt.

And he was leaving their goddamned town with enough money to keep the city coffers solvent, the tax rate low, and cushion life a bit for the likes of Lureen.

Hell, he was an absolute savior, he thought with a sour grin. He was even letting an old troublemaker like Leroy Peltner benefit, when it had been Leroy himself who wanted Luke sent to a juvenile detention center when he was caught stealing cigarettes from Peltner's general store. He was headed for prison, Leroy had always said. Might as well get him started.

But there was one person left in Coffin's Grove who wasn't going to benefit from Luke's ill-gotten gains. One vicious old lady who wasn't going to get one goddamned thing.

He liked his money easily transportable. He had money scattered in various bank accounts in

Switzerland, stashes of bearer bonds and hundred-dollar bills piled in various obscure places near the Retreat Center. Calvin had his own stash as well, which Luke kept supplementing. Calvin had been the only one he ever trusted, and he figured he owed him.

He owed Esther Blessing as well. She'd buried three husbands, and they were all probably relieved to get away from her. Harry Blessing had run the local hardware store, and rumor had it he liked to look at pictures of naked children, so Luke figured they were a worthy match. He was still alive when Luke made his first return visit to Coffin's Grove. And it had seemed somehow fitting to stash two hundred thousand dollars' worth of bearer bonds in the crawl space beneath Esther Blessing's old house.

He had to be careful, knowing the old lady's penchant for cleaning everything. But over the years, when he'd made his surreptitious visits back, the initial stash was always untouched, hidden beneath the house, and each year he added to it.

It was still there when he came for it that night. In the darkness Luke could hear the television blaring, but to his amazement it sounded like the news. Esther had never listened to anything more mentally taxing than game shows, unless she thought she was going to hear something gory.

The lights were odd too. The downstairs was

pitch-black, when he knew for a fact that Esther was paranoid enough to leave lights burning. There was a light in her bedroom, but none in the bathroom.

He still hated Esther with a childish passion that he'd never outgrown. More because of the way she treated his mama than the pain she'd inflicted on him. He hadn't done anything about it, afraid that his rage went so deep he wouldn't be able to control himself, and the idea of strangling an old lady didn't sit well. He was going to kill again, he knew it, deep inside, no matter how much he tried to deny it. He didn't want to, but it was going to happen, one more time.

He just wanted to avoid situations where he'd be sorely tempted.

But the house was too strange. Esther paced at night, but he could see no sign of her wizened old body at any of the windows.

It was easy enough to get back into the house the same way he had just last night. He moved through the rooms silently, unerringly aware of every little gewgaw and knickknack she had littering the place.

Despite the noise of the television the house felt still as death. He moved like a ghost, through the rooms where Esther had pinched him and slapped him and beat him, and ignored the cold sweat that crept between his shoulder blades.

He saw her silhouetted in her huge old bed, propped up against the pillows. He was ready to disappear, back into the shadows, when something struck him. She wasn't hacking and coughing.

He moved into the doorway, and she didn't turn. She was facing the TV, her frizzy gray hair standing up all over her head. For a moment he thought, he hoped, she was dead. But he saw the rise and fall of her shallow chest, the clutching movements of one clawlike hand, and he knew she was still alive. At least partially.

He walked into the room then, directly into her line of vision. She didn't move, but her eyes grew dark with silent rage. She must have had a massive stroke. He could see her life draining away even as he stood there, even as she tried to summon the ability to speak.

"What's wrong, Esther?" he murmured. "Aren't you happy to see your long-lost grandson?"

Her mouth worked, but no words came out.

"Well, never you mind," he said. "There wasn't any love lost between the two of us, was there? I was kind of hoping I'd be able to get some revenge, but it looks like fate has already taken care of it for me. Even if you recover from this stroke, another one will hit you, sooner or later, carrying you off. You're a dead woman, Esther. And there's not a damned thing you can do about it."

The old lady couldn't move. She could only glare at him.

"You've spent the last twenty years telling everyone I killed your precious Jackson, but you've never been able to prove it. And you've never really known for sure, have you, Granny?" He used the term mockingly.

He came closer. "Well, guess what? That old son of a bitch, and I mean that literally, was trying to blow his brains out that day. I came in and he had that damned shotgun in his mouth. He was so goddamned drunk he didn't know what he was doing, and I was going to sit there and enjoy myself, watch as he splattered his brains all over that house.

"But then he saw me. And I guess he must have figured he ought to take me with him, because he started to point the gun at me. And I knew if I didn't do something damned fast it wold be my brains for wallpaper.

"And you know something, Esther? I didn't want to die. God knows why, but I've always had an amazing capacity for life. So I grabbed the gun and just blew that cocksucker away. Just like you thought I did."

Esther's shriveled mouth worked in impotent

rage, but apart from one clutching hand, she couldn't move.

"Tell you what," he said softly. "Say hi to Jackson for me when you meet up with him in hell. It won't be too long now."

He should have felt purged when he left that house of death, with the old woman lying there. Cleansed, rejuvenated. Instead he felt like shit. He hadn't finished what he'd come to do. He'd accomplished more than he'd ever thought—nailing Rachel Connery, retrieving his stash of money, settling his accounts with the old harridan who still visited his nightmares.

But he still had one more thing to do.

It was night. The jet was stuck on the runway in Mobile, waiting for the fog to lift. Rachel stared out the window, watching the rain run down the layered glass, ignoring her own hollow-eyed reflection. There was always, she thought, the unspeakable possibility that she could get pregnant. Or AIDS.

She wasn't sure which disaster she'd prefer. If Luke Bardell had AIDS then he was doomed along with her, and dying was a small price to pay for a suitable revenge. If it came to that.

She wasn't particularly in the mood to die. She'd been a suicidal adolescent, but not a very adept one. She'd always taken just enough pills to make herself throw up, cut just deep enough with the razor to make it hurt. You couldn't even see the faint white scars crisscrossing her wrists unless you looked closely. And she did her best not to let anyone get close enough to look.

She wasn't quite sure when the desire to kill herself had left her. She'd missed it at first. When things got really bad she could always weave elaborate fantasies about her own death, and it made the world fade into relative unimportance.

But she'd lost it somewhere along the way. Suicide was no longer an option—she had to face the mess she made for herself.

And that was another unpleasant realization. She much preferred to blame other people, particularly her family, for the things that went wrong with her life. She seemed to have lost that ability as well, though that had left her more recently. She was coming to the unpleasant, unacceptable conclusion that she was responsible for her own life. Stella was dead. So was the past.

Still and all, she thought, she'd rather be dying than pregnant. Than be carrying Luke Bardell's bastard.

She didn't want children, she told herself. They got hurt too easily, and she couldn't stand to see a child of hers wounded. If she had a child she wouldn't be able to do a damned thing to keep her safe but love her, and that wasn't enough.

Or was it?

She couldn't remember when she last had her period—it was an inconvenience she tended to ignore. It might have been two weeks ago, it might have been longer. Of course she'd done nothing about birth control. Why should she, when she'd had no intention of ever having sex again, with anyone.

So much for good intentions. She wasn't going to think about it. About lying beneath him on the hard mattress, clinging to him. Crying.

On second thought, maybe death wasn't such a bad idea after all. At least then she wouldn't have to live with the demoralizing memory of her defeat.

That's what it had been, of course. And that's what he had wanted. He hadn't wanted to have sex with her. He'd wanted to finish her off, to show her just how helpless she was against the likes of him.

He'd done an excellent job of it. She could still feel his rain-slick, sweat-slick body against hers. Feel the hard metal side of the van as he shoved her up against it. She could still feel a faint tremor shimmering through her body at the thought of what had happened next.

People didn't get pregnant from a one-night stand. Or one afternoon stand. She was borrowing trouble, when she already had a plateful. If this goddamned plane would just get off the runway and take her out of this godforsaken state, then she'd be all right. She wanted to go somewhere cold.

It was too hot and muggy in Alabama. It was too hot and dry in New Mexico. She wanted snow, she wanted to wrap herself in sweaters and down comforters and keep herself safe.

It was a little late for that. Rather like locking the barn door after the horse was stolen. She'd known Luke Bardell was trouble the first moment she laid eyes on him, and if her usual defenses had been working right she would have kept her distance. Concentrated on keeping herself safe, and the hell with vengeance and money.

But she hadn't. She'd let anger, grief, and an anonymous letter make her forget everything she'd worked so hard to protect. And now her life was in tatters.

Right now she wasn't sure what she was going to do. Find someplace and see what she could do about healing. About putting her defenses back together, protecting herself from the harm Luke Bardell had done to her.

When she was feeling stronger, colder, fiercer, she would make a list. A plan. She would decide what she wanted from the messiah of the Foundation of Being, whether it was money or revenge or simply exposing him as the fraud he was. And she would go after that goal, and accomplish it, with no further distractions.

After all, how bad was it? So she'd had sex with him. Twice. So she hadn't been physically ill. That wasn't saying much.

All right, it was more than that. He'd been able to make her respond the way she'd never imagined, and she hated him for it. Because she already craved that feeling again, and it made her vulnerable.

But in the long run, maybe it would do her good. Maybe, eventually, she'd find a decent, loving man who would be a partner to her. Maybe she could live a storybook life in a white cottage with a picket fence and two point three children and a minivan.

And maybe pigs could fly.

She didn't want life in the suburbs, and she certainly didn't want a man. Despite Luke's efforts to convince her otherwise.

He'd simply been able to bring about a normal, physiological reaction that she hadn't experienced before. She could learn to bring it on herself—most women did. It was perfectly natural, and there was no reason she had to make a federal case out of it. Luke was used to manipulating other people, emotionally, physically, sexually. She should have realized just how dangerous he could be.

She knew now. She wouldn't go anywhere near him unless she was completely invulnerable, fortified against his insidious charm. He probably thought he'd managed to drive her away forever. He probably hoped he had. It was a small price to pay for twelve million dollars—one afternoon of enforced sex with an angry woman.

But he was mistaken if he thought he'd won so easily. This war was far from over. She would be back, stronger than ever. And she would win.

She suddenly realized the plane had started moving, taxiing down the runway. She gripped her armrest and closed her eyes, breathing a small sigh of relief. She wanted to get out of Alabama. She wanted to get away from her memories.

But most of all, she wanted something to eat.

Luke Bardell, savior of the world, prodigal son of Coffin's Grove, Alabama, leaned against the side of the ancient van and stared at the old house. He was smoking another cigarette, even though he didn't really want it. That was one blessing in his otherwise disastrous life—he just plain didn't have an addictive personality. He could smoke a pack of cigarettes in one day flat and then not even care the next day. He could drink one hundred proof whiskey from a bottle for weeks on end and switch over to mineral water at the retreat without a twinge. He could bang everything in sight and then settle in for a long stretch of celibacy with no great hardship.

Except, maybe, for Rachel Connery. He was already missing her. Wanting her. Lusting after her, which was damned stupid, considering she was so inexperienced in bed. He thought making her come would be enough of a triumph. Now he wanted to push it further than that. See if he could get her to make love to him. Climb on top and take him, maybe use her mouth . . .

He shoved himself away from the van with a muttered curse. If he had any luck left in the amount allotted to him by a disinterested creator, then she'd be long gone and he'd never have to see her again. Which would be the best possible thing for both of them.

He still had the scent of her on his hands. He could still feel her arms around him, hear her strangled cry of completion and despair. Hell, he'd probably screwed up her life more than she had his. She thought she knew who she was. He'd just taught her she didn't know shit.

She was one hell of a woman, he had to grant her that. Every time he thought he'd won, she'd come back with a new piece of ammunition. He'd be a fool to think she'd stop now, just because he'd managed to nail her. And his mama didn't raise no fools.

There were a couple of gas cans by the back door—he'd put them there several days ago. Dusk was closing down around him, and the mosquitoes were getting nasty. He took the cans, walking through the old house, sloshing the gas as he went.

He spilled some in his old bedroom, where he used to hide under the bed when Jackson would come looking for him. He spilled some in Jackson's bedroom as well, where the old man used to lie, drunk and snoring, with his fragile, frightened young wife beside him.

He drenched the bloodstain on the parlor floor. He could still see Jackson's body lying there, bits of brain and bone sticking to the wall. He'd stunk— his bladder and bowels had automatically emptied moments after his death, and Luke had just stood there, staring at the man he'd hated beyond reason. The man he still hated.

He dumped the empty can, then wandered back out to the van, humming under his breath, an old hymn his mama had taught him. "Leaning on the Everlasting Arms."

The engine started right up. It was well tuned— Coltrane saw to that when Luke wasn't there. Still humming, he put it into gear and jammed his foot on the accelerator.

He smashed through the front of the house, through one of the empty window frames, knocking down decrepit walls, until the van finally came to a stop against the chimney. He sat there for a moment, dazed, then climbed out of the van. Leaving everything behind.

"What a fellowship, what a joy divine, leaning on the everlasting arms . . ." he sang softly, pushing his way through the wreckage of the old house. He stopped at the broken doorway, looking back. "Safe and secure from all alarm . . ." He reached into his pocket and pulled out the crumpled pack of cigarettes, the ancient Zippo that had once belonged to an old, old friend.

"Leaning, leaning, leaning on the everlasting arms." He let his voice rumble through the gathering dusk. He lit the cigarette, took a deep drag, and stared into the dark house. And then he tossed the lighter inside.

He'd kind of hoped for an instant conflagration. The fire smoldered, then ran along the line of spilled gas. The place didn't explode until he was almost half a mile up the road.

He was on the third verse by then, the words emblazoned in his memory. The mosquitoes gave him wide berth, and the sun set low on the horizon. He was walking away from Coffin's Grove, and he wouldn't be back.

Maybe now he could rest in peace. With Jackson's house consigned to the fiery flames where

Jackson no doubt resided already. Sent there by his stepson's loving hands.

"Safe and secure from all alarm," he sang out loud, and the buzz of the mosquitoes sang counterpoint.

PART THREE

SANTA DOLORES, NEW MEXICO

18

"It's about goddamn time you got your ass back here," Calvin greeted him.

Luke leaned against the door, shoving a hand through his hair as he stared at the little man. Calvin worried too much about him, he knew that, but there hadn't been much he could do to stop him.

"Anybody ask about me?" he said, pushing away and walking into the living area of his supposedly ascetic retreat room. The wall of television monitors shimmered in the shadowy light of the room, and he headed straight for the black refrigerator, grabbing a cold bottle of beer.

"What do you think?" Calvin demanded. "I've been fighting them off in droves. Several of the Grandfathers want to discuss financial strategy with you. Catherine wants to talk to you. Bobby

Ray is whining about missing you. Everybody else wants to sleep with you." He stared at him with growing suspicion. "But you've already taken care of that little problem, haven't you? Who was it this time? Anyone I know?"

"Jealous?" Luke said lazily.

"Not particularly. You're not my type," Calvin shot back. "Why the hell didn't you change out of those black clothes? What if someone had seen you?"

"Then I'd be up shit's creek without a paddle," he said recklessly, draining half the bottle of beer and staring blindly at the security monitors.

"You may be willing to throw this all away, but I've put a lot of hard work into the last seven years. I'm not about to let it go up in a puff of smoke because you've gotten bored. Speaking of which, you stink of cigarettes."

Luke leaned back. "I'm planning on taking a shower."

"Who did you sleep with?"

"Why do you care?"

"I want to make sure it isn't some fool waitress who'll show up claiming to be pregnant and then I'll have to get rid of her. That sort of thing gets too damned dangerous."

Luke looked at him. He was tired, foul-tempered, and horny. It had been a week since he'd left Coffin's Grove, a week thinking about going after Rachel. He hadn't, but he hadn't been able to get her off his mind either. Calvin wasn't improving his mood any.

"Have you gotten rid of anyone before?" His voice was dangerously quiet.

Calvin's shrug should have been convincing. "Your paranoia's gotten out of hand, Luke. You seem to forget, everyone around here thinks you're the next messiah. Except for Stella's nasty little daughter . . ." He stopped, and his dark face paled slightly. "No," he said flatly.

"No, what? No, you haven't gotten rid of anyone?"

But Calvin wasn't about to be derailed. "You didn't sleep with Rachel Connery. Tell me you weren't that goddamned stupid and self-destructive."

Luke slouched in the comfortable chair, stretching his dusty, black-clad legs in front of him. "All right, I won't tell you," he said, draining the beer.

It took Calvin a minute to pull himself together. He came over and sat down at Luke's feet, looking up at him out of deeply troubled eyes. "Why, Luke?"

Luke just shook his head. "Hell, I don't know. I can give you a dozen reasons but none of them is the right one. Maybe it all boils down to the fact that she was there when I needed to get laid."

"Where?"

"Coffin's Grove."

"Shit! Are you out of your fucking mind? What was she doing there?"

"What do you think? She was trying to find out some new way to destroy me."

"Sounds like you gave her perfect ammunition."

Luke stretched back and closed his eyes. "She would have found her own. Besides, you don't seem to have much faith in me. Maybe I fucked her so well she's now madly in love with me."

"Maybe. If she were like most women. Knowing her, she probably still wants to kill you."

Luke found he could manage a small, cold grin. "Probably," he agreed.

"So where is she now? Telling the newspapers about it?"

Luke shook his head. "I doubt it. I expect she'll be showing up here sooner or later."

"The Grandfathers aren't going to like hearing about this. Sometimes I think they're just as in love with you as everyone else around here is."

"Except you, Calvin."

"Except me," he said flatly. "We'll have to do something about her. You know that, don't you?"

"You tried before. You do anything again and I'll break your scrawny little neck."

"Isn't that getting a little intimate? I thought you usually shot or stabbed your victims."

"You're annoying me, Calvin."

Calvin snorted in profound disapproval. "What are you going to do about her? Are you going to let her destroy everything we've worked so hard for?"

"Maybe," Luke said dreamily.

He could feel Calvin's frozen fury. Calvin was the only one who dared get angry with him, but somehow the charm had begun to wear off.

"I won't let you do that," he said.

Luke looked at him, very calmly. "You can't stop me," he said. And he closed his eyes again.

He hadn't wanted to return to Santa Dolores. It had taken him more than a week to make himself return, a week he'd spent bumming around the southern part of the country, drinking too much, smoking too much, too damned angry and horny to even bother jerking off. He had no idea where Rachel Connery had disappeared to, and he didn't care.

At least, he didn't think so.

He was so damned weary of the life he'd made for himself. He was sick and tired of saintliness and celibacy, he was sick and tired of feeling responsible for the hundred or so gullible souls who flocked to the meditation center and loaded the coffers with their disposable income. Siphoning off a generous proportion was too damned easy, and now Calvin had started making demands as well. Demands he didn't particularly feel like meeting.

He was going to disappear. He'd prefer to do it in full view of his faithful followers, vanishing in a puff of smoke, but unlike those deluded souls, he knew he didn't have any supernatural powers, or any tricks other than his powerful charisma. He'd have to make plans, careful plans. And he'd have to include Calvin.

He opened his eyes again. Calvin hadn't moved, perched at his feet like Satan's altar boy. "You're leaving, aren't you?" he said.

"Yes."

"Will you take me with you?" The question was simple and profound. Calvin had been by his side since Joliet; he'd been his confidant and his partner in crime for the last twelve years. Only Calvin knew the depths of Luke's particular scam. All the others believed.

Calvin knew where Luke kept the money he'd siphoned off, even though he didn't have access to it. Calvin had devised the original escape plan, when they'd been ready to ditch everything at a moment's notice, never imagining that the hokey Foundation of Being would grow so powerful or so profitable. Calvin was the best friend Luke had ever had. And the one he most wanted to escape.

"No," he said.

Calvin nodded, and his faint grin was lopsided. "I didn't think so. That's one thing I can always count on with you, Luke. You'll be straight with me. No matter what. When are you going?"

"I'm not sure." He leaned back, closing his eyes wearily. "When the time is right. I'll see to it that you get your share, you know I will."

"I'm not worried about that." Calvin dismissed it with a wave of his hand. "But the people here aren't going to just let you walk away. They don't just love you, they think they own you."

"Yeah," he said. "But they don't. And they can't stop me. They won't even know I'm gone until it's too late."

"What about me? Do I get any warning, or are you just going to disappear on me as well?" He sounded no more than casually interested.

"You'll have warning. It won't take them long to start suspecting things aren't quite what they seem, and you'll need to be ready to make your move as well."

"So this is gonna be the end of a beautiful friendship?"

Luke glanced down at him. As usual Calvin seemed remote and faintly cynical, accepting of what life had to offer him. "You know what they say about all good things," Luke said gently.

"Do me a favor? Give me a couple of days to

get a few things in order, will you? Don't just decide to walk out tonight."

It was a small enough request from a partner he was about to abandon, and Luke had no intention of denying it, no matter how much he wanted to. No matter how much he wanted to turn around and walk right back out of the meditation center, find himself a six-pack and a willing blonde and see if he could screw Rachel Connery out of his brain.

But he knew, at least for now, it was a lost cause. She'd taken possession of him, body and soul, and it was going to take more than one night to exorcise her.

"Sure, Calvin. I won't make any move for the time being. Everything else going okay? Apart from Alfred and Catherine trying to beat down the door?"

"Everyone's trying to get to you, but you've gone off on these meditation retreats before, so they don't suspect anything. As for everything being okay, I don't know. Something funny's going on, but the Grandfathers haven't felt like confiding in me," he said. He'd risen to his feet and moved away, busying himself with disposing of the empty beer bottle he'd taken from Luke's hand.

"Surprises?"

Calvin's face was impassive. "God, I hope not. I hate surprises."

Luke waited until Calvin left him before he moved, erupting out of his seat with a sudden excess of nervous energy that would have amazed his placid followers. The security monitors flashed on empty corridors, empty rooms. Everyone was asleep in their own beds, and the room where he'd put Rachel was still and dark. Empty.

His own quarters were carefully divided into private and public areas. To his followers and their benevolent Grandfathers, Luke lived in a large, barren room, sleeping on a pallet on the floor. He had a narrow, metal shower stall, a stone fireplace for heat, and absolutely nothing to distract him from his communion with the wisdom of the ages.

And if he needed even more privacy, his meditation chamber, off-limits to everyone, lay beyond.

Of course, that room came equipped with the security monitors, the beer-filled refrigerator, the king-sized bed, and the sybaritic bathroom. That was where he lived his life, where no one could see.

For some reason the self-indulgent luxury of that secret room rankled. He didn't want clandestine opulence. For the first time in his life his soul craved simplicity.

He banged his elbow in the narrow shower stall in the front room. The water was lukewarm, but he didn't care. He brushed the taste of beer and cigarettes from his mouth, finger-combed his long wet hair back from his face, and dressed himself in his white cotton clothes. He shaved without a mirror, and he told himself a few more days of sainthood might be good for him. And then walked out into the main room, in time to see a slender female in the pale yellow clothes of a penitent setting a tray on the low table for him.

The breach of privacy startled him. "I didn't ask for any food," he said.

She hadn't heard him come in. She dropped the tray with a noisy clatter, then slowly turned around to face him. "Catherine sent it," she said. "Catherine sent me."

It was Rachel.

He was so shocked he could do nothing but stare at her. He knew his automatic protective instincts would come into play—his face would be wearing no expression at all, and she'd be at a loss to guess his reaction to her presence.

"Does Calvin know you're here?" he said after a long moment, his voice even.

"No, but I think he suspects. Catherine thinks he might be dangerous. That he might still want to hurt me."

He moved into the room, slowly, seemingly at ease. She was watching him with a nervous intensity, the kind that might suddenly explode into full-scale panic, and he didn't want to frighten her away. Not until he found out what in hell had made her come after him. To this place, of all places.

"Whereas you think you're safe from me?" he asked idly, sinking down on the floor in front of the food tray. Lentils. When he left this place for good he would never let a lentil past his lips again.

She'd been avoiding his gaze. Now she looked at him, a certain amount of courage in her eyes. "Not particularly."

He nodded, picking up a piece of whole-meal bread and ripping it apart. "So why are you here? I assume you must have a good reason—I didn't expect you to ever willingly get within a hundred miles of me again. Are you planning to kill me?" He glanced down at the lentils. "Poison?"

She stiffened. "If I were going to kill you I wouldn't use something devious like poison. I'd probably stab you."

"In the back or in the heart?" He sounded no more than faintly curious.

"In the heart. So I could watch your expression."

It startled a laugh out of him. "Naaah," he said, leaning back on the thin cushions and staring up at her. "You'd use poison. They call it a woman's weapon. And whether you like it or not, sweetheart, you're very much a woman. No matter how hard you try to fight it." He let his eyes roam down her body. There was something different about her, though he couldn't quite figure out what. She looked stronger, more alive, than she'd ever looked before. Still frightened of him, but less fragile.

She took an instinctive step backward at his blatant surveillance. "Maybe I didn't come to destroy you," she said. "Maybe I came panting after you, maybe I can't get enough of you. Maybe I've become as hopelessly besotted as all the other people here, and I'm hoping so desperately that you'll make love to me again that I'm willing to endure any humiliation, just to be near you."

He had to laugh. "I may have underestimated your courage, Rachel, but I never thought you were less than brilliant."

"You wanted a challenge. You wanted to take a woman who hates you, your worst enemy, and turn her into your love slave. You've succeeded. Voilà."

He shook his head. "So you're my love slave, are you?"

"Of course."

"Why?" It was fascinating to see how far he could push her. He couldn't even begin to imagine why she was here, waiting for him, any more than he could guess why Catherine had let her back in. Then again, as far as Catherine knew he'd been holed up in his meditation room, accepting no visitors. Calvin said she'd been trying to see him. Maybe to explain her reasons for letting Rachel back.

Rachel stared at him. Her hair was different, and she looked less like a boy than the last time she came here. "Maybe you're irresistible," she said finally.

He didn't believe that for one minute. At least not where she was concerned. "Come here and show me," he said in a soft, taunting voice. "Show me how irresistible I am."

The panic was there, stronger than ever. For a moment it surprised him, but then it made sense. Before, she'd been frightened of the unknown. Now she knew for sure just how much power he could have over her.

"Catherine should be here any minute."

"I don't mind the risk," he said, his eyes daring her. "Come over here and put your mouth on me."

She stood there staring at him, and it was a battle of wills. One he would win, because there was no other choice. She was strong, and she could fight him. But she couldn't fight herself. She would come to him, and she would touch him, and he would make her remember what it had been like.

She had already taken one tentative step toward him when the quiet knock heralded Catherine's arrival. Luke didn't say a word, didn't even blink as rage and frustration rushed through his body. He quickly stilled his unruly response. Rachel was here. For whatever obscure reason, she was already back in his territory, of her own accord. Sooner or later he would have her.

"Blessings, Luke," Catherine murmured, poking her head through the doorway.

"Blessings," he said in response, watching the tension drain from Rachel's tight shoulders. He planned to make certain it was back the first chance he got.

Catherine stepped into the room, the dove-gray clothes of the Grandfathers draped comfortably around her compact body. She looked the same, elegant, mothering. Not the sort to have any unpleasant surprises in store for him. "You may leave us, Rachel," she said, taking a seat opposite Luke, the untouched food between them.

Luke gave her an inquiring look. It was unlike Catherine to give such a blatant order, and he was about to countermand it when he saw Rachel's lower lip tremble. She needed time alone to recoup her defenses. And he wanted her armed and ready for battle.

He nodded his approval in a deliberately gracious manner, enough to jar Rachel out of her distraction. If she were free she would have stuck her tongue out at him. But she wasn't free, she was wrapped so tightly in fear and uncertainty that all she could do was escape.

"What's she doing here?" Luke asked when the door had shut behind her.

"I tried to talk to you about it, but you weren't seeing anyone." There was no defensiveness in Catherine's voice. A woman with her background had no use for defensiveness. "It seemed a wise idea. She showed up here a few days ago, and I really had no choice. She looked shell-shocked."

"Did she tell you where she'd been?" He wasn't the slightest bit concerned about any possible confessions she might have made. He was more interested in Catherine's observations.

"No. And I didn't ask. She just said she needed to be here, and I accepted that. I decided it would be wiser if Calvin wasn't aware of her presence. He doesn't trust her."

"Do you?"

Catherine's smile was tranquil. "She's a troubled young woman who's recently lost her mother, and she's looking for answers, for someone to blame. I have complete faith in you, Luke. You can bring her the peace of mind she needs, no matter how hard she fights it."

He had a sudden vision of her, lying beneath him in the back of the van, fighting the response that was rippling through her body. Catherine wasn't likely to look at his crotch, but he was glad the table stood between them, hiding his immediate erection.

"What's she been doing?"

"Anything I tell her to. She's been doing kitchen duty, cleaning, meditating. I think she's finally ready for you, Luke."

The image was almost overwhelming, but not for a minute would he let Catherine see his reaction. "She could start with some basic instruction. See if you can find someone to handle it. Someone with a fair amount of patience," he added wryly.

Catherine's faded blue eyes narrowed in surprise. "I thought you would see to it."

"I've been in retreat too long. Calvin tells me the Grandfathers need my input, and I'm sure there are lots of other things that require my attention. Other people. There are any number of followers who can undertake Rachel's instruction," he said.

And what was most fascinating of all was Catherine's reaction. The brief darkening of her eyes. The faint tightening of her lined mouth. Then she smiled, and he might have imagined her sudden irritation.

"As you wish," she said. "I'll see to it." She rose in one fluid motion that belied her age.

"Blessings, Catherine," he murmured.

She was, after all, a Biddle. She stiffened her

upright back and bestowed her patrician smile upon him. "Blessings, Luke," she said. And as she turned to leave he caught the faint, shocking glimpse of a hickey on the side of her lined neck.

19

By the time Catherine left the room Rachel had managed to make herself scarce. It was a close call—everyone at the Foundation of Being moved very quietly, partly because of their unruffled pace, partly because of the soft shoes they all wore. But Rachel had used the last few days perfecting her eavesdropping skills, and once more she escaped detection.

Obviously she hadn't been as effective in working on her quiet, subservient manner. She thought she'd had it down pat, the lowered eyes, the quiet voice, the demure manner. One minute with Luke and it had shattered, and the raw emotions had come flowing back through her, anger and despair, contempt and an infuriating, grudging amusement. Something else as well, but that was a struggle that she knew was ongoing. It was the reason she'd come back.

At least it had seemed so very clear just a few short days ago, when she'd discovered that there really was no place to hide. Her body had healed—she'd washed away every trace of him, and the scratches, the marks, the faint swelling and bruises vanished almost too quickly. There was no sign that her life, her body, had undergone a significant upheaval. Except for the strange side effect of her appetite.

It wasn't anything interestingly extreme. She simply ate at regular intervals. She noticed she was hungry, and she would sit down and eat something. She didn't always clean her plate, but she managed to keep her stomach decently filled.

She spent two days convinced she was pregnant, convinced her sudden appetite was her body's way of telling her she was eating for two. The onset of her period wiped out that particular theory, but it didn't stop her partaking of regular meals. It seemed as if Luke had taken everything from her: her mother, her inheritance, her peace of mind, and her neuroses. She'd lost track of what she resented most.

If she'd been able to turn her back on Luke, on the Foundation, then she surely would have. There was no longer anything calling her back—she'd let go of her mother, her vain hopes for some kind of resolution. And Luke had taught her how very dangerous he could be—she would be far better off miles and miles away from him.

If it hadn't been for Bobby Ray with the angelic face and the warning letter. If it hadn't been for her mother's surprising death, the death of Angel McGuiness, the overwhelming sense that something wasn't right about the Foundation of Being. Her mother had been cremated—there was no way to discover whether she'd really died of cancer. Unless she found Bobby Ray and forced him to remember, to tell her what he knew.

So far she'd found absolutely nothing to substantiate her sense of impending disaster. She'd dressed in the clothes Catherine had insisted upon, she'd eaten lentils and bread and vegetables with surprising gusto, she'd done everything she'd been told to do, and she'd listened and watched. The Grandfathers moved through the hallways, usually in groups of three or more, their somber faces a match for their gray clothes as they talked in low voices. Catherine was kind and distant, soothing. Rachel slept on a pallet next to her narrow bed, and she lay awake at night, listening to Catherine's deep breathing, and wondered why she couldn't trust anyone, not even the motherly woman who was trying so hard to help her find peace of mind.

Four days she'd been in New Mexico, four long days, waiting for a sign that Luke had returned.

Four days waiting, and dreading. She was almost relieved to know the wait was over. Except that now it was time for action.

She couldn't hear a thing from the closed room, but that meant absolutely nothing. He moved silently—he might be pacing, he might be asleep. She knew one thing for certain—she wasn't ready to face him again, not quite so quickly. And Catherine would be wondering where she was.

She'd promised to be obedient, to do everything Catherine told her, and up till now she'd been able to keep that promise. She wasn't sure for how much longer, though, now that Luke was back in the picture.

She stepped forward, out of the shadows. The hallway was still and silent, the meditation center had shut down for the night, encased in darkness and sleep as it was encased in light and quiet during the day. She moved as silently as a wraith, past the door that led to the Zen-like garden.

She stopped for a moment, staring out the window into the black of the night. There was a flash of something white, a muffled cry, and like a fool she put her hand on the door, ready to open it, when the cry came again, and she recognized it for the frankly sexual sound it was. Someone was out there making love. Having sex. And the thought that it might be Luke chilled her to the bone.

She couldn't move. She could almost see them,

a blur of pale skin, the faint, grunting cries just carrying to her ears. Her stomach knotted, and she wanted to run, but she was glued to the spot, unable to move, scarcely able to breathe.

"If I'd known you liked to watch I could have arranged something." Luke's soft, drawling voice came from directly behind her, and she whirled around to stare up at him in shock. Her relief was so powerful it sickened her, and the need to touch him, to fling her body against his, was overwhelming enough to make her shake. But she didn't move.

"Who's out there?" she said finally.

"I don't have the faintest idea. I don't care— they're not hurting anyone. Anyway, I'm more interested in being an active participant than a voyeur."

She backed away from him, coming up against the metal door with a solid clanging sound. The sounds beyond stopped abruptly, and she had no doubt the lovers had been frightened off. They weren't the only ones who were frightened.

He was moving in on her, his body almost touching her, so dangerously close that she wasn't quite sure where her fear was coming from. "You still didn't answer my question," he murmured, and his voice was low and Southern, the seductive drawl of Alabama that she hadn't heard him use in this place before. "Why did you come back here?"

She looked up at him, and knew, with sudden terrible clarity, the answer to the simple question. She had come back for him.

It was a horrifying realization, one she was afraid he could read all too clearly on her face. "You owe me five hundred thousand dollars," she blurted out, desperate for an excuse. "We made a deal."

He didn't move. "I forgot about that," he said mildly. "Cash or traveler's checks?"

He'd managed to shock her even more deeply, so that she blinked, staring at him. "Whichever . . ." she began, but it was too late.

"Neither," he said. "And that's not why you're here, is it?"

Strength was flowing back through her. She didn't know its source, and she didn't care. "Of course not," she said, lightly sarcastic. "I came for sex. I'm absolutely panting for your touch."

"That can be arranged . . ." He reached for her, but her cynical bravado failed.

"No!" She wasn't going to cower from him, run from him, but with the metal door up against her back she had no place to go. He knew it. He put his hands on the door, on either side of her head, and leaned close. Not touching her. It was almost worse that way.

"You'll come to me," he whispered in a low, be-guiling voice that corroded her fear and resolve.

"Sooner or later you'll stop fighting. You know what I can give you, and you want it."

She rallied. "I'm sure I can find any number of people willing to provide me with sex and multiple orgasms," she snapped.

"I'm sure you can." He let the side of his face brush against her, and she could smell the shampoo in his long damp hair, the shaving cream on his skin, the mint of toothpaste. "You can find yourself a decent, honorable man, one to love you, respect you, cherish you. Someone with morals, with a decent job and a good future. That's what you think you want, isn't it? Not some white trash from Alabama. Not some ex-con who's running the scam of a lifetime. You're so good and decent, the very thought of me disgusts you, doesn't it?" His voice was low and seductive as he pushed the words at her.

She met his gaze with what she hoped was a fearless one of her own. "Yes," she said.

"Then tell me, Rachel," he said, letting his hand toy with the loose neckline of her tunic, "why aren't you out somewhere, fucking your little gentleman's brains out? Why are you here with me, quivering when I touch you?" He brushed his mouth against her cheekbone, moving toward her ear, and his hypnotic voice was barely a whisper. "It's a hot night, Rachel. Why are your nipples hard?"

"You're a monster," she said in a low, furious voice.

"No, I'm not. I'm just a man. Even if you think they're the same thing."

It was enough. He knew her too well. Her breasts were tight and burning, her stomach twisted, and she was hot and damp between her legs. She could either fight or admit defeat. And she was a born fighter.

She put her hands against his chest and shoved him as hard as she could, taking him by surprise. He fell back, and she took off, refusing to look back, half expecting him to call after her. He didn't say a word, but it wasn't until she turned the second corner in the long, narrow hallway that she felt safe.

She hadn't exactly been running—she hadn't wanted to give him any more proof of just how much he unnerved her. But she gradually slowed her pace, taking deep calming breaths, telling herself that he wouldn't come after her, he didn't really want her, he just delighted in upsetting her, disturbing her, throwing her off balance.

She turned another corner and then stopped abruptly, staring at the dead end, and the realization came to her with crushing force. She had absolutely no idea where she was. There was a door at the far end of the closed corridor, and her choice was simple. Either she could go back the way she had come, and risk running into Luke again. Or she could go through that closed door that led to God knew where.

She was drained, exhausted, and one more encounter with her nemesis would finish her off. If the solid metal door in the dark corridor was locked she would simply curl up outside it and go to sleep.

It wasn't locked. It didn't need to be. There was a sign in small, neat letters. NO ADMITTANCE. DANGEROUS MATERIALS. The good little scouts of the Foundation of Being would never think of going against orders, whether they came from Luke himself, the Grandfathers, or an anonymous sign.

Rachel wasn't troubled by any such scruples. The heavy metal doorknob opened easily enough, and she slipped inside, into the darkness, pulling the door shut behind her.

It was some sort of utility room, with machines humming a steady drone. There were storage shelves lined up against the cement walls, boxes and plastic canisters, metal containers with warning signs on them. She glanced around her, guessing that one giant piece of machinery provided the air filter and conditioning that made Santa Dolores habitable in the summer. The other complex system must provide the water.

She moved past the equipment, searching in

the murky darkness for another way out. There were utility lights at scattered intervals, and she didn't dare look for anything more powerful. A door shouldn't be that hard to find.

If the lights had been on she probably wouldn't have tripped over the round plastic canister tucked out of sight. If she hadn't gone sprawling her face wouldn't have come in proximity with the pesticide label on the can. She shrugged, scrambling to her feet, ignoring the odd feeling that assailed her. Something wasn't right, something wasn't making sense.

But then, she'd always felt that about Santa Dolores, from the first moment she'd set foot on the premises. Even before, when she'd read everything she could find about the place. The reality seemed so peaceful, accepting, warm. But beneath the benign, smiling faces something dark and rotting lurked.

She'd always wanted to blame that sense of nameless evil on Luke. He was the center of the Foundation, the heart, the brains. If there was evil, who else would it come from?

But that sense of evil had felt stronger than ever before when Rachel arrived back in New Mexico. And she knew, better than anyone, that Luke wasn't anywhere around.

She'd scarcely seen anyone in all that time.

Catherine had explained to her that most disciples came for a two-month stay, to cleanse their bodies and souls. Rachel had a pretty strong suspicion it cleansed their bank accounts as well. Then they returned to their lives to earn more money to give to the Foundation. Only the Grandfathers and a few long-term followers were always in place. She'd spied Calvin from a distance but she'd instinctively ducked out of the way, justifiably nervous. But, oddly, Bobby Ray Shatney was nowhere to be found.

She had just managed to summon her flagging courage, to work her way back along the deserted hallways and risk running into Luke again, when she heard the sound of voices. She immediately ducked behind a wall of boxes, lying on the cold cement floor, barely daring to breathe.

She hadn't the slightest idea what she was so frightened of. She only knew that she was utterly terrified.

The sound of Catherine's gentle voice reassured her, and she was almost ready to pull herself to her feet, to confront the newcomers, when she recognized Alfred Waterston's magisterial tones. The words made no sense, but Catherine did little more than make noncommittal noises.

"No need to take on new cancer patients," Waterston murmured. "We managed three of them this last go round, and I imagine that'll keep finances in good shape. You were probably wondering why I sent most of the caregivers away. They'll need to be replaced. We can't continue our work and expect them not to notice. It's a foolish man who underestimates the intelligence of his staff. Some of those nurses are damned smart. They know phony test results when they see them, and they've seen enough people succumb from the real thing. No way I can trick them into thinking every case at Santa Dolores is an anomaly."

"Whatever you think best, Alfred," Catherine murmured.

"We'd be wiser to hold off for a month or two. No need to be greedy. Besides, we've still got that Connery girl causing trouble. I can't imagine why you let her back in."

"That's your problem, Alfred, too little imagination," Catherine said smoothly. "We're much better off knowing where she is and what she's thinking."

"You know what she's thinking?"

"I can make a very good guess. Luke's managed to get to her."

"Why should that surprise you? He gets to everyone, sooner or later."

"He hasn't done a very thorough job of it, though. She may think she's half in love with him, but she hates him more than ever. I'm certain we can use that to our advantage."

"You're very good at using everything to your advantage," Alfred murmured, and there was an odd note in his voice. Rachel rose slightly, unbearably curious, and was shocked to see the pompous Dr. Waterston groping Catherine.

She didn't look pleased by the attention, but she endured it with her usual elegant grace. "Alfred," she said gently, "I thought we had a reason for coming down here."

"I wanted some time alone with you."

"It isn't safe," Catherine said gently.

"But it took me so long to find you! Besides, what were you doing out in the garden with that sick young man?"

"Billy Ray sees me as a maternal figure."

Alfred snorted in amusement. "Better watch out," he said. "Remember what he did to his own mother."

"I can handle Bobby Ray."

"And Rachel Connery as well?"

"Haven't you noticed how docile the little dear has become? At least as far as we're concerned. She may still hate Luke, but she's being seduced by the Foundation. She's just as willing as the rest of the followers."

"Then get rid of her. We don't need her here. The fewer witnesses the better."

"That's where you're wrong," Catherine said firmly. "A martyrdom is always more effective if the martyrdom is public. Rachel stays. I have plans for her."

"If you say so," Alfred said testily. "Maybe we can talk her into giving him the coup de grace. There'd be a nice dramatic resonance to that."

"I don't want Luke murdered by a spurned lover, which is what the press would make it. I prefer to keep his death an act of spiritual insanity."

"Then how are we going to do it?"

"Leave it to me, Alfred. You've always trusted me to handle the practical side of things, just as I've trusted you to handle the cancer research."

Alfred's snort of laughter was eerie. "Research. That's a good one."

"Be patient, Alfred. Trust me. I have things well in hand."

"I do, my dear. I do."

Rachel almost didn't notice that they'd left, closing the heavy metal door behind them, closing her into silence once more. She lay facedown against the cold concrete and shook in horror and disbelief.

Bobby Ray had been right. Patients weren't dying of cancer at all. They were being murdered. By pompous Alfred Waterston, the world-famous oncologist. No wonder no one suspected. No one but Bobby Ray, who'd then been drugged into oblivion.

And then there was Catherine, the epitome of gray-haired sweetness. Catherine was planning Luke's murder.

She lay on the floor and shook, chilled to the bone, afraid to move. Afraid to walk out the door and face someone, anyone. They all knew too much, and there was no way she could look them in the eyes and pretend everything was all right. They were going to kill Luke. And she wouldn't be surprised if they were planning on killing her as well. The only question that remained was where and when.

And why did a group of new age disciples, vegetarians who practiced healthful living and organic gardening, have a huge amount of cyanide-based insecticide hidden in the storage room of the meditation center?

She rose to her feet, slowly, her body aching for no sensible reason. She walked over to the heavy metal door, trying to still the fear inside her. Catherine and Alfred would be long gone. She had to get out of there, to find help, somewhere.

She put her hand on the cold metal knob and pushed. It was, of course, locked.

With a tiny moan of despair she sank down on the floor, shoving a fist in her mouth to still her panic. There was no way out. Not unless someone found her, and then the two old ones would know she had overheard them. They would kill her.

And she didn't want to die.

20

Luke had never been a stupid man. He wouldn't have made it to his fifth birthday if he hadn't possessed more than his share of intelligence, coupled with a gift for observation. He knew Rachel's blind, panicked run would take her nowhere but the main utility plant, and there was no way out. Sooner or later she'd have to come back this way, and he was fascinated to see how she would handle herself. Whether she'd gotten back her bitchy, you-can't-hurt-me persona.

It was simple enough to vanish back into the shadows when Alfred appeared. He wasn't in the mood to start fussing about entailments and mutual funds and the like, particularly since none of that had anything to do with him. Alfred hadn't the faintest idea that he only retained control over forty percent of the Foundation's massive income.

And that the rest had already found its way into Luke's pockets.

He didn't expect Catherine to wander in out of the garden, however, brushing twigs from her scattered gray hair. So she'd been the one sounding like a cat in heat. Who would have thought it of one of the Philadelphia Biddles? The notion filled him full of cynical amusement. Catherine hardly seemed the type to be enjoying the pleasures of the flesh, and indeed, there'd been a recognizable amount of pain in those cries of pleasure. He wondered idly who her partner had been.

He listened to the Grandfathers' hushed conversation for a moment, but it was nothing of particular interest. Something to do with the medical facility, which he left in Alfred's more than capable hands. He heard Catherine mention the water supply, but he ignored it as he ignored most mundane matters. The only thing that interested him was that they were heading in Rachel's direction.

He would have liked to hear her excuses. She didn't babble with anyone but him, a small tribute to the effect he had on her. She'd probably come up with a perfectly reasonable response for wandering into a forbidden part of the retreat center. Catherine would probably chide her gently and impose some sort of penance, and Rachel would have safe conduct back to her rooms.

He needed to find out where she was sleeping.

He needed to stop thinking about sex and think about how fast he could get out of here. His money was safe, escape was relatively easy. He'd promised Calvin enough time to get his affairs in order, but now that he'd made the decision to go every minute was torture.

He'd be taking Rachel with him. Whether she was glassy-eyed and pliant, or kicking and screaming, he wasn't leaving her behind. No, he wasn't going to let go of Rachel until he was good and ready. This time he wouldn't let her run away. This time he'd take her, calm her, tame her, until she was smart enough and brave enough to walk away, without looking back, and to hell with him.

There was no sign of Calvin in his rooms. He moved to the inner room and sat silently, staring at the bank of television monitors. He saw Catherine and Arthur as they returned from the utility complex, but there was no sign of Rachel. She must have managed to hide from them, though he couldn't imagine why she would. She adored Catherine—he'd seen to that. And Alfred Waterston was the epitome of the slightly pompous, genuinely kind older man, well aware of his worth in this world, but willing to care for others as well.

Very interesting. Even more interesting was the fact that he could see who Catherine had been dallying with in the garden, and he found that even he could, occasionally, be shocked. Things were very, very odd at the Foundation of Being. Maybe he'd tell Calvin he was getting out tonight.

He waited. Too long, he realized, as the hour grew later. It was almost ten o'clock, and there was still no sign of Rachel. The security system he and Calvin had installed couldn't possibly begin to cover all the spread-out areas of the retreat center, but it gave him enough of an overview to know that Rachel had not yet returned from her fearful dash. And he had no choice but to go in search of her.

He didn't expect to pass anyone in the narrow, dimly lit halls leading to the utility rooms, and he didn't. Someone had locked the door to the plant, which was very strange. He hadn't thought there were any locks in the place, except in his own rooms, and only he and Calvin knew about those. He could have picked the lock in less than a minute if he'd had anything with him, but he had no pockets in the loose-fitting pants and tunic, and he was barefoot.

He was also very strong, and he knew without reasoning that Rachel was beyond that heavy locked door. He simply kicked it, using all his strength, and it slammed open against the far wall with a crash.

The room was dark, but the light from the hall

pooled into the shadows, and he could see her, curled up in a little ball against the far wall, staring at him. It was too dark to read the expression on her face, and besides, he'd probably seemed like the wrath of God, coming out of nowhere and smashing open the door.

He walked over to her, ignoring the fact that his bare foot hurt like hell, and stared down at her. "Curiosity killed the cat," he said.

"Are you going to kill me?"

It was questions like that that made him want to smack her. He wouldn't, of course. He'd never hit anyone smaller or weaker than he was in his life, and he wasn't about to start, no matter what the provocation. He'd seen enough of that. But damn, she was annoying.

"Not at the moment," he drawled. "You want to spend the night on the cement floor or are you coming with me?"

"Do I have a third choice?" Her voice wavered only slightly, and he realized she'd been scared to death, locked up in this room.

He grinned slowly. "That's my Rachel," he murmured. "Still fighting. You can come with me and I'll escort you to your quarters like a good Southern gentleman. I won't even touch you. How does that sound?"

She didn't say anything. He wasn't vain enough to suppose she was reconsidering her options.

"Can I sleep somewhere else?" she asked in a quiet voice.

"The place is practically empty. Take your pick. What's wrong with the rooms Catherine put you in?"

"Actually I was sharing a room with Catherine. I just thought I might like my own space, and I'm sure she'd appreciate the privacy."

It sounded so reasonable. It was a lie. He tilted his head to one side to survey her. "What do you know, Rachel?" he asked in his softest, most insinuating voice. The voice that could make strong men weep for his approval. "What aren't you telling me?"

But Rachel was stronger than anyone he'd come across yet. "Nothing," she said with a bright smile. "Absolutely nothing."

He looked at her for a moment longer, then nodded, half to himself. He reached down and caught her arm before she could flinch away, hauling her up. He resisted the impulse to pull her against him. It might be a way to get to her secrets, or it might merely strengthen her gathering defenses.

"You shouldn't smile when you lie, Rachel," he said, releasing her arm. "It's always a dead giveaway. About the only thing that could bring forth an honest smile from you would be my head on a platter, and I'm not about to oblige."

"I'll just have to hope someone takes care of it for me."

He almost kissed her for that. Things were in a sad state when a woman's fond fantasies of his decapitation made him horny, but Rachel did that to him. She was unpredictable, and he wanted to push her up against the wall and kiss her.

"You can have your old room," he said. "It's empty."

"How do you know?"

"I know."

They walked in silence, down the hallways. It was late, and through the high-set windows he could see the brightness of the desert moon. A clear night, he thought. The wolves would be running.

He stopped outside the cell door. It was closer to his quarters than Catherine's were—a decided advantage. "Do you want me to tell Catherine where you are? She'll probably worry."

"Yes, please."

"Shall I tell her where I found you?"

The fear in her eyes was unmistakable and utterly fascinating. She was now afraid of Catherine, one of the calmest, most together of his varied band of followers. What had happened in that storage room?

"Please don't," she managed in a subdued voice. "When she let me come back I promised to be an obedient disciple. That room was off-limits."

"What did you think you'd find? My dead wives?"

"No, I imagine they'd be in Coffin's Grove," she said, rallying.

He stared down at her mouth, pale and full. It had yet to touch his body, and he wanted it. "There's nothing left in Coffin's Grove," he said.

And he turned and left her.

Bobby Ray had been waiting for Rachel to come back. Catherine suspected something was up, and she'd told him to keep watch for her. He was good at that, watching other people. Catherine had taken his drugs away from him, though she'd told him he still had to speak slowly, to keep his eyes unfocused. She told him she didn't like it when he was too calm.

He hadn't been calm for a long time.

Catherine liked pain. The more he hurt her, the more pleasure she got. He liked pain as well, but not as much as he liked death. But he'd learned, early on, that once you kill them there was no more pleasure to be had.

Maybe she'd let him kill Stella's daughter. She'd promised she would take care of his needs, and he knew that getting rid of Rachel was important. He could make it last a long time.

She was going back to her old room. That's what Catherine had thought she would do. She'd said that if Rachel did go there, it meant she knew things that she shouldn't be knowing. And there'd be no harm in telling her even more, since there'd be no way she could escape.

No locks on the doors at Santa Dolores. Nothing to keep him from Rachel Connery. And no one to care if she screamed.

Odd, Rachel thought, that her tiny cell would feel familiar, safer. She was still confused, disoriented from the time spent locked in the storage room. She was mildly claustrophobic—she didn't mind dark, enclosed places as long as someone was with her. Alone, unable to escape, she'd felt a panic so deep in her bones that she'd begun to doubt what she'd heard. It was odd that she hadn't had that reaction in the darkness of Luke's converted van. Of course, she hadn't been alone. And then she knew exactly what she was afraid of.

She still couldn't believe what she'd heard. The full horror of it was appalling—falsified test results, patients dying. He hadn't come right out and admitted that he was murdering patients, falsely diagnosing them with cancer and then making certain they succumbed to the disease.

But he'd said enough to convince her that Bobby Ray's wild suppositions had been right all along.

And they were talking about killing Luke. Had she imagined that? Or maybe it was wishful thinking. The Grandfathers made Luke the center of their lives—why on earth would they want to kill him?

Except for the word that lingered in her mind. Martyrdom.

The Grandfathers weren't the spaced-out yuppies who comprised most of Luke's followers. They were smart, experienced, sophisticated men and women. People capable of committing great evil. They must have suspected that Luke wasn't the plaster saint he presented to the world. They must know that their cushy little retreat center was living on borrowed time.

Not if Luke was killed, however. Martyred. A dead saint would bring the followers, and their money, flocking. If they could orchestrate it properly they would have an even bigger gold mine on their hands, and no dangerous live wire like Luke to send it all sky-high.

Maybe they weren't completely evil. Maybe they believed in Luke's new age mumbo jumbo, maybe they thought they were doing this for the greater good of humanity. It didn't matter. They were going to kill Luke.

And she had to decide whether she was going to do anything to stop it.

"Rachel? May I come in?" The voice was soft, hesitant, and she looked up in surprise, into Bobby Ray Shatney's sweet, handsome young face. He wasn't a Grandfather—maybe he wasn't part of the conspiracy. Or maybe he was. He'd warned her before. Could she dare trust him again? She wasn't sure.

She managed a faint, unwelcoming smile, stalling for time. "I'm really tired, Bobby Ray. Could we talk tomorrow?"

He pushed the door open and came in anyway, closing it quietly behind him. He looked so young, so innocent. What was it Alfred had said about his mother?

"It can't wait, Rachel," he said earnestly, and his voice was different, higher-pitched, and his eyes were clear and oddly emotionless. "I need to talk to somebody, and you're the only one I can trust."

"What do you need to tell me about? Is it something about Luke? Is he in some kind of danger?"

To her surprise he shook his head. "He's fine. No one would want to hurt him. They all believe in him, they think he's a god. Why should anyone want to hurt Luke?"

"Then what did you want to tell me?"

"I found out the truth," he said with a shudder

that shook his lean young body. "The truth about the cancer, the truth about your mother. They've been killing people. Telling them they have cancer, giving them drugs and radiation, cutting their bodies apart until they die, and they haven't been sick at all. We were right all the time."

Rachel didn't move. "I know," she said in a dead voice.

He stared at her in shock. "How?"

"I overheard Alfred and Catherine talking. I got locked in the storage room, and they came in. They didn't spell it out, but it was pretty clear what they were saying."

Bobby Ray had an odd expression on his face. "What are we going to do about it?"

"I don't know."

"You can't just ignore it. It happened to your mother. It didn't make sense, her getting so sick, so fast. And then just dying like that. Leaf is my friend, and I told her what I suspected, and she checked the records, and it's true. It's all true. They keep killing people, and no one can stop them. And now Leaf's disappeared, and I think they know we've found out. I had to tell someone before they get rid of me, too."

She stared at him in sick horror, wishing it were all a nightmare, that she didn't have to believe him. It was too horrifying—the thought of healthy men and women systematically destroyed for a lie and a pile of money. "Does Luke know?" she asked finally. "Is he part of this?"

Bobby Ray lifted his head, tears streaming down his sweet face. "That's what's stopping you, isn't it? You've fallen under his spell, just like everyone else, and it doesn't matter that he's condoned murder. Even the murder of your mother. Of course he knows, Rachel. It was his idea in the first place. Dr. Waterston just does the dirty work. He'd do anything for Luke. Anything for the Foundation. We have to stop them. Kill them."

The nausea was back. She wanted to throw up, to scream, to throw things. She didn't move, frozen.

"And Catherine?" she managed to ask.

Absently Bobby Ray reached up and touched his neck. There was a deep, nasty scrape there, and his hand came away wet with blood. "She's part of it as well," he said heavily. "She deserves punishment."

"We've got to get help," she said, her voice numb.

"No one will believe us."

"It doesn't matter. I've got to go to the police, get them to come here and—"

"That's not all, Rachel."

She didn't want to hear any more. But Bobby Ray was looking at her so expectantly, like a little puppy, that she couldn't move. "What else?"

"We have to move fast. They're going to kill everyone."

"Don't be ridiculous!" she snapped.

"Catherine's going to put poison in the water system. Cyanide. Like those people that drank poison Kool-Aid. Everyone will die, and she and the Grandfathers that are in on it will disappear with the money. And no one will ever find them."

"I don't believe it. She couldn't . . ."

"She has help. She has a lover who'll do anything she orders him to do."

For a moment Rachel was silent. The room suddenly stank of sweat and fear, sickness and evil. She had been right about the Foundation. All her paranoid instincts had been right.

She'd been right about Luke Bardell. He was even more of a monster than she'd ever imagined, a creature so horrifying she couldn't even comprehend. And she had let him touch her. She had wanted him to touch her again.

"I'll go for help," she said flatly. "They won't suspect me."

Bobby Ray nodded, a faint, approving expression in his colorless eyes. "If you go now you could probably make it. It's seven miles to town, but you should be able to do that in a few hours. Go out through the garden and over the wall there. No one goes out there—no one will even notice until it's too late."

"Why don't you come with me?"

"They keep a close eye on me. I've already been here too long. Be careful," he said, heading for the door. "There are very bad people out there. People who like to cause pain."

She looked up into Bobby Ray's soulful face. "You be careful too," she said, and touched her fingers to his cheek.

Bobby Ray was shaking so hard he wasn't sure he could stop himself. Catherine hadn't told him he could have her so soon, but he couldn't wait. That touch on his cheek was the deciding factor. He slipped out into the garden, glancing up at the faint sliver of moon that hung overhead. Not a full moon, and yet he felt like a werewolf. He had no knives tonight, but he didn't need anything. He would use his hands, his fingernails, his teeth. And he would dance naked in her blood.

21

Luke leaned back, staring at the television monitors. He'd moved Rachel back there on purpose. It was too expensive and too boring to watch each bedroom in the retreat center. Only a few came equipped with surveillance equipment, and he wanted Rachel where he could see her. He'd had every intention of placating himself with the distant pleasure of watching her undress. He hadn't expected her to welcome Bobby Ray Shatney into her room.

He should have had the place bugged as well, but he hadn't bothered. So far no one at the retreat center had secrets from him—if he wanted to find out something he simply asked.

But he'd sat alone in the darkened room and watched the sick horror wash over Rachel's face, and he knew things were moving too fast.

It could have been something relatively simple. Bobby Ray was kept in a docile state through the judicious use of tranquilizers, but that didn't mean he'd forgotten. He might be telling Rachel about the night he systematically, savagely destroyed his entire family in the name of some arcane satanistic message. Bobby Ray had told him, his voice soft and slurred, his innocent face dreamy and peaceful as he recounted horrors that shocked even Luke, who prided himself on having seen everything.

If he was telling Rachel about washing his hands in his mother's blood, it was no wonder she was looking sick.

No, that couldn't be it. She'd be more than sick, she'd be puking her guts out, as Luke had once Bobby Ray had finished his cheerful confession and left.

Bobby Ray had kept his back to the surveillance camera during most of the time he'd spent in Rachel's room, and Luke had little chance to see his expression. For a moment he wondered whether any of his devoted followers had come to suspect he might be watching them, then he dismissed the notion as Bobby Ray turned away and headed for the door, touching his cheek lightly where Rachel had impulsively touched him.

His eyes were sharp and clear and, unseen by

Rachel, he was smiling. And Luke knew that the monster had been unleashed.

There was no sign of Calvin, no sign of anyone as Luke rushed into the main room. It was close to midnight, and everyone would have gone to sleep hours ago. Calvin had his own rooms, at the far end of the compound—they'd planned it that way so that he could keep an eye on things. Luke tried the cellular phone, but there was no answer. Another anomaly. Calvin kept his miniature cell phone with him at all times. He was never beyond reach.

He had no choice but to go and find him. He went out into the hallway, just in time to see Bobby Ray disappear into the garden, the door closing silently behind him.

Luke paused, uneasiness washing over him. Maybe he was simply waiting for Catherine to return, so that they could continue their kinky games. Or maybe he had something else, something worse in mind.

The answer came a few minutes later as Rachel tiptoed down the darkened corridor, holding her soft-soled sandals in one hand to keep her advance even quieter. The lights had been turned way down, as they were every night, and she had no idea he was watching her surreptitious approach. Odd, he would have thought she'd start to develop a sixth sense about him. As he had about her. He knew when she was nearby, he sensed her. Apparently she was better at fighting the obsession.

Obsession. An ugly word, but curiously apt, and Luke wasn't one to shy away from ugliness. Yes, he was obsessed by her. Too damned bad he couldn't have chosen someone a little easier to fall in love with.

He jerked, startled at his own inadvertent mental slip. Obsession was one thing, sick but unavoidable, like most of life. Falling in love was stupid, childish, weak, and impossible.

She saw him then, just as she was reaching for the door to the garden. If she made it through the door Bobby Ray would have her, Luke knew it with a sudden terrible clarity. He would kill her, without compunction, with pleasure and lingering agony. He didn't know why things had suddenly come to this pass, but they had.

He caught her before she had the door halfway open, slamming it shut again, slamming her back against it. "Where do you think you're going?" he demanded in a dangerous undertone.

She was looking up at him in utter horror. He thought he'd grown used to that expression on her face; for some reason she kept thinking he was evil incarnate, and he was getting damned tired of it.

"For a walk in the garden," she said after a

long moment. "I'm having trouble sleeping. Do you have a problem with that?"

With Bobby Ray lying in wait. "Yes, I have a problem with that," he said softly.

"All right. Then back off and I'll go back to my room."

"I don't think so."

"What do you mean by that?"

"I mean that I'd feel better if I kept you with me."

"I wouldn't."

"Too bad."

She glared up at him. "I don't want to be with you," she said in a loud, clear voice.

"Then why did you come back here?"

"Not for your dubious physical charms," she snapped.

He couldn't help it, he laughed. He knew it would only enrage her further, but rage kept her off balance. Besides, he preferred her anger to her fear.

"It's a package deal," he said. "I *am* the Foundation of Being. Make up your mind, Rachel. It's your choice. Do you want to sleep with Catherine, or do you want to sleep with me?"

Her reaction fascinated him. He was an experienced fighter, all his life he'd had to defend himself in schools and alleyways and bars and prisons. He felt her muscles tense a bare second before she went for him, mistakenly hoping the element of surprise would enable her to escape.

Instead her knee glanced painlessly on the outside of his thigh. He caught her flailing fists in one hand, threading the other through her hair and yanking her against him, pinning her between his body and the wall. "Are we going to have a wrestling match, Rachel?" he whispered in her ear.

"I'm going to kill you," she panted furiously.

"Is that what they want you to do?"

She froze.

"Shit," he said. And then he dragged her, kicking and struggling, down the deserted hallway to his rooms, one hand over her mouth to muffle her furious screams. Not that he thought anyone would come to her aid if they heard her, but he wasn't sure how badly things had deteriorated. He was a supremely dirty infighter, a believer in taking any unfair advantage he could find, but he wasn't sure how good a match he was for Bobby Ray Shatney's homicidal insanity.

He didn't even pause in the outer room. Clamping her flailing body against his, he pushed the buttons that released the secret door, and the moment it slid open he shoved her through, so that she went sprawling on the huge bed. He risked turning his back on her as he punched in the security code, but she'd temporarily lost her fight, too astonished to do more than stare around her in shock.

He leaned against the panel and looked at her. He liked seeing her on that bed, where no one had ever lain except him. Her face was pale, her hair wild, and he was so damned hot he had to keep very still so that he wouldn't dive onto the bed with her. He needed answers first. And he was going to get them from her, by any means he could.

"This is a secure room," he said. "Soundproofed, locked. There's no way anyone can get in, no way you can get out unless I choose to let you, and no way anyone can hear you."

She rallied, as he knew she would, scrambling into a sitting position on the rumpled white sheets. "So no one can hear if you murder me."

He closed his eyes for a brief, weary moment. "I'm getting sick and tired of you accusing me of murder. Frankly there are times when I'd like nothing more than to wring your neck. You're annoying, you know that? You're paranoid, humorless, irritating, and too damned skinny."

"That's hardly any reason to kill me."

"Exactly. For some strange reason I don't make a habit of killing people, even those who irritate me. I don't make a habit of sleeping with them either, but you seem to be an exception."

"Why are people dying of cancer?" she asked suddenly, as if afraid of his answer.

He blinked, momentarily confused. "How the hell should I know? Ask a doctor, ask Alfred, don't ask me. I suppose it's a combination of genetics and environment and God knows what else. Why? Are you afraid you're going to get what your mother had?"

She was staring at him like he had two heads. "I mean why are so many people at the retreat dying?"

He couldn't move. "What the hell are you talking about?"

"Why do healthy, rich people show up here, get diagnosed with cancer, and then die, leaving all their money to the Foundation?"

"Just lucky," he snapped.

"Are you part of it?"

"Part of what?"

"Do Waterston and Catherine follow your orders? Was it your idea to convince these people that they were dying, to hack away at their bodies with drugs and radiation and needless surgery until they died? *Did you kill my mother?*" Her voice rose to an anguished cry, and her eyes were haunted.

At that moment he didn't give a flying fuck about her eyes. "You're as crazy as Bobby Ray Shatney," he said flatly.

"What do you mean by that?"

"Bobby Ray Shatney is a grade-A nutcase. He slaughtered his entire family when he was thirteen, insisting Satan told him to do it. I believe he ended up drinking their blood. He wasn't tried as an adult, and he got out four years ago when he was eighteen with a clean record. He's been here ever since, and Alfred keeps him suitably drugged so he's no danger to anyone. Or at least, he used to be."

"He told me about the people dying."

"And you believed him?" Luke scoffed.

"Yes. I still do."

And the damnable thing was, so did he. It all made a horrible kind of sense. The growing list of people who had died so damned quickly of sudden, virulent cancer. His own willing agreement that Alfred should help them along at the end, to finish their unnecessary suffering.

"Fuck it," he said in a low, sick voice, turning away from her. Now he was the one who wanted to puke his guts out, as he saw the faces, the hands that he held as death claimed them, the scores of people who died because of his greed.

He'd sworn he would never kill again. Jackson's stinking corpse haunted his dreams. And now he had countless souls on his conscience.

She'd risen, approaching him tentatively. He could feel her standing behind him, too close, and he wanted to lash out. "You really didn't know, did you?" Her voice was infinitely gentle. He hadn't thought she was capable of it.

He reached for the door panel and began to push buttons. "Get out of here, Rachel. Now."

But she put her hand over his, stopping him, and he let her. "They're going to kill you," she said. "I overheard Catherine and Alfred talking when I was in the storeroom. They're afraid you're going to abandon the center, and they need a martyr."

He turned to look at her, leaning against the heavy door. She looked different. Troubled, not so sure of herself anymore. "That should suit you just fine then, sugar," he drawled. "Haven't you wanted me dead for ages?"

"Don't!"

"Don't?" he mocked, pushing her. "Not quite so bloodthirsty when it comes right down to it, are you? No longer so interested in seeing my head on a pike? Or are you just afraid your head's going to be alongside of mine?"

"I don't care about you."

"Of course you don't," he said, moving away from the wall, watching her back away from him. "You don't care about anyone or anything. So why did you come back? Why are you looking at me like that?"

"Like what?"

"Like you want me to lay you down on that bed and put my mouth between your legs again."

"I don't!"

He smiled, a slow, dark smile. "That's good, sugar. Because I'm not going to do it. This time it's your turn. You're going to use your mouth on me. You're going to be on top, and I'm to watch you as you take my cock inside you. I'm going to watch your face when you come."

She stared at him.

"Want to run," he said softly, "Or do you want what you really came for?"

She didn't even glance at the door panel behind him. "Sex is a game to you, isn't it? Some sick, twisted game of domination and victory?"

"No," he said in a slow, deep voice, letting desire take over his body, washing everything else away. "It's much more simple than that. It's about pleasure. It's about sweat and come and bodies rubbing up against each other; it's about aching and hurting deep inside and then finally feeling whole. It's about love and a dark kind of joy that you can only begin to imagine. You're the one who sees it as a battle. You're the one who sees it as sick."

She stared at him, mesmerized. "Love?" she said, unerringly picking out the word as he knew she would. "What the hell has this got to do with love?"

"Get on the bed," he said, "and I'll show you."

It was too much to hope for twice in a row. She just stood there at the end of the bed, and he came right up to her and began to unfasten the stupid ties of her cotton clothing. He wanted to rip it off her, but the cotton was strong and he didn't want to hurt her. She didn't stop him, she just looked up at him out of somber eyes.

She didn't look quite so scrawny when he pushed the tunic off her shoulders, letting it fall to the floor. Her ribs didn't stand out as sharply, and her breasts were fuller. He wondered idly if she was pregnant. He didn't think so. He wondered if he could make her pregnant tonight.

"You've gained weight," he said. "You must have been eating." He slipped his hands inside her drawstring pants and pushed them down her legs. He'd done this before, when she was unconscious, lying like a virgin sacrifice in the main audience room. The drugs had left her responsive, dreaming, and the pleasure he'd taken in her body had haunted him ever since. Until he'd finally had her beneath him in the back of that broken-down van, scratching his back and weeping with pleasure and sorrow.

"I'm not pregnant," she said, her voice shaky.

"I didn't think you were." He didn't touch her naked body, much as he wanted to. Instead he cupped her face, tilting it up to look at his. "I want to make you pregnant."

Her eyes lowered for a moment, then lifted. "Yes," she said.

She stood in front of him, naked, willing, and he didn't give a shit about anyone else.

He kissed her, so very gently, and her mouth was soft, lifting to his, pliant. She slid her arms around his neck, drawing him closer to her, and he had no doubt she could feel him pressing against her. He'd been waiting for this for so damned long he wasn't sure if he cared what she did. Right then he wanted to push her down on the bed, free his cock, and shove it in her. He wanted to fuck her like an animal, hard, merciless, intent. Everything she was afraid of. Everything he needed.

"Get on the bed," he said hoarsely, amazed to realize how very tenuous was his self-control. "I won't hurt you. I won't do anything you don't want me to do."

She looked up at him and for a moment he couldn't read her expression. It took him a moment to recognize it, because it was entirely new to her. There was a definite glint of amusement in her eyes. "But that's half the fun," she whispered, brushing her mouth against his.

He almost lost it then. He didn't know what the hell was wrong with him—he'd endured celibacy for a hell of a lot longer than the few days since he'd been between Rachel Connery's legs, and he felt as helpless as a fifteen-year-old in sight of his first piece of tail.

Or more so. He wanted her more than he'd wanted Lureen O'Meara; he wanted her more than he'd wanted anyone in his entire life. She was looking at him as if she could read his mind.

"What do you want from me, Rachel?" he asked suddenly.

She took a step back, up against the low bed, and her voice was oddly calm. "What you promised me," she said.

"And what's that?"

"Love," she said. "And a baby." And she waited for him to come closer.

22

He didn't make a move toward her. Everything had tilted sideways in the last few hours. All Rachel had ever believed had been knocked out from under her. She looked at Luke and tried to imagine the villain, the murderer, the heartless, ruthless con man.

He looked weary. He looked lost. He looked unutterably sexy, and she knew she wanted him. Knew it with a certain calmness and delight. She wanted to touch him, kiss him, take him. The thought of sex with anyone else still filled her with bone-shaking disgust, but with Luke it was different. It was that simple, and that complicated.

Love, he'd said, when he thought she wouldn't pick up on it. She had, of course. He wasn't a man capable of love, and she shouldn't expect it of him. She wasn't even sure she believed in it.

And yet, deep inside, beyond cynicism or rationality, she felt it. The tie between them, crazy and fiercely strong. It made no sense, but it was there, burning through her fears, burning through his distance. It was there, and there was no breaking it apart.

His loose cotton tunic tied at the waist. Her fingers fumbled as she unfastened it, but he made no effort to help her. He just watched her out of hooded eyes, no expression on his face. The room was dark, lit only by the flickering light from the wall of black and white television monitors. The bed behind them was huge, low, covered with rumpled white sheets and nothing else. White. Everything pure and white in this place of unutterable evil.

She pulled the shirt off him, staring at his chest in the dim light. She didn't know whether his physical beauty made things easier or more difficult. He had a lean, strong body, covered with golden skin, a flat stomach, and subtly defined muscles. His long hair was swept behind his back, but his eyes were cool and mesmerizing, watching her, daring her, and she wished she could back off, lie down and close her eyes and think of England. Wasn't that what he had taunted her with?

She put her hands on his chest, tentatively, letting her fingers trace the curve of muscle that patterned him. He let out the faintest of sounds, but his expression didn't change, and he held himself very still as her hands danced across his hot, sleek skin.

She wanted to taste it. Without thinking she leaned forward and put her mouth against his nipple, using her tongue. He jerked, then stilled again, but she could feel the sudden racing of his heart as she slid her tongue against him.

She kissed his stomach, feeling the tightness of the muscles beneath her mouth. The drawstring pants rode low on his narrow hips, and she put her hands on them, feeling the boniness, caressing with her fingers. He made a muffled sound, but his hands stayed at his sides, clenching, as he waited.

She knew what he wanted her to do. She knew what he needed. She closed her eyes and pressed her face against him through the thin cotton, feeling him jerk and leap against her touch, and she let her mouth dance across the thick ridge of his erection beneath the layer of cloth.

He swore then, and she didn't know if it was a prayer or a curse. He lifted his hands to touch her head, to guide her, but then dropped them again. He was leaving it up to her. Her choice, no force. She kissed his hipbones above the loose waistband of the drawstring pants, slowly, lingeringly. She put her mouth against the rough hair she exposed as she pulled at his clothes. She put her lips on his sex, pushing it deep into her mouth, taking him.

She felt his hands in her hair, gently, and it was like a benediction. She backed off slightly, tasting him, and then sank down again, and her eyes closed as his body began to tremble.

She wanted this. She wanted him. She knelt at his feet, naked, and took him in her mouth, and everything around her faded. It came down to pure sensation, to need and longing, taste and pull, reaching and clawing, and she could feel the power build inside him, and she knew her own was beginning to match his, and when he tried to pull away from her she clutched at his hips in a desperate attempt to keep him there.

"No," he said in a hoarse voice, stepping back.

She didn't move from her position on her knees. "I want you to come in my mouth."

"No," he said, and she could see the ripple of reaction sweep up his strong, beautiful body. "Next time. If there is a next time." He hauled her up against him, lifting her, so that her feet dangled off the floor. "That's not the way to make a baby."

The bed was soft beneath her back, and he was on top of her, leaning over her, his long hair a curtain around them. She caught it in her hands and sucked it into her mouth, she pulled him down to her with it and kissed him. He put his hands over her breasts, and a tight, furious spasm of response shot through her, an unbelievable sensation that shocked and shook her. He squeezed her nipples lightly, and she cried out, convulsing, reaching for him, needing more, her body suffused in longing, in trembling, aching need as she tried to wrap her legs around him.

"No," he said again, a faint thread of laughter and despair in his voice. "You do it." And he rolled over onto his back, waiting for her.

She wanted to scream in frustration. She didn't move, and he caught her arms and dragged her body across his, so that she straddled him, her knees on either side of his lean hips.

She was shaking, whipped by a longing so fierce she thought she might dissolve. "Help me," she said, trembling. "I can't . . . I don't know . . ."

He caught her hips in his big hands and lifted her so she was positioned over his cock. He was huge, and she knew it. She'd taken it in her body, in her mouth. He was hot and pulsing against her, and she needed him so badly she thought she might fly apart.

"Take me," he said in a harsh voice. "Slowly. Don't rush it. Don't hurt yourself. Just sink down on me. Let your body lead you. Just slide down over me, like that. Yes . . . like that. Slowly . . . slowly now. Yes . . . that's it. All the way. So deep that you can feel me in your throat. More, Rachel. Deeper. Push. God, yes!"

She was panting, trying to control the reactions that surged through her body. She shifted, taking him in deeper still, sinking down fully onto him, and he was huge, filling her, possessing her.

For a moment she couldn't move. All she could do was tremble. Her body was dripping with sweat, and she could hear his words. It wasn't about battles and fear, it was about hurt and longing and an aching that had to be filled. About love and a deep dark joy, and she needed more.

His hands were still cradling her hips, and she could feel the strength in them, the tension of a fierce control that threatened to break free. He moved her hips, lifting them, then letting them sink back, so that she began to feel the rhythm of it, the sleek, sliding joy of it. "You can figure out the rest of it. Ride me, Rachel," he whispered. "Make me come."

She moved carefully at first, afraid of pain, afraid of making a mistake. But she was wet, sleek, and even though he felt larger still as he filled her, she took him with an ease that made her tremble inside. As if she were made for him. Her movements were meek, tentative, but he made no effort to hurry her. In the flickering light of the television monitors he lay back with his eyes closed, absorbing the feel of her.

He put his hands on her breasts, and she grew more adventurous, faster now, harder, trying to force a response from him. She couldn't catch her breath, her skin was burning, and she leaned forward, bracing her hands on either side of him, pushing, taking him, needing more, always more.

He slid his hands down her body, cupping her hips again, as if he could no longer restrain himself. He surged up into her, slamming against her, hard, and she welcomed it with a glad cry, needing him so desperately, meeting his thrust, enveloping him, again, and again, tiny strangled cries bubbling out of her throat as she began to shake. She wanted him to touch her, to put his hands between her legs, to help her, when suddenly there was no need. Her entire body convulsed—her breath caught, her heart stopped, her skin burst into flames, and all she could feel was the pulse of him, flowing into her, through her.

He caught her hands in his, entwining her fingers with his long ones, braiding them together in a fierce, strong grip that couldn't be broken. She cried out, but she didn't know what she was saying. She didn't care. It lasted forever, an endless spasm of lust that shattered into love, and when it was over she collapsed on his strong, sleek body, too lost this time to even weep.

She slept. With his arms around her, she slept.

* * *

She was awake, and she didn't want to be. The room was dark, only the flicker of the television monitors disturbing the darkness. She was alone.

She rolled over on her back, slowly, taking stock. She felt achy. Sticky. Strange and sensuous. And then her eyes focused on the one screen that held any movement beyond the flickering of black and white.

It took her a moment to recognize the front room, the room he'd dragged her through. With the sparse decorating most of the retreat tended to look the same. She could see Luke, dressed only in the white drawstring pants she'd taken off him ages ago, leaning over a bundle of clothing on the floor. There was a river of darkness around his feet, and her eyes narrowed as she sat up, focusing.

On the black and white monitor the dark river was blood. And as Luke stepped back she could see the huddled figure of a body. A corpse—no one could live with so much blood flowing around them.

She scrambled out of the bed, pulling the sheet around her body, and stumbled to the door. It was locked, and she had no idea what the electronic combination was. She punched at the buttons in hysteria, banging at them, and in the monitor she could see Luke lift his head, turning toward her. His face was absolutely expressionless. And there was blood on his hands.

She had no choice but to watch. She was trapped in that room, imprisoned, with nowhere to look but the mesmerizing flicker of the television monitors. She watched in numb horror as Luke simply stood there. And then she began to hunt for her clothes, scrambling into them in desperate haste, ready to take the first chance for escape she could find.

She was still struggling with the ties of her tunic when Luke came back into the room, the door skimming shut behind him before she could leap for it. In the dim light of the room she could see the deep red of blood on his hands, his feet, soaking into the hem of his pants. She could smell it.

He looked at her, still that strange, expressionless caste to his beautiful face. "Dressed already?" he said calmly. "I thought we might manage a replay. Unless you have an aversion to blood." He moved over to the bathroom and began to wash his hands, not bothering to shut the door. Not that she had any chance of escape.

"What did you do?" she asked in a sick voice.

He looked up at that, his eyes narrowing. "I didn't kill him, Rachel. I was too busy being gloriously fucked by you. Someone else did it and left him as a little present for me."

"Who?"

"Who did it? Probably Bobby Ray. He has a

talent for such things, and I kept him from getting to you. He was waiting for you in the garden, and he was probably pissed as hell when you didn't show. So he took it out on Calvin."

"Calvin?" she echoed, stunned.

"I'm not sure I made the right choice between the two of you," he said casually, stripping off his bloodstained pants. "Calvin was probably the best friend I ever had. He shouldn't have had to die for me."

He yanked on a pair of black jeans that had been hanging in the bathroom, then came back into the room. "I'm getting the hell out of here," he said. "I've got more than enough money to keep me happy, as long as no one catches up with me." He pulled a black tank top over his head. The wreaths of thorns stood out clearly around his wrists, and his long hair flowed down his back. That quickly he'd gone from a saint to a devil, and Rachel could do nothing but stare at him in shock. He began to stuff clothes into a black leather duffel.

"You can't go," she said finally.

He paused, looking at her. "Why not?"

"Because they weren't going to stop with killing you. They're going to kill everyone. It's going to be a bloodbath, like Jonestown or that cult in Switzerland or Waco."

He didn't look even vaguely curious. "How do they intend to do that? And who are they?"

"Catherine. Bobby Ray. I don't know who else. They're going to put cyanide in the water system."

"Bullshit."

"I saw it in the storage room. Canisters of the stuff. Why would a place that believes in organic gardening have high-powered, cyanide-based insecticides?"

He didn't move for a moment. And then he shrugged. "What do you expect me to do about it?"

She stared at him in disbelief. "Stop them."

"Easier said than done. I suppose I can call the police and give them an anonymous tip once we're out of the state."

"That will be too late."

"Maybe. But that's not my problem, is it?"

"Isn't it?"

He shook his head. "If you'd paid any attention you'd know that everyone's responsible for their own shit in the Foundation of Being. Their own life, their own karma. If they're supposed to die from poison administered by a kindly old woman, then so be it. We can call the police once we're out of here but that's the end of it."

"I'm not going anywhere with you."

She didn't expect tears of disappointment, but

the absolute blankness of his expression was somehow more devastating. "Suit yourself, sugar. You
gonna stay here and fight the good fight?"

"Yes."

He hoisted the leather duffel to his shoulder.
"All right. I'm outta here. No one ever gave me a
goddamned thing in this life, and I figure I don't
owe them anything in return." He started past her,
paused, and leaned toward her. She tried to jerk
away, but he caught her arm in a grip that hurt.

"You're a monster," she said.

"So you've told me. Let me just give you a little
hint." He paused. "Don't drink the water."

The door slid shut behind him, silently, and it
took Rachel a moment to realize she was still
trapped. She looked up at the television monitors, only to watch them flicker and then plunge
into darkness. The room was inky black, with no
light from any source.

She wanted to scream, but she didn't. Instead
she sat down on the low bed, her fist in her
mouth, trying to still her panic. She remembered
the stories, the television reports, the newspaper
accounts. She could see the pictures, the piles of
bloated bodies, the flames destroying the buildings, the charred remains. She didn't want to die.
And she didn't want to burn to death in this
tomblike room that so recently had seemed like a
haven.

Don't drink the water, he'd said, his voice light and mocking. If she could feel the flames coming to get her that was exactly what she would do. She had no idea whether death by cyanide was a gentle one or a painful one, but nothing could be worse than burning to death.

She scooted up to the head of the bed, pulling a pillow against her for some sort of creature comfort. The bed smelled of sex. It should have made her sick. Instead it made her weep.

How could he have left? How could he have turned his back on everyone? He would have taken her with him, and maybe the Rachel she used to be would have gone. She hadn't considered that she owed much to the people around her—she'd felt just as used and abused as Luke did.

But she couldn't stand by and let them be murdered.

She lost track of time. It was possible she slept, she wasn't certain. In the pitch-darkness and unending silence she could feel death moving around her to swallow her in a black embrace, and she slowly came to the conclusion that her noble stance had been a waste of time. There was nothing she could do to stop what was happening. She had simply offered them another helpless victim.

It was the pounding that woke her from her nightmare-laden sleep. The splintering of wood, and suddenly she was blinded by a pure shaft of light, pinning her to the bed. She covered her eyes in an instinctively protective gesture.

"There you are," Catherine said in her elegant, motherly voice. "I'd wondered where you'd gotten to. I suppose Luke's taken off?"

There was no other answer. "Yes."

"Well, not to worry. It would have helped if he'd been around to cooperate, but we can always go on to plan B."

"Cooperate?" Rachel echoed. "Cooperate with his own murder?"

"My, my, you have been a busy little girl, haven't you? Bobby Ray said you'd overheard something, but the boy's brain has been so addled by years of drugs that I've never been quite certain what to believe. Which makes things difficult when you're planning something as complex as this."

Rachel's eyes were slowly adjusting to the pool of light cast by the high-beam flashlight. She could see the gun in Catherine's hand, and there was no comforting tremor.

"I'm sure you could rise to the challenge," Rachel said sarcastically.

"That's what I like about you, Rachel. You aren't one to underestimate a woman's ability. Though it does surprise me that you managed to crawl into bed with Luke. I thought you weren't interested in sex. Of course, Luke could manage to seduce an eighty-year-old mother superior if he set his mind to it. Come along, Rachel. The others are waiting."

"The others?"

Catherine sighed audibly. "The timing is off, of course. But it will have to do, I suppose. I had Bobby Ray dismantle the generator too soon. It's still quite early and this place is damnably dark. I was almost going to leave you trapped in here but I couldn't resist. I'm afraid I do like an audience. One of my little weaknesses."

"A minor failing," Rachel said faintly.

"I'm afraid I'm also troubled by an unhealthy addiction to money and power. Though that's not that unusual. After all, aren't they what rule the world?"

"What about love?"

Catherine's laugh was bone-chilling. "You disappoint me, Rachel. I wouldn't have thought you'd be so foolish as to believe in love. Sex, perhaps. But that's far less interesting than money and power." She gestured with the gun. "Get up, dear. The others are waiting for you. Time to become one with the infinite. As the Native Americans say, it's a good day to die."

Rachel's muscles coiled in readiness, and her hand tightened around the heavy brass lamp that stood by the bed. "I don't think so," she said gently. And hurled it in the direction of the bright beam of light.

23

Rachel didn't consider herself particularly gifted, but she had been good at softball. She could throw, and she could connect, and the heavy metal lamp slammed into Catherine with a satisfying clang.

There was no way Rachel could tell if the gun went flying as well as the flashlight, but she had no choice. She dove for the opening of the door, trampling Catherine as she went, and took off into the murky darkness.

Something was slippery beneath her feet, and she knew it was Calvin's blood. She didn't stop to think about it, she simply kept running, for the nearest escape she could think of. The garden.

It was early morning when she stumbled into the fresh air. The magic hour, just past dawn, with a faint, damp breeze and the sound of birds overhead. The door slammed behind her, shutting out the evil, and she scrambled across the sparsely landscaped trail, slipping and scraping her knee through the wretched cotton trousers.

She heard the metal door slam in the distance, and she knew she wasn't alone. She could think of no place to hide in the Zen-like stillness of the place, and once more she cursed the static simplicity of the Foundation of Being. Someone was coming after her, someone intent on killing her. And she had no weapon, no defense left.

She didn't look where she was going, and she slammed into him, and not for one moment did she make the mistake of considering him safe. She looked into Bobby Ray's empty eyes and knew that Luke had told her the truth. Here was evil of such monstrous proportions that it wiped everything else out.

"There you are," he said, his fingers tight on her upper arms. He didn't look that strong. "I've been waiting for you a long time. You knew that, didn't you? Luke took you away from me. I don't understand it." There was a faint, fretful whine in his voice. "I've always done what I could to protect Luke. He knew I would do anything for him, and there wasn't much I needed or asked in return. I just wanted to hurt you," he said with a bewildered expression. "I wanted to make you bleed. I don't see why it was any business of his."

"Because he was sleeping with her." Catherine had appeared, breathless, her long gray hair falling loose from the bun at the back of the neck. In the early daylight she looked eerily normal—the gentle soul who comforted the afflicted.

"No," Bobby Ray said flatly. "Luke doesn't do dirty things. Not like you and me."

"Of course he does," Catherine said. She'd retrieved the gun, holding it loosely in one blue-veined hand. "He does just what you do to me, only he does it much, much better." She smiled sweetly. "He knows just how much to hurt me. He never stops too soon."

Rachel took a tentative step away from them. Bobby Ray didn't notice. Catherine was playing him like a master, and his once-expressionless face contorted with shock and rage. "No," he screamed. "He wouldn't . . ."

"He's your father, Bobby Ray," Catherine said bluntly. "And I'm your mother. And he puts his hands on me, and he hurts me in ways you can't even imagine, but the one thing he won't do is hurt you the way you want it. Will he?"

With a raging howl Bobby Ray leapt for Catherine. Only to be stopped, cold, as three successive bullets shattered his forehead.

Catherine crossed the short distance to his body, nudging it with her sandaled feet. Then she looked up at Rachel and smiled. "A lesson for you, dear," she murmured. "Choose your tools well, and be ready to dispense with them when they're no longer needed."

"Why?" Rachel asked in sick horror.

"Because I don't like to share," Catherine said simply. "Will you do me a favor, dear, and drag his body into the pool? I'm afraid he'll draw buzzards if you don't."

She made no move to comply. She couldn't bring herself to look at the corpse with the shattered head, much less touch it. "What about me? Are you going to shoot me as well?"

Catherine glanced at the heavy gun in her hand, then back at Rachel. "I don't think so," she said. "I do like watching people die. It's fascinating to see the moment of cross-over. I'm quite addicted to watching. Your mother fought it, of course. Despite the pain Alfred was manufacturing she didn't want to choose the easy way out. She kept thinking something would save her. Some new treatment would be discovered in time to wipe the cancer from her body. Of course, dear, she never had cancer."

"Of course."

"Did Luke tell you she called for you as she was dying? Did he tell you she wanted you by her side in the last minutes of her life?" Catherine moved closer.

"No."

Catherine's smile was gentle. "Good. Because she didn't. Trust Luke not to give the easy lies. She kept screeching about how unfair it was. I didn't even know she had a daughter until Luke told me to call you. I should have realized any child of Stella's would be a troublemaker."

"But you're not going to shoot me?"

"No, dear. I'd rather you drank some of our fresh spring water. Cyanide poisoning is fast but very painful. I expect the others have gone by now. Alfred will have seen to it."

"And then you and Alfred will run off with the money?"

"Oh, no. Alfred thinks we're all going to die. He'll have had his glass of water as well. I imagine he's sitting in Luke's special chair like some tragic King Lear, a cup of poison clasped in his hand."

"You monster," Rachel said.

"Still fighting," Catherine said, shaking her head in dismay. "Life is so much easier if you stop fighting, my dear."

"I don't expect life to be easy."

"Then don't expect your death to be easy. Are you going to dump Bobby Ray's body in the pool?"

"No."

Catherine shrugged. "I don't suppose it matters. Come with me, dear. There's a faucet by the

door. You can get a little drink there. I think I'm
being very kind, actually. It would be far nicer to
die beneath the New Mexico sun than trapped in
some room with a bunch of new age flakes."

"You don't believe?"

"I believe in nothing, dear. Nothing at all." She
gestured with the gun. "Come along, Rachel."

The morning air was brisk, almost chilly, belying
the heat that would settle down around the place
later in the day. Of course, Rachel would feel no
heat. Her body would be cold, stone cold, and even
the summer sun of New Mexico wouldn't be able
to warm it.

She moved ahead of Catherine on the path
back to the center, careful to avoid Bobby Ray's
body. Her feet were already stained with Calvin's
blood, but for some reason it was important not
to mix them. Calvin must have discovered what
they'd planned, and therefore had to be sacri-
ficed. She already knew there was no place to run
between the pond and the heavy metal door. And
she didn't want a bullet slamming into her back.
If Catherine was going to kill her, then she would
have to do it while she looked her in the eye.

The faucet was there, hooked up to a hose.
Catherine leaned over and turned it till there was
a faint trickle of water, then held it out toward
Rachel. "I know it's dreadfully phallic, dear, but I
think you can manage. I dumped the insecticide

in the water system several hours ago, and by now it's all the way through it. Just a few moments of exquisite agony and then it's over."

Rachel just stared at the hose. "And if I don't?"

"Then I'll do what I did with Calvin when he made the mistake of trying to stop me. A nice execution-style killing, a bullet in the back of the brain at point-blank range. Messy, but I think the water's safe to shower in . . . And Bobby Ray was the only one likely to lick my skin," she added with a soulless chuckle. She waved the limp hose at Rachel with its faint trickle of water. "Come on, dear. Pretend it's Luke."

"No."

"He left you. Of course, that surprised me. I thought he'd gotten quite irrationally sentimental about you. I never thought he'd abandon you just for the sake of money. I was sure I'd find the two of you entwined like Romeo and Juliet when I opened that door."

"Sorry to disappoint you," she said politely.

"I should have known Luke was too cold-blooded to care about anyone."

"Yes," drawled Luke from directly behind Rachel. "You should have known."

Catherine must have seen him coming. She bestowed her best lady-of-the-manor smile on him as he moved past Rachel with a glance in her direction. "But you did come back," she said.

"Not in time, however. Did you plan some heroic gesture?"

"No," he said.

"You came back for your true love?"

His look at Rachel was dismissive. "No."

"Then why . . . ?"

"I came back because I didn't like the idea of you and Alfred sharing the money I brought into this place. I've managed to skim a fair amount off the top that I've got stashed away, but I figured there was no reason for me to stint myself."

"But look at it this way, Luke. Thanks to me you won't have to share your money with Calvin."

"Thanks to you," he echoed softly, without emotion.

"And if you really don't care about your little whore, why don't you let her have a nice refreshing drink of water? Or do you want to stop her?"

He shrugged. "Hell, no. The tidier things are the better. Let her have a drink."

Rachel listened with growing numbness. It didn't matter, she told herself. It didn't matter that she looked at his almost unearthly beauty and still wanted him. She was already dead, and she didn't care.

She took a step forward and caught the hose from Catherine's hands. Luke made no move to stop her, watching her with distant curiosity. She held the stream of water to her mouth and drank. It was cool, faintly metallic, and she filled her mouth with it. And then she spat it at Catherine.

Catherine chuckled, wiping the water from her face. "Silly child. There's so much cyanide in there that it'll kill you anyway. It will just take longer."

Rachel stiffened, waiting for the first cramp to hit her, tasting the deadly water in her mouth. And then she lifted her head. "I thought cyanide was supposed to taste like burnt almonds," she said.

Catherine shrugged. "I don't know, I've never had any." And then her insouciance began to fade as she peered more closely at Rachel.

"She's right," Luke drawled lazily. "And the body smells like burnt almonds afterward. They go into cyanotic shock, and they turn a faint shade of blue before they collapse. Why aren't you turning blue, Rachel?" he asked gently.

She turned to look at him. "There's no cyanide in the water system?" she said.

"That seems a logical guess. Someone must have dumped the insecticide and replaced it with something harmless. Like lime. I wonder who would have done such a thing? He ruined all your plans, Catherine."

Catherine's face contorted in ugly rage. "No!" she screamed, her voice filling the morning skies.

"No." The gun in her hands was shaking as she pointed it directly at Luke's face. "No!" she screamed again, but Rachel had already moved, diving at her legs, knocking her sideways.

The gun spat into the air, a fast volley of bullets as Catherine's hands clamped around the trigger. She knocked Rachel away, and Rachel fell against a rock, momentarily stunned, watching with horror as Catherine launched herself at Luke, the gun pointing in his face.

He caught the crazed old woman, clamping one arm around her flailing body. And then he put his other arm around her head and jerked it, quickly, efficiently breaking her neck.

He dropped her body onto the dusty ground where it sprawled awkwardly. He lifted his head to look at her with empty eyes.

"She's dead," he said needlessly.

Rachel felt dazed from the blow on her head. She stayed where she was, huddled against the artfully, damnably placed boulder. "I gathered as much," she said faintly.

"That makes three people I've killed," he said. "Jackson Bardell, Jimmy Brown, and Catherine Biddle." He looked at her. "I don't want to kill again."

She moved then, ignoring the pain that racketed through her body. She pushed against the rock and stood, stepping over Catherine's body.

She took his hands in hers, hands that had dealt death too many times. "You won't," she said. She lifted his hands to her mouth and kissed them. The palms, the wreath of thorns that encircled his wrists.

And then he pulled her into his arms, shuddering. And she went, holding him tightly.

"We have to get out of here," he said after a moment. "Alfred called the police and told them they'd find a bloodbath. I suppose three dead people will qualify, but poor Alfred's going to feel like a major asshole when he realizes they've got a confession and all he has is a stomach full of lime water." He tilted his head back. He looked old. Haggard. And infinitely dear.

"Why did you come back?"

"Do you want me to tell you it was for you?"

"No," she said.

He managed a faint smile. "You were the major reason. But I figured maybe I couldn't just let the rest of them die."

She answered his smile. "Maybe you're going to turn into a hero after all."

"I doubt it. Let's get out of here. I don't know where the hell we're going, but the sooner we split the better. Somewhere out of the country, as fast as we can get there."

"What will we do when we get there?"

His faint grin was a ghost of his bad-boy smile.

"Live off my ill-gotten gains. I tend to be very resourceful—we'll figure out a way to spend our time."

"So I should give up everything and follow you?"

"Yes," he said. "Come away with me, Rachel. Lose everything, give it all away. No defenses, no safety, no margin for error. Just you and me."

She looked at him. "Just us?"

"We need a good place to grow fat and raise a family. You need a daughter, Rachel. A daughter to love. I want you pregnant."

"Barefoot and pregnant," she murmured.

"Again and again. Will you come with me? Will you give up everything?"

She looked up at him. "I know a little town on the coast of Spain," she said.

He closed his eyes for a moment, and then smiled brilliantly, the haunted look beginning to fade. "I've always wanted to live in Spain," he said.

And by the time the nine police cars arrived at the Foundation of Being at Santa Dolores, they were long gone.